WINNING BACK
HIS DUCHESS

Amanda McCabe

MILLS & BOON

First Published in Great Britain 2022
by Mills & Boon, an imprint of HarperCollins*Publishers* Ltd,
1 London Bridge Street, London, SE1 9GF

www.harpercollins.co.uk

HarperCollins*Publishers*
1st Floor, Watermarque Building,
Ringsend Road, Dublin 4, Ireland

Winning Back His Duchess © 2022 Ammanda McCabe

ISBN: 978-0-263-30161-8

03/22

MIX
Paper from
responsible sources
FSC™ C007454

This book is produced from independently certified FSC™ paper
to ensure responsible forest management.
For more information visit www.harpercollins.co.uk/green.

Printed and Bound in Spain using 100% Renewable Electricity
at CPI Black Print, Barcelona

Prologue

~~~~~~~~~~~~

A Lady in Society Tells All: bi-weekly in the Daily Londoner

Such news today, my dears! One of the lovely and so very gold-plated Wilkins sisters is to be married.

The charming eldest, Miss Lily, you say? Hardly a surprise. Alas, no, though a tiny wee bird whispers she might very soon be, to that sun-browned wanderer the Duke of L., no less, but not quite yet.

No, the Wilkins lass about to catch a whiff of orange blossom is the very youngest, Miss Rose, to the Duke of B.'s second son, Lord James.

This Author confesses that she would have thought His Lordship—a true Oxford don if ever there was one; alas for him that

he was born a duke's son—too buried in his studies to notice a fair lady.

Congratulations to him for having such discerning taste and best wishes to her for a new life on English shores. We feel she may need them. And we look forward to seeing where the Beautiful Couple lands in the future.

1873

Rose Wilkins paced to the end of the terrace, outside the noise and chatter of Lady Gregson's ball, and then swirled around to hurry back and peer in the glass doors. Where was he? His friend had delivered the message asking her to meet him here and she had been so eager, so filled with fizzing excitement. He wanted to see her! Talk to her, alone. *Her*, Rose Wilkins.

Had she been a fool? Was it a joke of some sort? She had fallen for such a thing before, to her burning shame. But Jamie was so very different. Wasn't he?

'Perhaps I should go back,' Rose whispered and pressed her gloved hands to her cheeks. Despite the cool night breeze, she felt so warm, as if feverish.

Maybe that was it. A fever. She'd certainly

not felt quite like herself ever since she met Lord James Grantley—Jamie—at that garden party. Ever since she'd peeped up into his dark eyes, glimpsed his slow, sweet, lazy smile, felt his hand on hers. Heard his voice, that deep, rich, dark-as-chocolate sound that seemed to flow all through her. He was not like anyone else she had ever met, especially not like…well, that person she had vowed never to think of again, after what happened in Newport. Jamie was… he was…

He was marvellous. *Too* marvellous for her, a lady too young for serious romance, too shy, too uncertain. An American, tossed into this strange English society to flounder and dream. Maybe she had let herself dream too much about Jamie.

She shivered and wrapped her arms around her waist. She couldn't stay there, waiting like an idiot, but she couldn't quite make herself go inside, either. She caught a glimpse of herself in the glass and for an instant she didn't recognise herself—she looked like a ghost in the novels she loved to secretly read, where maidens had to battle haunted castles and mysterious, dark men with deep secrets. In her white satin dress and pearls, her wide hazel eyes in her heart-shaped face, her deep red hair piled high, curled and braided, too heavy for her slight figure, she *did* look haunted. Sad, even.

Which was silly. She had escaped what haunted her before! She was not sad—what did she have to be sad about, as her mother so often snapped at her whenever she thought Rose was too quiet, too dreamy? Her father was one of the richest men in America and he was never stingy with his family in anything but his time and attention. She hadn't seen Coleman Wilkins in months and months, since their mother had brought them to Europe for 'culture', but they all really knew it was to find an old title for Lily to marry. She had the best sisters in the world in Lily, and in Rose's own twin, Violet. She had books and music, which she had shared with Jamie in these last wonderful weeks. He knew so much! He understood her as she was sure no one else ever had.

Jamie. Rose bit back a little smile to remember those precious moments together: strolling through the British Museum, sitting next to each other at the opera, reading Shakespeare in the park. His smiles, the touch of his hand. How wonderful it all was! How glorious to share so much with someone. Someone so very handsome.

Yet still he hadn't appeared tonight. She had dared to hope that he might feel about her as she did him. She sometimes caught him watching her in secret, an unreadable expression on his face.

She went up on the toes of her satin shoes to study the bright, crowded ballroom. Dancers flowed through the cream and gold flower-bedecked space like a kaleidoscope, the men in their dark evening suits setting off the ladies in their rainbow silks, their flashing jewels. Rose heard the swirl of the music. Was sure she could practically taste the champagne and the sweet ices. How she wanted to be a part of it all! To dance there with Jamie, only with Jamie, and know they were admired, seen. Part of something.

She saw Lily, so beautiful in her pale blue satin gown, standing with their mother and her friend Lady Heath, smiling and nodding serenely as several suitors stopped to talk to her. Rose didn't see Violet, who hated such stuffy events and usually crept away to look at the host's artwork when she had to attend. Violet was too intelligent, too vivid and quick and full of fun for such staidness as a mere ball.

Rose felt shy at such parties, even as she longed to know how to be a real part of them. And ever since she had met Jamie, she had felt…well, not free of that plaguing shyness, but lighter under its weight. No longer alone in a crowd. She looked forward to any event her mother let her attend, hoping he would be there. She couldn't dance yet, being too young, so mostly there were just teas and garden parties, a few large events like this one, but they were all made brighter by Jamie.

She couldn't glimpse him anywhere in the ballroom. Had she misunderstood? Taken polite conversation for something else? Something more?

She smoothed the skirt of her gown and straightened her shoulders, holding her head high. She would go back inside, smile and smile, and never think of Lord James Grantley again…

'Rose. You came!'

Rose spun around to see Jamie standing there on the terrace steps, smiling at her. The lantern light of the garden shimmered on his glossy dark hair, the cut-glass angles of his high cheekbones, his blade-like nose, his smile. At last, at last! She forgot her resolve to march away; indeed, she almost ran to him and flung her arms around him.

She stopped herself from being quite *that* silly and curled her gloved hands into fists. 'James.'

He came closer, the light casting shadows over his shoulders, his panther-like slow movements, so strong and elegant even though he had a reputation as scholar. 'I'm so sorry I'm late, I forgot old Lord Gregson sets his clocks back. So strange.'

'D-does he indeed?' she managed to choke out. She felt even more shy now that he was here. She wished she was like Lily, always serene, always certain of what to do, or like daring, confident Violet.

'Something about having more time for shooting. As if anyone is tracking down pheasants in London.' He stepped closer, his smile widening, and she was touched by the intoxicating scent of him, lemons and books and the fresh breeze and something dark and mysteriously Jamie-like. 'Once I remembered about the ridiculous clocks, I rushed out here, hoping you would still be waiting, that I could be so fortunate—and here you are. You look so beautiful, Rose.' His smile shifted, changed, became something more intense and wicked that it made her breath catch. 'So very beautiful.'

'So do you. Look—look handsome, that is,' she whispered. She found she couldn't quite think straight when he was near. It was dizzying.

His eyebrow arched. 'Do you think so?'

'Of course!' She laughed nervously, wishing beyond wishes she knew what to do. What to say. Her only other tentative foray into romance had ended so very badly. Her one real guide to such situations, the heroines in novels, usually shrieked and fainted, and she had no desire to do that. She didn't want to miss a moment with Jamie. 'You are—you are…'

Perfect.

'Oh, Rose. Sweet, darling Rose. How lucky I am to have met you, to have found you at last.' He reached for her hand and drew her closer, closer, until they were alone in the shadows beyond the lights of the ball, wrapped up together in the night.

Rose dared to wrap her arms around his neck and hold him. His dark, caramel-streaked, waving hair, longer than was the fashion, curled around her fingers, clinging to the silk of her gloves. She buried her face in his shoulder, inhaling him deeply into herself.

'I've never known anyone like you,' he whispered roughly. 'You are an angel.'

Rose knew that certainly was not true. But to hear him, this brilliant, wonderful man, say such a thing—she was dizzy with delight. How had such a marvellous thing as this moment come to *her*?

Then he tipped her face up and his lips touched hers, a soft, sweet touch, and she gasped at the sensations of it. It was nothing like in the books, when the wounded, mysterious man 'claimed' the sobbing heroine's lips in a fierce, 'punishing' embrace. This kiss seemed to burst the world into sunlight, warm and bright and glorious, and seemed to make everything come to life at last. All colour and heat and delight. When he kissed her again, Rose met him eagerly, parting her lips to try to kiss him back.

'Sweet, darling Rose,' he growled and his arms closed around her so tightly, awing her up into another, all-consuming kiss. The whole world shifted beneath her, cracking open, made entirely new. A place where there was only the two of them.

She never wanted to leave it, never wanted that moment to end.

'Rose.' Jamie leaned back from her, his arms still around her, holding her safe. 'Rose, my darling. I was going to wait, going to be patient—but I can't. Marry me. I need you so much.'

Rose gasped, shock and delight and joy and fear flooding through her. She was sure that, if he wasn't holding her, she would shoot up to the moon. 'Yes!' she cried. She knew her answer was not as graceful as a lady's should be, not demure or proper or hesitating.

His proposal had not been studied, either, as if it had flown out of him before he could think about it. Yet that didn't matter. Nothing mattered but the fact that she would be his wife. She didn't have to worry about anything in life ever again, or ever be alone. It all opened out before her, perfect and beautiful. Perfectly happy.

'Yes,' she said again, giggling with sheer, dazzling delight. Her whole body felt like a smile. 'Yes, Jamie, I will be your wife.'

'Rose!' He smiled, too, broad and filled with joy, and she couldn't believe she had found such a glorious thing here, now. He kissed her again and she knew, absolutely knew, it was happily ever after from now on.

Chapter One

A Lady in Society Tells All

This Author has been perusing the newest crop of photographs in the stationers' windows, and she must confess to being quite bowled over by the Celestial Beauty of our English ladies!

Lady Randolph Churchill, Mrs West— and the most beautiful of all, of course, the Duchess of Byson, the former Miss Rose Wilkins. Such eyes, such hair, such a tiny waist and elegant wrist! Such clothes... Parisian, naturellement.

All of London, from Their Royal Highnesses to the chimneysweeps, are in love. If only her reclusive husband could say the same, alas...

1876

Rose watched as her sisters' children, Lily's son and daughter and Violet's toddling twins, also a son and a daughter, scampered over the carpet laid out on Lily's lawn, their dark and golden and auburn heads shining in the autumn sun, their laughter caught on the breeze like snatches of the sweetest song. Their mothers and nannies chased after them, while Rose laughed at their antics and fanned herself and sipped tea and wondered if it was too early for champagne.

She adored her nieces and nephews, loved them fiercely, and these days with her sisters were sometimes all that sustained her now, all that held her upright and kept her moving. Yet sometimes, when she looked on at their exuberant joy, she had to use all her strength not to burst into tears.

'Oh, Little A., do help your sister stay still for a moment!' Violet beseeched Lily's eldest child, Little Aidan, as she stood behind her camera and tried in vain to take an image of all the children. Rose thought it a brave endeavour, though perhaps a hopeless one.

Like so very many things in life.

She took another sip of tea and smiled at Lily as her older sister dropped into the wicker chair next to Rose's. Her cheeks glowed pink, her smile was radiant and Rose wondered if Lily might be expecting again. Another adorable addition to the Roderick Castle nursery. Lily took a drink of the cooling oolong and pursed her lips against a pang.

'Donat!' Lily called to the butler. 'Can we have a bottle of champagne, please?'

'You absolutely read my mind,' Rose said.

'We shall need fortification if we're to keep up with Violet,' Lily said. 'Where *does* she get all that energy?'

'I wish she would share a bit of it.'

'Oh, yes, indeed.' Lily sighed and snapped open a painted silk fan. She waved it vigorously, stirring the damp curls at her temples. 'And *you* must share some of your beauty secrets, Rose darling! I vow, you get lovelier by the week. Even Princess Alexandra seems envious.'

Rose laughed, trying not to squirm in embarrassment. She didn't know why society had decided she was a beauty; she still felt like the shy, awkward girl she had once been, the uncertain young bride. 'Latour almond cream and violet soap from Paris. And dancing!'

Lily studied her closely over the lacy edge of her fan, until Rose actually did fidget a bit. Her older sister always seemed to see far too much, in her quiet, concerned, mothering way. It was ridiculous for a grown lady like Rose, married for years, separated from her husband for many months now, to feel like such a schoolchild!

'No, it's not soap, not even Parisian soap,' Lily said. 'Though I will certainly buy some now! It's *you*. We saw your last photograph in the papers, so beautiful. By Nadar, the last time you were in France?'

'Yes, he is quite the genius. Not as good as Vi, of course, but such a wizard at making everyone look quite glorious.' Rose turned away to hide her warm cheeks, straightening her ribbon-bedecked hat. She hadn't quite become accustomed to everyone seeing her in the papers over their breakfast table, her smile peeping out from black-and-white pages, her gowns and hats and parasols copied. It still made her want to laugh. But at least it gave her something to do every day, something to think about besides the wreck she had made of her life. Her heart. 'Perhaps it really is Paris making me look better!'

'Paris can do that. Especially at Christmas, I imagine. The French must be so *très elegante*.'

'Indeed they are. You should see the lights along the Champs-Élysées! A modern wonder.' Rose had not meant to be gone quite so long as she had, over Christmas and into the spring until the political situation looked too much, and then there'd been the summer, visiting friends in Nice to watch the boating. She usually adored the holidays with her family, listening to the children sing and watching them tear about with their new toys. Seeing her sisters kiss their adoring husbands under the mistletoe. She hadn't quite been able to face it all with a smile that time, so she'd stayed in Paris and danced instead.

And tried so very, very hard not to wonder what Jamie was doing.

The separation, where there might be a glimmer, no matter how small, of finding happiness again, should surely make her own life feel lighter? Feel more…certain? She had to keep dancing until it was true, which would surely be any day now.

Surely.

Donat appeared with a tray of cut-crystal glasses filled with bubbling golden liquid, as well as a pitcher of lemonade, and Rose gratefully took a glass as a welcome distraction from

Lily's worried scrutiny. Distractions were always good these days.

'Delicious,' Rose said after a large sip and sat back to watch Violet. Her twin had given up on taking the group photograph and was chasing the children across the grass as they shrieked in delight. Violet had lost her hat and her red-tinged curls fell from their pins. The hem of her green-and-white-striped dress was stained with grass and photographic chemicals. Violet never seemed to care, nor did her grand, formidably handsome ducal husband. Violet was always exactly and only herself.

Rose felt such an aching, envious pang as she watched her sister, even as she had to laugh. How glorious it would be to know you only had to be yourself to be loved!

'Princess Alexandra has asked me to go to Baden with her next month, when she takes the waters for her rheumatism. She never has quite got over that fever, the poor lady,' Lily said. She served as an occasional lady-in-waiting to the Princess of Wales, a great honour for an American and one Lily excelled at. 'Why don't you come, too? My duties won't take up nearly all my time. I've heard the waters there are quite wondrous and the casino a great deal of fun.

You could collect even more admirers! Not that you need them.'

Rose laughed and tried to brush away Lily's worries. She knew her sisters thought she had grown too thin of late and perhaps she had, but she wasn't sure the Baden waters were the answer. As for admirers—Lily didn't need to know about Paul. Not yet. 'Indeed not! No more admirers. In fact, I need someone to take a few of them off my hands. I would certainly love to spend more time with *you*, dearest Lily, but I'm not really sure the Princess likes me so very much.' Whenever Rose went to a party at Marlborough House with the Wales's set, as she often did, she usually caught the beautiful Princess watching her quizzically, as if she was trying to figure out whether or not Rose was one of the Prince's flirts. Rose certainly was not.

'Oh, but she does! She often compliments your gowns and hairstyles. She doesn't usually speak to anyone except a few at parties, her hearing has become so difficult. And there is…' She trailed away and waved her fan harder.

'I assure you, Lily, the Princess's husband is not among my admirers, except for a bridge game or two,' Rose said firmly. It could be that the Prince might be more, if she gave him any encouragement. Bertie admired all women. But Rose was firm—no married men.

'Well, yes, of course,' Lily said. Strangely for unflappable Lily, she seemed somewhat flustered, as she poured out a glass of lemonade for herself. 'You are above reproach.'

'A lady who lives apart from her husband? Above reproach?'

'Indeed. Everyone admires you; no one gossips about you, for they know there is nothing to gossip about. And you *are* a duchess. That counts for much.'

Rose almost laughed. She always forgot that she was a duchess now, like her sisters. The Duchess of Byson. First Jamie's father had passed away and then her brother-in-law, Jamie's older sibling, a man she barely knew, had died last year in a riding accident, leaving no wife or children. It had happened soon before the separation and had hardly seemed real to her. She couldn't picture Jamie, Jamie who lived in his own world of books, with the weight of such a title on him. And she'd certainly never felt duchess-like. 'Perhaps I will go with you to Baden, Lily, or somewhere else very soon. I feel the need to leave London again, it becomes so dreary. Mother has asked me to Newport...'

Though she couldn't imagine ever going back to Newport. Not after what happened there. It still made her feel queasy.

'Oh, no, Rose darling, you can't be *that* desperate to get away! Better come with me to Baden.'

'I shall think about it. It sounds quite restful.' And elusive rest would be a marvellous thing.

Lily leaned back with a teasing smile. 'You must recover your energy from dealing with all those bouquets left on your doorstep! Ah, the travails of being a famous beauty.'

Rose laughed obligingly. 'Yes, it is quite dreadfully exhausting!' Living a life that didn't feel like her own—yes, it was tiring. But she would fix that all very soon, one way or another.

Violet shooed the children towards their toys and nannies and joined her sisters in their shaded chairs, reaching for a glass of champagne. 'Oh, Lily, you are a genius of hospitality! I am completely run ragged by these wild children.'

'Only because you let them run you ragged, Vi.' Lily laughed. 'You love to let them chase you about. Not that I am complaining, you tire them out so they fall into bed like little lambs.'

'Well, I shan't be able to outrun Little A.

much longer, he's growing like the proverbial weed,' Violet said, happily sipping her drink.

Lily gave a beatific smile as she watched her children tumble over pulling their hobby horse across the grass. 'He *is* going to be tall, like his papa. And he and Honoria are so smart! You should have heard what they said to me at tea yesterday...'

Rose had to turn away as her sisters chatted about their children. Even after so very long, she couldn't quite face it head-on. Couldn't move entirely past it, as she knew she should. She poured out another glass of champagne and took a gulp.

Violet seemed to sense Rose's discomfort, for she gently touched her hand and said smoothly, 'But what were the two of you whispering about when I came over? Am I left out of the gossip again?'

'You're only ever left out of the gossip, Vi, because you aren't at all interested,' Lily said. 'You're too busy with your Solar Club and your Photographic Society and such.'

Violet gave a satisfied smile, as well she might. The Solar Club was the most exclusive photographic society in England and few women were admitted. Violet's work was becoming very well known. 'They do keep me rather busy. But I always want to know what my sisters are doing.'

'I was trying to persuade Rose to come with me to Baden. Mother is trying to lure her to Newport.'

'Oh, no, Rose! You cannot go to Newport,' Violet cried. 'But why should you go anywhere? You only returned from France not so long ago. Just because James has—' She broke off and looked away to take a long drink.

'Because James—what?' Rose whispered. Her sisters never spoke his name, but she was sure they heard things about him. What was happening to him now?

'Has been such trouble to you in the past, of course,' Violet said hurriedly.

She saw her sisters exchange a quick glance, before Lily gave her a gentle smile. It was often thus. Lily and Violet protecting Rose, the youngest—younger than Violet by twenty minutes—the baby, the vulnerable one, as they saw it. And she *had* been fragile at times, a young bride in a world she didn't understand, with a husband she hadn't really fathomed.

She wasn't that girl any longer, but Violet and Lily couldn't always see that.

And she did fear what they might say. Maybe James was drinking to excess again? Maybe they would say he had a new love. Divorce was easier now than it had once been. He was a duke now; he needed an heir. The heir they couldn't have. Maybe he was tired of living in their twilight world.

So was she. She hadn't seen Jamie in so long. They couldn't go on as they were for ever, navigating their separate but parallel lives. She had thought that Paul might be able to help her, steady, sophisticated, funny Paul, who had been wooing her so gently for some time. Yet this time by herself, discovering who she might be beyond that young bride, had been strangely comforting.

Rose shook her head. She had no real answers for her dilemma, not yet. She only knew the time for a resolution would have to be soon. She needed to visit Jamie and talk to him herself.

'I'm off to a Saturday-to-Monday at Pryde Abbey in a few days,' she said. Paul would be there and perhaps a resolution of sorts would present itself. Even if it didn't, she loved her time with the Madewells at rambling old Pryde Abbey, their casual ways and beautiful gardens, their artistic friends. There were always fascinating painters and writers and eccentrics to talk to and they liked to have Rose there as a 'muse'.

'Oh, you lucky ducky!' Violet exclaimed. 'I haven't seen Lady Madewell in ages. I would love to see her sister's new paintings. But I have to go with Will to some boring Court reception.'

'I will write you all about it,' Rose said. Maybe she would even have a bit of personal news for her sisters, too. But first, she had to talk to Jamie, whether she liked it or not.

'What do you think, Vi?' Lily asked after Rose departed. She absently nibbled on a cream cake as she watched the children race about.

Violet glanced up from her camera. 'About what?'

'Rose, of course. Do you think she looked happier? I was so hoping Paris would really do her some good.'

'Paris does everyone good,' Violet said. 'And I think she is happy enough. A bit pale still.'

'Yes.' Lily and Violet had become worried about Rose, ever since it became too apparent that she and Jamie were not as happy together as they should have been. Ever since she'd lost her baby. 'I do wish she would forget about Jamie!'

Violet shook her head sadly. 'I'm not sure she can ever entirely forget him. He was her perfect prince and he so disappointed her with his drinking, his neglect of her, especially after the miscarriage.'

'So he did. Poor, sweet Rose. Yet I fear she still cares about him. The look in her eyes...'

Violet sat down in the chair next to Lily's, her face creased in worry. 'What do you think we should do to help her? I hate that she carries such a burden with her.'

'As do I. I've turned my mind over and over, trying to see how to help. I suppose all we can do is what we have already done—be there for her. Tell her we love her, no matter what.'

Violet nodded sadly. 'If only...'

'Yes,' Lily whispered. 'If only.'

Chapter Two

Rose peeped out the carriage window at the house waiting for her. She hadn't been to the Russell Square town house for so very long and it looked exactly as it did in her memories. Pale stone, rising four storeys, with a glossy black-painted door and shutters, gleaming iron railings, immaculate and quiet and all that was proper. Hiding behind its windows.

She twisted her handkerchief between her gloved hands and took a deep breath. The house might be the same, but *she* was not. She was far from the nervous, love-dizzy girl who had first gone up those stone steps and into the marble-floored hall. She had nothing to fear.

She rapped on the carriage door and her footman opened it and helped her alight to the pavement. She straightened her feathered hat, smoothed the jacket of her blue velvet walking suit and marched up the steps to the front door.

Someone must have been watching her, for it swung open before she could reach for the brass lion's head knocker. Makepeace, the butler, stood there, his faded eyes startled but kind under bushy white brows.

'Your Grace,' he said with a bow.

Rose made herself give the careless, bright smile that had become famous in her photographs and breezed through the door. The hall was the same, too, she noticed as she tried to distract herself from what she was about to do by gazing around. The black-and-white floor, the gilded balustrade soaring up to the drawing room, the alabaster-topped table holding a large blue-and-white Chinese vase and a rather drooping bouquet of white lilies.

'Hello, Makepeace, I hope you're doing well,' she said, tugging off her gloves.

'Very well, Your Grace, thank you. Do you have an appointment?'

She waved her hand, the faint light from the brocade-draped windows catching on the diamond-studded ring she still wore. 'Oh, no, I won't be long at all, I just have a teensy question for His Grace. No need to make an announcement.'

Assuming Jamie would be in his library, she hurried up the winding staircase. The green carpet under her feet muffled her steps, while various Grantley ancestors stared down with astonishment from their portraits hung on the green-striped wallpaper. Maidservants peeped out at her, wide-eyed from behind doorways, feather dusters in hand, dropping hasty curtsies. She smiled and waved at them, astonished to see that they, too, were the same faces from before she left. She had hired them herself.

'His Grace said he cannot be disturbed, Your Grace,' Makepeace called, starting creakily up the stairs behind her. Rose was quicker.

'Shan't be a moment, Makepeace,' she said and pushed open the library door at the top of the stairs.

Jamie *was* there, of course, as he usually was, unless he was off in some museum or dusty archive. The cavernous room was dimly lit, the velvet curtains half-drawn against the daylight, the soaring bookshelves cast into shadows. Over the carved oak mantelpiece hung a portrait— Rose in her creamy satin and lace wedding gown, wide eyes so hopeful and unaware that this moment would come.

She turned away from her own gaze…and saw her husband. She nearly fell back a step, almost turned coward and ran, but she knew she couldn't.

Jamie sat at his desk amid an unruly pile of books and papers, the lamplight outlining him in amber-gold, as if he was a painting himself, a Renaissance prince as she had often imagined him. He wore no coat or cravat and his waistcoat was unbuttoned to reveal the thin white muslin shirt beneath, the collar loose at his throat, the sleeves rolled back to reveal his corded forearms, his elegant hands. Those hands that had once caressed her so gently, so enticingly, drowning her in such delight…

Rose swallowed and glanced sharply away from the sight. She could *not* think of that now, could not remember those long, glorious, giddy nights of their young marriage. The delight and wonder and wild, wild love she had known then. It was gone now. She was no longer that Rose.

She peeped back at him and found him watching her with stunned eyes, as if she was a mirage which had suddenly appeared in the middle of his sanctuary. His hair had grown longer, falling over his forehead in unruly dark waves that he impatiently pushed back, making his cut-glass cheekbones, his elegant features even more classically handsome. His skin was lightly golden, as if he had been somewhere far from misty London.

She felt a pang that she didn't have any idea where that could be, that she didn't know anything of his life now. Unlike her, he seldom appeared in *A Lady in Society Tells All*. Jamie was contained within himself, something that had always frustrated her even as she'd admired it. She well remembered sitting in this very room, novel or embroidery in hand, watching him as he was absorbed in his work. The play of emotions over his face, the way he drove his fingers through his hair, leaving the waves awry. The way he would suddenly burst into joyful laughter at some discovery and catch her in his arms...

'Rose,' he said hoarsely. 'What a surprise.'

The out-of-breath Makepeace appeared in the doorway. 'I am sorry I could not announce Her Grace, Your Grace.'

Jamie shook his head and seemed to recover from the shock of seeing his estranged wife in his library. He smiled that slow, lazy white smile she'd once longed for so much. 'That is quite all right, Makepeace. It is her home, after all. Perhaps we could have some tea?'

'I won't take up much of your time, Jamie,' Rose said, forcing herself to stay light, breezy. A fluttering butterfly, never still for long, never lonely for long, as she had learned to live her life. It helped keep reality, real emotion and fear and longing, at bay. She wasn't sure it would work right now. She went to the window and tugged back the curtain, letting in a bit of pale daylight.

'Tea anyway, please, Makepeace,' Jamie said, and the butler bowed and left, shutting the door behind him. She wondered how many of the maids would be gathering to listen there.

Rose studied the room to give her a moment before facing her husband. Jamie rose to his full, lean height and took off his spectacles, fastening his waistcoat and reaching for his coat. Unlike the rest of the house, she had never touched the decoration and arrangement of the library, it was always Jamie's alone, and it hadn't changed at all. The same dark red and chocolate-brown carpet, slightly faded under her feet, the same piles of books everywhere. The same velvet armchair by the fireplace, where she had once sat and watched him.

Jamie was known as a great scholar of literature and history, not only in society—which marvelled that a man of the *ton* would *read* so much, instead of hunting—but among other intellectuals all over the Continent, many of whom he corresponded with frequently. It was true he would have made an excellent Oxford don.

Rose had loved that about him, the way he made poetry and plays and history come alive for her, the beautiful way he saw the world. He had made her see it, too, and he never, ever made her feel foolish or silly. He spoke to her as he did to his scholarly friends. She was never little, fragile Rose who needed protecting, as she was in her own family.

It had been so glorious. Until it all came crashing down around them and the shimmering vision had burst like a bubble on a summer's day.

Rose bit her lip, forcing herself to remember this was *now*. Their days of poetry and passion were gone.

'I'm sorry to disturb your work,' she said stiffly. 'I was paying a call nearby and I thought

I would stop here for a moment. I wanted to talk to you about something.'

'You know you are welcome here at any time, Rose,' he said gently. 'I meant what I said—this is your home.'

Rose wasn't so certain it had *ever* been her home. She studied the room: the dark, worn upholstery on the heavily carved furniture, the faded carpet, the shelves and shelves of books, the smell of dust and lemon polish in the air. This room had certainly never been meant for her. Yet her little house in Portman Square, arranged as she wanted it, every inch of it, didn't quite feel like home, either. She stepped closer to the desk and ran her fingertips over the pile of books. *Servant of Two Masters*... *Man of the World*... *The Shrewd Widow*... *Memoirs of Goldoni*.

'Goldoni?' she asked curiously. 'The eighteenth century seems late for your work.'

'Yes, it is, generally,' Jamie said, running his fingers through his hair again, leaving the thick waves unruly. Rose curled her hand into a fist to keep from reaching out to smooth them, as she once had so often. 'I saw a production of *The Fan* last year and was quite enthralled. I'd been corresponding with Signor Mastrelli in

Florence lately and he invited me to visit his archives. I've just returned.'

So that was why he looked sun-touched. He had been in Italy. Rose wondered with a pang if there had been a dark-eyed *signora* while he was there, a woman of greater wit and intellect than herself. She reminded herself that was none of her business any longer. No more than her own arrangements were *his* business. And that was why she was there.

'Italy…' she sighed '…how I should like to see it. Properly see it.' With her mother, before Rose was married, it had been a quick whirl of paintings and palazzos and Baedeker before they headed to England to look for suitable husbands. A gloss of culture. Nothing at all as she was sure it would be with Jamie, a deep dive into beauty and books.

'You would adore it and it would suit you perfectly,' he said, and Rose remembered how he had once compared her to a Veronese Madonna, serene and smiling and pale and perfect—and then he would kiss her silly, the two of them swept away in each other.

'I confess a bit of sun would suit me right now. As it has you, obviously.' She dared to let herself give in to temptation, for an instant, and reached up to touch his cheek with her fingertips. His skin was smooth and warm under a faint prickle of whiskers and he leaned into her touch.

'Rose...' he whispered with that old, rough longing that used to reach out to her like magic, drawing her closer and closer. Until she was burned.

She stepped back and laughed. 'You've become adventurous, Jamie.'

'Italy is hardly the veldt. I'm off to Venice soon to finish some research,' he said, looking away.

Venice. Once they had talked of going there together, of what they would do among those ancient, romantic stones. 'How lovely for you.' She straightened a stack of books and glimpsed a half-full coffee cup on the desk. Once, there would have been brandy or whisky.

Jamie seemed to notice her gaze and he tapped his long finger on the rim of the cup. 'I became quite a connoisseur of coffee in Italy.'

Rose nodded and turned in relief as a maid came in with the tea tray. 'Thank you, Mary,' she said as the girl arranged it on a small table near the window. 'How is your mother these days?'

'Oh, ever so much better, Your Grace,' Mary said. 'She uses that cordial you sent her every week.'

'Very good. I'll have some more made up.' After the maid curtsied and left the room. Rose sat down and reached for the teapot. Antique Sèvres, painted with delicate roses and twining ivy touched with bits of gilt, a wedding gift from some business associate of her father. She was surprised it was still used there. 'I know it's not Italian espresso, but it seems properly brewed. Lemon?'

'Thank you.' He sat down across from her, carefully, slowly, watching her warily, as if he was sure she would fly away any second. And she wondered if she should. Having afternoon tea together after all this time, as if nothing had ever happened, felt most peculiar. It felt almost as if, for a moment, the whole world didn't lie between them. 'You are looking very well, Rose.'

'Am I? I do feel well. It must be the new hat.' She patted at the feathered and beribboned, tip-tilted confection on her head.

He laughed and for a moment he sounded like the old Jamie again. Bemused and full of wonderment at her. 'It *is* fetching and I'm sure it's in the height of fashion...'

'So it is, though I'm surprised you noticed.' He had never really noticed her clothes at all, no matter how fashionable and expensive they were. He always seemed to prefer she be *out* of them as quickly as possible.

'I may not notice fashion, but you do always look beautiful. The loveliest lady in any ballroom. But I don't think it's the hat. It's—well, it's just *you.*'

'You look well, too,' she murmured and he did. The paleness that had haunted his handsome face during the worst of their times had been banished, his eyes dark and sparkling like a starry night. 'Italy clearly agrees with you.'

'I've been making a few changes.'

She took a long sip of her tea. 'Like drinking coffee?'

His lips crooked in a smile. 'Among other things.'

'My sister has asked me to go to Baden with her. I may have to try it, since travel does seem so transforming.'

'With the royal party?'

'Princess Alexandra, yes. I haven't yet decided if I should go.'

He reached for the dish of lemon slices, his hand brushing hers. It felt like a quick, darting touch of lightning and she shivered. 'Did you come here to consult me about travel arrangements?'

Rose blinked at him, confused. They hadn't consulted each other about such things even at the end of their time living under the same roof.

'You said you have something to talk to me about, yes?' he said, and Rose remembered. She'd forgotten in the confusion of being here again in this house with Jamie. In a moment of no quarrels, no chilly silences. It was—nice. Better than nice, it felt like the contentment she had craved for so long and which still eluded her.

Now she remembered. Gathering her resolve, she set down her cup, and said, 'Yes, indeed. I have been thinking a great deal, you see, Jamie, and I know we cannot go on as we have. I think we should consider divorce.'

Jamie wasn't sure he'd heard Rose correctly. Divorce? Had his sweet, shy, soft-hearted wife just calmly stated that they should throw themselves into scandal?

She gazed back at him coolly and he remembered sharply that she was no longer *that* Rose, his wide-eyed bride. She was a famous beauty, an independent woman on her own. She had gathered a hard, glittering shell around herself, a beautiful shield against the world, and he couldn't blame her at all. Not after the horrible mistakes he had made, the drinking, taking her for granted, taking *them* for granted.

He had held a perfect pearl in his hand and like the biggest fool he had dropped it. Lost the most wondrous gift ever. Now it seemed gone for ever.

Yet as he stared at her now, all his words snatched away, he thought he saw a glimpse of his Rose in her hazel eyes. A tenderness. Or perhaps he only imagined it, something from his dreams, in the sparkling diamond Rose had become.

He shook his head. Why had Makepeace let her in at all? Why had she even shown up, instead of sending him one of her usual short messages on her rose-scented blue stationery? She hadn't come to the house since the day she'd left it, stepping into her sister's carriage and driving away. Out of his life.

She took another sip of tea and glanced away, and that soft spark of the old Rose was suddenly gone again. There was the shining society beauty in her ruffled velvet and lace walking suit, that daringly tilted hat of blue and amethyst feathers on her shining deep red curls, a tiny blue lace veil flirting over her brow. Amethyst drops sparkled and winked in her ears, sending light into the dusty room, drawing him closer. She peeped up from beneath that veil and he was caught again in the glory of her beautiful eyes, like at that garden party where they'd first met so long ago.

'Well?' she said, as if she had asked him about the weather. 'What do you think?'

He put down his cup with a sharp click. 'I'm surprised a lady who moves in royal circles would want such a scandal tainting her life.'

She laughed, a bright, hard, tinkling sound. 'I am entirely peripheral to royal circles, you know. It hardly matters if I'm asked into the Royal Enclosure at Ascot, or forbidden to enter Windsor Castle. It is a small price to pay for freedom.'

'Do you not have freedom now? I would never curtail anything you do.' He had no right to do so, after the way he'd behaved. The way he'd marred what could have been such a perfect life together. He owed Rose at least that.

'No. But it's not *true* freedom, is it? You are a duke now, after all. You will need an heir and…' She looked away, her eyes suddenly very bright. 'And you know the doctor said he was almost certain we could never have another.'

'Rose…' he said softly, instinctively reaching for her hand. The sadness and misery of those dark days seemed to lower over them again.

She slid farther from him and gave him an even more brittle smile. 'We can't go on like this for ever.'

A sudden idea, chilling, struck him. 'Is there—have you met someone?'

'I meet a great many people, but no one I would care to tie myself to right now. We have both been living in this halfway world too long, it can't last for ever.' She glanced at his desk. 'Perhaps there will be a suitable lady for you in Venice? Someone far more intellectual than me, who will be a good match for you.'

'I never wanted anyone but *you*, Rose,' he said, the truth bursting out before he could chase it away, as he always did now. Pushing his emotions, his grief, down into his work, burying it all until it came to haunt him in the silent darkness of the night. His beautiful sweet wife, lost to him because he had been an utter fool.

He wasn't a fool any longer. He had worked hard to become the man he once was again, to be someone worthy of winning her back. But now he looked into her eyes, her cool, unreadable eyes, and had the icy sensation it was all too late.

No, he thought fiercely. It couldn't be too late. Not when she was so close he could reach out and touch her again, could smell her summer rose perfume.

She carefully set down her teacup and gathered up her gloves and reticule. 'Do think about it, Jamie. You will see I'm right. It won't be easy, of course, but I'm sure between us and our solicitors we can see it done in a timely manner. You can write to me when you have decided.'

She rose to her feet in a rustle of velvet and lace, and Jamie instinctively reached out for her hand. She was so warm and soft under his touch, her wrist as delicate as a little bird. Her eyes widened and she shivered, as if she felt the current between them at even that small touch.

'Stay. Please,' he said hoarsely. He wished suddenly he *had* spent more time with people and less with books of long ago, that he could read human nature as well as he did an ancient poem, could persuade them, show them what he saw. Could convince Rose to listen to him, if he could only find the right words to say to her. He couldn't let her walk away from him for ever. 'We can talk of whatever you like, anything at all.'

Her expression softened, but she shook her head. 'I'm going to a house party at the Madewells' house in a few days and I have errands to do before that.'

The Madewells, her dashing new friends. He knew well about their house at Pryde Abbey, a gathering place for artists and writers and free thinkers, a place which surely suited this new Rose very well. 'More portraits to pose for?'

She laughed and turned away to hurry out of the library. Jamie followed, compelled to stay with her as long as he could. 'I doubt there will be time for new portraits in a Saturday-to-Monday.'

'I saw Violet's photograph of you at the Photographic Society exhibition,' he said. He paused at the top of the stairs, not trusting himself to go further.

Rose paused in the hall below, adjusting her hat in the looking glass. He thought of how many times he'd watched her do that in the past, the tilt of her head, the soft curve of her neck.

'The one where I posed as Diana? I rather liked that one. Vi's talent grows all the time. She always makes me look rather pretty.'

Rather pretty. His Rose looked glorious. He had coveted that photograph, the image of Rose posed in a forest glade, clad in a white robe, crescent moons and stars in her loose hair, a bow and arrow gracefully raised in her hands. But he had been told it was not for sale.

Rose was always the most beautiful woman he had ever seen, no matter where or when. He remembered the first time he ever saw her... at that garden party he had been so sure would be dull. Her slim, small figure in pink against the glossy green of the hedges, her shy smile, her wide eyes.

'You are always, er, rather pretty, Rose,' he said.

She glanced up at him through her veil and for an instant she was that girl again. 'Thank you, Jamie. Do think about what I said. Good afternoon.'

She turned and swept through the doorway. Jamie had to curl his fists hard on the carved banister to keep from running after her, catching her in his arms, locking her in with him. That was hardly the way to convince her he had changed, that he would never hurt her again. He forced himself to stay where he was, to let the door close behind her and the house be shut in shadows and silence again.

When Rose lived there, it had always felt full of flowers and laughter and music, her embroidery and novels, tea trays scattered about, her fingers tripping over the piano keys, her sisters and friends coming and going. So much life. He had never understood *why* she wanted company like that, why she enjoyed parties and gatherings, but he enjoyed watching her take pleasure in it all. Until he'd ruined it.

But surely what was broken could be mended? Not as it was, but perhaps it could be even better. Stronger. He had to decipher how. Convince her not to divorce him.

Jamie sat down heavily on the step, staring at the spot where Rose had just been. He could still smell her perfume and was sure the very air shimmered. He set his jaw determinedly. He had to decide how to persuade her to come back to him again.

Chapter Three

~⧫~

A Lady in Society Tells All

Now, this Observer would never believe it if she had not seen it with her own shocked eyes!

The Duchess of B., always acknowledged as the Greatest Beauty In London, was seen departing from the Duke's own house! A doorway she has not darkened in many a day.

Can true love be in bloom again for this American Rose? Or is All at an End for real this time?

Stay alert, my dear readers. This story will surely only grow more fascinating...

Rose watched in the dressing table mirror as her maid Jenny dressed her hair. She had looked forward to the ball, one of the last before absolutely everyone fled town for their country estates and places abroad, but now she felt unaccountably nervous. Fidgety. Her visit to Jamie had thrown her quite off her social stride and into a confusing whirl. And after she had worked so hard to build this life for herself! To forget her old dreams and try to find something new.

She picked up a silver-capped powder pot and put it back down. It was only because she hadn't seen Jamie in so long. She'd known it would not be easy to be in a room with him again, but asking for a divorce was no business for a letter. She'd thought she was prepared, that the hard shell she'd created so carefully around herself would hold together—until she was there, in the reality of her old home. With *him*.

And he had looked more handsome than ever, blast him. She dropped the powder pot and reached for a lace fan, opening and snapping it shut, the tiny sequins sewn on the cobwebby threads shimmering. As she waved it in front of her warm face, she saw him again, his dark eyes startled to see her there, his elegant, ink-spotted fingers reaching for the tea, his smile. She hadn't been able to attend the musicale she was invited to that evening. All she could do once she left their house—his house—was sit by the fire and let the memories wash over her. The good and the bad, the terribly sad. The laughter and kisses and the fiery delight of lovemaking, the tears and loss and pain. The terrible disappointment.

That was no way to live, she knew that very well. It was why she seldom let herself dwell in the past, but kept running forward, to the next ballroom, the next regatta or horse race, the next portrait sitting. If she looked back too much, she would be lost.

Seeing Jamie again had made her stumble. Badly.

The only good thing was that he was unlikely to be at Lady Baddely's ball. Jamie had always hated large parties. But maybe Paul would be there, to dance and laugh and joke with her, bring her champagne and ices, make her forget her broken heart for a few minutes. He really was a darling.

'What do you think, Your Grace?' Jenny asked.

Rose glanced up at the mirror. Jenny had twisted her hair up into glossy ringlets, bound with ropes of pearls and wreathed with roses, like some classical goddess. 'Lovely, Jenny, as always. You are such an artist.'

Jenny beamed. 'The pink satin, then?'

'Yes, that will do nicely.' Fashion was far from her mind at that moment, but she knew Rose Byson, Famous Beauty, could never let the side down. Descriptions of her gowns and jewels would be in all the social papers tomorrow and hostesses counted on the mentions of their soirées.

As she tucked one stray curl back into its pin, she wondered if Jamie ever glanced at the social columns, saw her name there. Maybe he might have wondered how she felt then, even wished he was with her...

No. She'd given up such futile thoughts long ago. Their lives were too far apart now.

She stood up to cast aside her dressing gown and let Jenny help her into one of the new Worth creations she'd brought back from Paris, a pale pink ballgown trimmed with white tulle like drifts of snow and silk rosebuds beaded with tiny crystals that shivered and shimmered when she moved. Every detail, as always, was perfect, and suited to her slim figure and heart-shaped features. She never wanted to be the gauche, silly American girl, pushing her way around

English ballrooms. She never wanted to embarrass her husband, even now. Thinking of divorce showed her how very desperate she had become.

She twirled around to examine the small train, pink brocade edged with more tulle, and she remembered that Jamie had said he was going off to Venice soon. She had always longed to see Venice, but only with him. She imagined strolling beside a misty canal as the moonlight shimmered on the domes of St Mark's, that pink train drifting over the stone stairs, her hand held tightly in Jamie's. He smiled down at her, so tender and filled with longing, before his lips found hers in a hungry kiss, his arms coming around her, Venetian bells ringing out in jubilation…

Stop this now! she commanded herself sternly. She'd made a mistake seeing him again. It made so many old hopes bubble up inside of her again, ones she'd thought long since turned to cold ash. She had to shove them away again. It was why divorce, a true, final break, seemed the only option for them now.

Jenny fastened her pearl necklace around her throat, triple strands interspersed with diamonds, her parents' wedding gift to her. Her sisters, duchesses when they married, had received tiaras whether they'd wanted them or not, but

Rose, only Lady James then, was given a beautiful pearl parure. She seldom wore them now, as they brought back memories of her mother's face as she handed Rose the leather box on her wedding morning. That shining pride in having all her daughters settled in the English nobility. *My most beautiful baby*, Stella Wilkins had sighed.

But Jenny said only the pearls could possibly go with this gown and Rose couldn't argue with that. Jenny had been her maid ever since she married, and her eye was impeccable.

Rose was glad she looked her best when she made her way into Lady Baddely's orchid-bedecked ballroom and saw Paul waiting for her.

Lord Paul Adelman was a younger son, as Jamie once was, and he took full advantage of his lack of real responsibility. He was a good dancer, a fine card player, a graceful rider and funny conversationalist, easy and charming to be around. Nothing whatsoever like her complex husband. It was why Rose appreciated him.

'My dear,' he said, bowing over her hand, the sweep of his golden hair shining in the gaslight. His perfectly trimmed moustache tickled her fingers through her thin kid gloves and his blue eyes crinkled in a grin. 'You do look exactly like a delectable summer rose tonight. You should wear this colour all the time. May I claim the first dance?'

'Of course.' Rose took one of the glasses he caught from a footman's passing tray and studied the ballroom over the gilt edge. It was all as gloriously abundant as Lady Baddely always conceived her parties: the yellow-silk-papered walls banked with ivy, ferns, gold baskets of orchids, roses spilling from tall crystal vases. Only a half-open glass terrace door gave a breath of fresh air in all the cloying sweetness.

An orchestra played in a gallery high above the coiffed curls and feathers of the guests and everywhere around her was a swirl of bright satins and silks, flashing diamonds and rubies, men in their black coats and pomaded hair, laughter and chatter and the snap of fans. 'Quite a crush this evening.'

'Ah, yes, no one would miss the last ball. And Lady Baddely is quite the hostess. They say royalty may appear later—is your curtsy in order?'

Rose laughed. 'Oh, my. Shall it be the Queen?' she teased. 'That *would* be a coup, though I fear it would rather put a damper on the fun.'

'Pack up the baccarat room, *tout suite*, the Widow of Windsor appears! No, no, it will be Bertie and his fair princess, I should think. Or maybe Mrs Langtry?'

'My sister Lily says she is set to go to Baden with the Princess soon. Lily, not La Langtry. She wants me to go with her.'

'My darling, you can't! It's too dreary. Everyone's maiden aunt playing bridge.'

'Oh, I don't know. I think I should like to get away for a while.' And if she couldn't be in romantic Venice, maybe playing bridge in a spa town would do.

'It would be too lonely without you. But no matter what, we must dance first.'

Rose laughed as he handed her empty glass to another footman and swept her into his arms, twirling her on to the crowded parquet floor. It was a mazurka, light, quick, fun, hopping and spinning around until she giggled. Paul was a very skilled dancer, never letting her trip or miss a quick turn.

She suddenly froze as Paul spun her around again and she glimpsed the newest arrival at the ballroom door. A tall, lean figure in plain but perfectly tailored black evening dress, bowing over their fluttering hostess's gloved hand. *Jamie*—at a ball!

As the crowd around the dance floor saw him, a wave of whispered speculation went up like a hot air balloon; everyone was as surprised, as curious, as Rose. The Duke of Byson seldom appeared at society parties now and never balls. Rose used to coax him to dances sometimes, for he was a lovely waltz partner and she had so relished spinning in his arms, but since they had parted she had never seen him on London's dance floors. Yet here he was, now, tonight.

She realised that *she* was also an object of sudden interest, of speculative glances over fans and wine glasses. Surely everyone wondered how she would react to her husband being in the same room. She knew she had to keep smiling, keep her cool-headed wits about her, as in her photos and portraits.

Or she could let them have the satisfaction of knowing their old opinions of 'wild Americans' were true after all and have a fit of temper in the middle of the ballroom. But she knew herself too well to think she could carry off something like that, no matter how fun it might be in the moment. She had learned how to cover her shyness, but not to eradicate it.

'How astonishing,' Paul said tightly. 'Who would have thought he could tear himself away from his books for an entire evening?'

'He's studying Goldoni now. Maybe it has lightened his thoughts a bit,' Rose murmured, watching Jamie as he made his way through the room, answering greetings, bowing, nodding. He looked solemn, but not uncomfortable.

Paul glanced down at her, his blond brow arched. 'How do you know this?'

'I called on him a few days ago. We had some matters to discuss.' The dance ended and Paul led her to the row of gilt chairs along the yellow silk wall before he left to find a fresh glass of champagne. She whipped open her lace fan, but it was not distraction enough when she turned and found her husband standing before her.

He bowed, his expression watchful, wary, though a polite smile touched his lips. That tiny dimple she had once loved, so rarely seen, peeped in his sun-gold cheek. He smelled lovely, of sea salt, soap, lemons and warmth. Lily waved her fan faster.

'May I have this dance?' he said, his tone something of a challenge.

Rose glanced around uncertainly. Everyone seemed most interested in their little scene, though they pretended not to be. Even Paul, starting back towards her with glasses in hand, watched her as if he was in a theatre. She thought again of wild Americans and dramatic scenes, and sighed.

'Yes, very well,' she said. 'Why not?' There were so many people around—what could really happen? She had kept her calm under much more trying moments. She rose and took his offered arm, trying to pretend he was merely one of her many admirers, her casual dance partners, but her heart would not be fooled. It pounded and stuttered beneath her silk bodice, until she feared she might faint. And that would be a good source of gossip for at least a sennight.

It was a waltz, once her favourite dance with Jamie. As the lilting music began, she slid her hand on to his, glove over glove, and stepped closer into the circle of his protective arm. She knew at once it was a great mistake. They stood the proper distance apart, surrounded by other couples, but she could sense, feel, only him. The familiar thrill of his touch, the intent way he looked down at her, the way their bodies moved together in the circling steps, as perfectly matched as they always had been.

As they flowed and swayed and turned to the music, Rose was struck by how very *easy* it all was, as if they had danced together only yesterday.

'You have caused a stir, Jamie,' she said, staring at his waistcoat, the antique cameo stickpin in his cravat, rather than looking up into those eyes. Perhaps she was afraid of what she might read there in his gaze. The memories that would drown her. 'Attending a ball, imagine that!'

He laughed, rueful and teasing and merry all at once. 'I cannot become predictable. That would be too dull.'

They spun again, her train wrapping around them for a second and then swirling free. 'Predictable' was one thing Rose had never considered Jamie. 'But surely you wouldn't want gossip?'

He shook his head. 'I never hear gossip, you know that. My dusty old poets never repeat it in their crumbling pages.'

'I seldom hear it, either. Even in the middle of parties. There are far more interesting things to think about.' Like the way Jamie's hair curled over his ears, the way his smile was crooked at the corner…

'Very wise, I am sure.' They turned again, a double spin that made her giggle and hold on to him tighter. 'Oh, Jamie! Do slow down a bit, you're making me quite giddy.'

'We can't have you feeling faint,' he said teasingly. He spun her to a halt near the half-open terrace doors, her pink skirts swaying, the cool breeze catching at her hair. 'Shall we take a stroll, a breath of fresh air?'

Rose glanced out the doors to the beckoning night, the lanterns strung along the marble balustrade. She remembered too well that other terrace, when she had been that other Rose, and he that other Jamie. When they'd first kissed, so giddy with the bubbling, joyful knowledge that they would be together always, that the future stretched before them in blue skies and sunshine, love and family. All the old demons would be banished.

How little she had known then…how young and blind she'd been. If she had known what was really lying ahead of them…

Would she have done anything different? She wasn't so sure.

She sensed eyes watching them and suddenly

needed to escape. She nodded and drew away from Jamie's arms to slip outside.

She hurried to the far, shadowed end of the terrace. More lanterns were strung in the garden beyond, making the flower beds and lawns shimmer, the leaves tossed in the wind throwing shadows on the couples who walked past, giggling softly. The air smelled fresh for London, the breeze sweeping through, catching on flowers and sending their scent towards the terrace.

Rose spun around, her brocade train twining at her legs, and found Jamie watching her, very still, very intense. It made her shiver.

'Why did you really come here tonight, Jamie?' she said through stiff lips.

A frown touched the corner of his mouth. 'To see you, of course, Rose.'

'Why? If you wished to agree to the divorce, you needed only to write to me. No need to torment yourself with parties.'

'That is just it. I do not wish to agree. Not yet.' He took a step closer, then another step, the soft wool of his sleeve brushing her bare arm. She was surrounded on all sides by that delicious sea salt, soap and lemon smell of him.

Rose stared up at him in shock. 'Wh-what do

you mean? Why would you not want to move forward with your life?'

'Because I—I still care about you,' he said, so simply, yet so very complicated.

Rose stared at him in the heavy night silence that fell around them. Even the music from the ballroom seemed hazy, distant, as if she was hearing it while underwater. Indeed, she felt as if she had tumbled down with cold waves closing over her head. She'd thought she could manage anything that came her way now, that this new Rose was a woman of the world.

She clearly was not.

'You—what?' she choked out.

His hand rose towards her and dropped again, and he shook his head. He looked as if he, too, could hardly believe what he was saying. 'I care about you and I miss you, Rose.'

'I also miss you. But you know we cannot live together again. It would become a misery for us both.'

'And that was my fault. *All* my fault. I was a fool, a blind, stumbling fool. But in these months on my own, I've learned so much about myself. I'm not the same man now as I was then, Rose.'

For one mad, whirling moment, she longed to

believe him. When she'd fled their home, hadn't she lain awake for so many nights, crying, praying? Longing for him to come to her, put his arms around her, declare these very words? Yet even then, even in the midst of her anguish, she'd realised it wouldn't, couldn't, happen. She had to guard her heart now from further pain because she surely wouldn't survive it.

She turned to look out over the garden. A couple kissed in the shadow of a tree, the lantern above them swaying, the silver moon watching it all. 'It's no good, Jamie. That was all gone, finished with so long ago.'

'Perhaps it might not be.'

Rose shivered and she heard a rustle, felt a warmth settle all around her as he laid his evening coat over her bare shoulders. 'Jamie…' she protested.

'You are cold,' he said simply. 'It's just a coat, for a moment.'

Rose swallowed hard and nodded. She remembered all the times they had done just that very thing, him wrapping her in his coat as they sat on their terrace, watching the night, talking about poetry and plays and history and their own blissful future. Cuddling close, kissing, so warm, the two of them. 'We are different people now. We've made new lives,' she choked out.

'And I don't want to take anything away from you. Never again.'

Rose studied him carefully in the half-light, trying to read his thoughts, his feelings. Yet he was still as much a mystery to her as ever. His handsome face could have been carved by a classical master and displayed in a museum. She remembered when they first married, her eager, romantic ideas of being together always, partners and allies in life. Things had not happened at all as she'd expected. *She* hadn't become the person she'd expected.

'Remember when we first married?' he said gently, as if he, too, felt suddenly brushed by those few golden, sweet days.

'Of course.'

'What would that Rose have wanted from romance?'

Rose blinked up at him. 'I—what an extraordinary question. I hardly remember what that girl wanted, what she dreamed of.'

Jamie leaned on the stone balustrade next to her, so very close, and gave her that slow, teasing smile she had once loved so very much. The smile that once made her feel such a throbbing tingle down to her very toes.

No longer, of course. His smile had no effect on her now. Well, not very much. Only for a moment, only until she thought she would giggle and blush like that old Rose, who was… Just like…

Oh, blast him!

Rose turned sharply away, staring out into the night.

'That girl existed not so long ago,' he said, his arm brushing against hers, his voice low and rough, enticing. 'What did she want?'

Rose thought hard, forcing herself to open doors she had slammed shut and locked. To walk those deserted corridors once more. She had now taught herself to live in the real world, the bright, brittle place where that old, shy, tender Rose had no place.

'I suppose she wanted what we all want,' she said slowly. 'To be respected for herself. Respected for being Rose—not Old King Coal's heiress daughter.'

And that was true, or at least part of the truth. So few people saw her as Rose, not her rich father's daughter, one of her mother's levers into grand society, her duchess sisters' little sibling.

Jamie saw *her*, he always had done, and that was a true part of their story, one she had clung to even in the midst of her turmoil. He cared nothing for her family and their money, nothing for how society saw her. She glimpsed that in him still, as he stood next to her in the darkness, his gaze so steady and intent only on her.

But it was not the whole truth. Deep in her most secret heart, she had longed to be loved. Adored. She knew now how silly that was.

'I suppose she wanted a loving marriage,' Rose said quietly. 'A real family. And—and…'

And that bright, delicate dream had been so horribly shattered.

'Oh, Rose.' He touched her hand, gently, like the old Jamie. 'You have always had that from me. You were—are—like no one else I have ever known. Just because I have been a fool, that can never erase *you*.'

Could it not? She had certainly felt *erased*, so very many times as her life had crumbled around her. One ideal after another—marriage, love, motherhood, a place as a duchess—all gone. She felt the horrible prickle of tears at her eyes and turned her head to dash them away with the back of her hand. She would not cry, not now! She had been done with tears, so long ago. And she definitely couldn't let Jamie see her cry.

'What does *this* Rose want?' he asked. 'Right now?'

She drew in a ragged breath. 'Respect, still, I suppose. Peace. And time.'

'Time?'

'Time to know herself. To think carefully. The old Rose never had that. Never wanted it, I suppose. But this Rose knows that it is essential.' The old Rose had thought she knew so much, knew everything, when she'd kissed Jamie. She'd been so sure he was her prince, that their life together would be perfect. She'd been young and naive.

'We've been apart for so long,' he said. 'Is that not time enough?'

Rose looked at him and she couldn't help but smile. He did still look like her Jamie, young and slightly baffled, his hair tousled by the wind. 'Oh, Jamie. You study things hundreds of years old, plumb knowledge hard-won by centuries of thinkers. Of course there has not been enough time. I've barely come to realise—certain things. A few tiny things.'

'What sorts of things?' he asked, his tone deeply interested.

Things like—she was stronger than she'd once imagined. Her life was worth living in peace. Love should not hurt. And that everything was so very, very confusing.

'Things such as being able to rely on myself, of course,' she said. 'Learning to see the world as it is, not as I wish it would be, and making my way through it all, by myself. Learning—learning not to feel pain, or cause it, any longer.'

'Rose. Oh, Rose, my dear.' He gently, slowly, took her into his arms. Rose stiffened for an instant, afraid she would cry, would cling to him, but she relaxed into his warm strength for a moment, letting herself be absorbed by him again. 'I never wanted to give you an instant of pain. I had no idea how to be married, either…how to be in this real world you mention. But I should have known. I was handed a precious jewel and should have guarded it with everything in me. I should have told you every moment how gloriously beautiful you are, how I treasured your kind heart, your laughter…'

Rose ached at his words, the very words she had once longed for so much. She shook her head.

'Give me a bit of that time, Rose, and I will show you,' he whispered.

He lowered his head, slowly, so slowly, as she stared up at him, mesmerised by his velvet-dark eyes, those eyes she knew so well, had once been so utterly lost in…

At last, his lips touched hers. Slow, soft, almost gentle, as he brushed his mouth back and forth over hers, pressing little, questing kisses to her lower lip. Those slow caresses, though, the kisses she had always loved so much from Jamie, ignited something deep inside of her, some need she had thought she'd successfully buried. She curled her hands into his coat and pulled him closer.

He groaned deeply, his tongue twined with hers, his arms around her. She could sense, though, the tension in his lean body, that he was still holding back after all that had happened between them.

But Rose feared she did *not* want him away from her! She still craved what they once had, craved *him*. Even though she was quite sure this was a terrible idea, she couldn't stop herself.

His lips slid from hers, down along her cheek, unerringly seeking out the tiny, sensitive spot below her ear that always made her shiver, as he well knew. She gasped and sought his lips again.

Barely had their lips touched again when

something did break through her delightful haze—the memory that this was *Jamie*. Her husband. Her estranged husband.

Rose stumbled back, all her hard-won stillness and peace, that sparkling shell she'd built so carefully, piece by piece, starting to crack. She couldn't let it. She *wouldn't* let herself be vulnerable to him again. It would spell disaster for her.

'I must go,' she gasped. She handed back his coat and suddenly all the chill of the night, of the whole world, rushed at her again. She dared not stay a moment longer, or the old Rose, the Rose who'd craved Jamie's love so very much, might surface again. She spun around and ran towards the glass doors, towards the lights and music and the blessed distraction of the ball.

'Rose!' he called hoarsely, but she didn't look back. She had to keep moving forward, ever forward, no matter what.

He was the biggest damn fool that ever lived.

Jamie made his way back down the terrace steps to the shadowed, lantern-shaded garden, avoiding the people who strolled there. He doubted he could make any sort of light conversation at the moment. His mind was all in pieces.

He ran his fingers through his hair, leaving the waves disordered. He had kissed Rose. *Rose!* His wife, the woman who had haunted his dreams for so many months, the woman he had stupidly allowed to slip through his fingers.

Yet she had tasted as sweet as ever, just as intoxicating. And something deep inside of him, something he'd thought had died when she left him, had burst back to fiery life. Powerful and primitive and wonderful.

He kicked at a stone in the pathway with a muttered curse. When he touched her, kissed her, he hadn't been thinking at all—that burning lust he had always felt for Rose completely took over and he'd *had* to taste her. And then— oh, glorious, awful moment—she'd kissed him back.

What was the right thing to do now? How could he ever win her back? Did he dare even think such a thing was possible? He had to dare. It was the most important chance he'd ever had to take in his entire life.

Chapter Four

A Lady in Society Tells All

Did you see the new hat the Duchess of B. wore to Lady L.'s tea yesterday? I am sure you did, as did this Author.

Everyone will be wearing just such a chapeau next week, of course. The American Rose always sets the style. I dare say even the Duke of B., buried in his dusty tomes, shall take notice...

'I'm not sure about this one. What do you think, Rose? You're so much more *au courant* about these things.'

Rose sipped at her tea and watched as Lily examined herself in the mirror of Madame Varens's exclusive millinery shop, turning this way and that to make the plumes dance. Once upon a time, when Stella Wilkins would drag her daughters behind her to every couturier in New York, Rose hadn't enjoyed shopping at all. It was tedious and confusing and she'd always ended up with frocks and hats she didn't like. But now that she could make her own choices, now that she had learned about the construction of gowns and hats, she found it all a fascinating challenge.

It was also a fun distraction, especially when her sisters joined her. They could happily spend hours in the shops, teasing each other, laughing, making all the proprietors happy with large orders so they were eager to see the Wilkins sisters again.

Lily pursed her lips and tweaked critically at a ribbon. 'Is it quite suitable for Court events, do you think? One must be stylish while accompanying Princess Alexandra, of course, as she is such a great *noticer* of hats, but one must never be *more* stylish than her.'

'You have the best taste, Lily,' Rose said and it was very true. Lily had made Aidan's crumbling old castle into a showplace of quiet elegance and her gowns were always among the prettiest at any party. But she was never a show-off or flashy bright.

Violet laughed and popped a bonbon into her mouth. 'I notice you didn't ask *me*, Lily! Perhaps you're afraid I would recommend that green-and-yellow taffeta monstrosity in the case over there.'

'Madame la duchesse!' Madame Varens protested. 'That is the very latest style from Paris.'

'Oh, I meant no insult. Indeed, I am very tempted to try it on myself,' Violet assured her. 'I needn't worry what the Princess thinks, or anyone at all really.' And Violet never did have to worry, Rose thought with a sad little pang. Her William always thought her the most beautiful lady in all the world, who could do no possible wrong.

As Violet hurried across the salon to try on the hat, Rose turned away to take a sip of the tea. It had grown cool and a black silk-clad assistant jumped forward to hand her a fresh cup. Even after all this time, Rose was amazed at how a duchess was treated in every shop where she showed her face. It must be how it had felt to be Cleopatra.

'It's a very pretty hat on you, Lily, and you should take it,' Rose said.

'If *you* say so, then I certainly shall,' Lily said. She handed off the feathered confection to be packed in one of Madame's pink-striped boxes and sat down beside Rose to take up her own tea.

'Will La Duchesse de Byson not try something on?' Madame Varens asked hopefully. The last time Rose had worn one of Madame's creations, an adorable little purple silk tricorne trimmed in net, every lady in London had besieged the store wanting one.

Rose sighed as she thought of the rows and stacks of hatboxes in her wardrobe room. She didn't need another; if she and Jamie did divorce, she wouldn't ever have to worry about impressing the Princess again. But Madame Varens did look so hopeful, Rose hadn't the heart to say no.

'Of course, *madame*,' she said. 'I would love to see your very newest creations.'

As Madame Varens and her assistants hurried away to fetch the new hats, Lily and Rose watched Violet spin around in the bright chapeau. Even the garish colours looked amazing next to her vivid beauty.

'I think I shall take it!' she cried. 'It will look astonishing in a photograph, with the ribbons like so.'

Lily and Rose laughed. 'I shouldn't really advise it, Vi,' Rose said.

'La, I should not go against the American Beauty Rose when it comes to fashion,' Violet giggled, relishing that silly new nickname from the gossip columns, naming Rose after the brand-new blossom a French botanist had created.

'I heard the Baddely ball was quite—interesting,' Lily said quietly, gesturing for more tea. 'Did Jamie really show up there?'

'Jamie at a ball?' Violet gasped. 'Wonders will never cease.'

'He did show up there, yes, and we danced,' Rose murmured. 'It was all very civilised.'

'Had you spoken to him about—about your idea for the future?' Lily said.

'Yes, but not at the ball. I haven't become that much of a hoyden,' Rose answered. 'I went to the house earlier and we had a conversation.' She took a long drink, thinking about that visit, about being in the memory-haunted house again.

'You went to the house?' Violet said, pursing her lips in concern, but Madame Varens returned then, followed by several assistants carefully bearing feathered, flowered creations.

'We haven't finished this conversation,' Violet whispered ominously and Rose sighed. She adored her sisters, but they never did let anything go. She hardly knew what to tell them, when she barely understood her own thoughts.

After the hats were purchased and packed for delivery, Rose and her sisters set out towards their favourite tea shop. As it was a sunny day, and not far away, Lily sent her carriage ahead so they could walk and window-shop, but they soon regretted that decision. Someone recognised Rose and a small crowd grew around them, staring with wide eyes.

'My, but it *is* a pretty jacket she wears!' someone whispered loudly. 'But she's such a wee thing. You wouldn't think that from the photographs.'

'I should find me a hat like that.'

'Ain't she pretty? So young and fresh! How can her husband ever be like that to such a lass?' The woman called out cheerfully, 'You pay him no mind, luv! Plenty of fish in the sea, eh?'

'You're too good for him, Duchess dearie,' an old lady declared stoutly, banging her stick on the frame of her window.

Rose didn't know whether to laugh or sob.

She gave them a little half-smile, a wave, and took her sisters' arms tightly as they hurried on their way.

'Is it like this every time you go out, Rose?' Violet asked.

'Only when I walk,' Rose said. 'And forget my veiled hat.'

'That *A Lady in Society* nonsense,' Lily said with a tsk. 'Spreading silly gossip all over the place.'

'Well, they're not entirely wrong, are they?' Violet said acerbically.

'That there *are* plenty of fish in the sea?' Rose laughed.

'Well, yes. Of course there are. Though Aidan is a pretty salmon and my Will is more of a trout,' Violet said musingly. 'You deserve a prize Dover sole, Rose, and if Jamie can't be that and can't appreciate the great jewel he has in you, then you should pay him no mind any longer.'

'Violet,' Lily said, half chiding, half approving.

They reached the tea shop at last, still trailed by a few admirers, two or three of whom dared ask for autographs, until they ducked inside. The rosy-cheeked, motherly proprietor, Mrs

Antheil, who knew them well, quickly ushered them to their favourite table in a quiet, curtained alcove. Rose sank down gratefully in the pink-cushioned chair, breathing in the cinnamon-scented quiet and the dim light that covered her blush. She knew she would have to become accustomed some day to gossip and speculation, especially if she and Jamie formally, publicly separated, but she would never like the attention very much.

Not that gossip about her was anything new. Not with such a rich father, not with two sisters who had snatched up two rare eligible dukes, not with her own youthful marriage, then becoming a duchess herself. She wondered what a new life, a *really* new life, might be like. A quiet place in the country, or maybe abroad somewhere, France or Italy or a sunny little Greek island. A place where she wasn't American Beauty Rose, where she could just be *Rose*. Whoever that was. What would she be again without the newspapers and gossips and photographs?

A pink-aproned maid brought the tea, an elaborate tiered tray of sandwiches and cakes and sweets. Violet eagerly reached for a cucumber sandwich and put one of Rose's favourite raspberry tarts on her plate to tempt her, but Rose found she had no appetite. As so often lately, all her worries seemed to tighten around her stomach and she could barely swallow anything.

'You should try to eat a few bites, Rose darling,' Lily said gently. 'Maybe a cucumber sandwich? Something light.'

Rose gave her a bright smile, one of her masks. 'In a moment, of course. Right now I need some tea and to catch my breath after such a dash.'

Her sisters nodded. After a few minutes of light chatter about hats and parties, Lily poured out more tea and said, 'Rose dearest, if you are so very unhappy you must, of course, do whatever you possibly can to change that. Aidan and I, and Violet and William, shall always stand by you.'

'And whatever fishes I might catch?' Rose teased, but she felt rather sad. She bent her head and took a quick drink of tea to cover the sudden sheen to her eyes.

Lily's lips quirked. 'Yes, them, too, even a humble perch. But perhaps Jamie could use one more chance.'

Rose glanced between her sisters, remembering how fond they had once been of Jamie. How his love of art had appealed to Violet; the two of them could talk of paintings and light and composition for hours. And Lily had liked his kindness and easy-going ways, his love of poetry—before it all changed. 'Do you really think so?'

Lily gently held up her hand. 'I know he has not been all that you deserve in a husband. You were once very happy with him though, yes?'

'Yes, I was. Once.' Rose stared into the dark swirls of her tea and let some of the memories she had so ruthlessly pushed away flood back over her. Laughing with Jamie, sitting in the sunshine holding hands, the sweet hours wrapped in bed together. Kisses and caresses.

How had it all ended so badly?

'And now he even shows up at balls to see you!' Lily said. 'Did he behave well?'

Rose thought of twirling around the dance floor with him, standing in the night silence wrapped in his coat. Their passionate embrace. 'Yes, of course. Jamie is not a boor, you know. He never mistreated me physically in any way. He says he is sorry, that he's changed. But...'

Lily smiled. 'Perhaps, then, if it was made very clear to him that he has only this one chance to make things right, he could indeed make it happen. If he still loves you, as I am sure he must.'

'He would be an utter fool not to love Rose,' Violet declared. 'But if he has behaved so badly, he does *not* deserve her!'

'No, indeed. Violet is entirely correct,' Lily said. 'Yet if he sees his mistakes, if he makes proper amends—perhaps he could have one more chance?'

Rose glanced again between her sisters. Lily looked hopeful, Violet doubtful. Just as she herself felt with Jamie, always caught between hope and doubt. It was true Jamie was never physically threatening; it was not like Newport all over again, that one terrible night which still haunted her. But he had scarred her heart nonetheless.

'I shall give it some thought while I am at Pryde Abbey.' She always seemed to be able to think more clearly there, in the quiet and the freedom.

'If you *do* give him one more chance and he dares behave badly again,' Violet declared, 'then he shall have to deal with *me*.'

Rose laughed. It was true—no matter what happened, she always had her sisters.

* * *

'Byson? Oh, it *is* you! How fascinating to see you here. Though I suppose you often come to Hatchard's, of course.'

Jamie glanced up from the book he was perusing to see a lady beaming at him from beneath an enormous, flower-bedecked hat, blue and white and pink like her lace-trimmed, loose Aesthetic dress. 'Lady Madewell?'

Everyone knew Lady Madewell, of course, the mistress of Pryde Abbey, patron of artists and writers and free thinkers of all sorts. Jamie knew that she was friends with Rose and was thus rather surprised she would be smiling at him in such a friendly fashion.

He gave her a bow. 'How very nice to see you again. It has been too long.'

'Oh, yes, Lord M. and I recently returned from a Tuscan sojourn! We brought back the most delightful sculptures for our gardens at Pryde.' She tilted her head, watching him speculatively. 'In fact, we are having a little house party to show them off and it should be such fun. You must come!'

Jamie was startled. Pryde Abbey was not a place for men like him. 'How kind you are. But I fear…'

Lady Madewell waved her lace-gloved hand as if to brush away his words. 'No, I shall not accept a refusal. Your mother and I were such friends as girls, you know, and I have longed to see more of you for years. Your own scholarly work is so fascinating. You would fit right in at my home.' She smiled slyly. 'And Rose will be there. Such a grand surprise for her.'

Jamie was not at all sure Rose would find his appearance at the party a 'grand surprise'. He had heard of her new life among the artists and poets, the way they idolised her beauty. He had no right to interfere in her happiness. Yet ever since their kiss on that moonlit terrace, he had not been able to stop thinking about her. Of the scent of her perfume, the taste of her lips, the way she'd moved under his touch. How very much he'd missed her.

'We *are* very fond of Rose,' Lady Madewell said emphatically. 'All of us. Such a darling girl. And she has so many admirers…'

Admirers better for her than him? 'I am not at all surprised by that.'

'No. I suppose you would not be.' She gently touched his arm for an instant. 'Well, I shall send you an invitation to our little party. Perhaps there would be a chance for you and our

Rose to talk, away from all this London hubbub. The rest, Byson, I fear shall be up to you. I shall leave you to your books. Good day.'

She wandered away, calling greetings to friends, leaving Jamie looking after her in astonishment. He wasn't sure what had just happened, but he did know he would not let this opportunity slip away.

Chapter Five

A Lady in Society Tells All

*And where is the handsome Lord J. G.?
This Column's sources say not at home
with his fair lady, even after she was
rushed so very swiftly from a grand ball
last week so pale that all nearby feared
greatly for her. Nor at his usual haunt in
the British Library.*

*It's all a great mystery, is it not? Or
perhaps a lesson for our young men of
old family name—American brides might
be attractive on the honeymoon night, but
not to preside over ancient halls of This
Sceptred Isle...*

Rose dropped the gossip column to the carpet,
her fingers suddenly numb, and rolled over in

the rumpled sheets of her bed. If only she could be done with all that, give away the Sceptred Isle and just have the one day Jamie had taken her walking in the park after that fateful garden party. As they'd laughed and held hands, and he'd kissed her cheek under the cover of her parasol. In that moment, all the world had seemed to stretch before them in golden, beautiful promise. She would have all she dreamed of—love, a place to belong, a place where she could be herself.

If only they could start again, move forward only from that moment! But they could not. It had only been a dream, after all, and she was heartily sick of the life it became. The loneliness that had crept up between them, the misunderstanding and silence. She didn't know how to fix it, not now.

She slid back down under her blankets. It was so dark outside her window, a bottomless black it was so late. Yet when Jenny tried to close the curtains, Rose wouldn't let her. The night brought a strange comfort, quiet and invisible and lonely. She thought of all the parties she'd once rushed to, seeking that forgetfulness in music and champagne and laughter.

She pressed her hand to her stomach, so

flat again beneath her nightdress. The bump that had been there, bringing her such joy, was gone. Lost in pain and blood and Jamie hadn't been there. Not when she'd first felt the cramps at that wretched ball and Aidan and Lily had rushed her home; not when the doctor had come and shaken his head. Jamie had been off somewhere with his scholarly friends, students who gathered at pubs, drinking and arguing about poetry and history. She was alone with that hollow ache, the cold knowledge that she had failed in her duty.

She knew she couldn't go on like this much longer. She felt as if she was made of glass and would crack in the heat.

Suddenly, she heard a sound from downstairs, a crash, a muffled voice, so loud in the silent house. Rose carefully climbed out of her bed and reached for her dressing gown. She slowly inched her way out to the staircase landing and peeped down at the hall.

Jamie sat sprawled on the lower steps, candlelight flickering over him. He had knocked over a pier table, scattering the silver card tray, the Chinese vase and the Roman bust on to the floor. He studied the mess with a strangely sad expression on his handsome face. For a mo-

ment, he looked like the man she had married. Yet now he was thinner, greyer, his eyes dull, his hair too long. Could he possibly be tired of this life, too? Could they maybe start again? She still dared to hope; she couldn't help it.

She took a step down the stairs and Jamie glanced up at her. He did look like her old Jamie, stark, young, sweet, but then he gave a crooked, wild grin that was not Jamie-like at all.

He pushed back a wave of tousled black hair and held out a shaking hand to her. There was a blotchy wine stain on his cuff and, as she tiptoed cautiously closer, she smelled the sweet, acrid scent of wine hovering like a cloud around him.

'Rose! My lovely, lovely wife,' he cried.

'I couldn't sleep,' she answered. In truth, she hadn't slept in days. She wanted her husband; she wanted her lost, tiny daughter back. She knelt beside him and smoothed his hair. He tugged her closer, kissing her hard, hungrily, but not like her husband's usual kisses. This one was desperate, tasting of sour wine. She drew back.

He fell back on to the floor. 'You should have come with me. Our friends missed you.'

'Our friends?' She barely knew most of the

people Jamie met now and they did not know her, not really. She wasn't a scholar and they didn't know what to make of her. It wouldn't get better any time soon; she felt so shy outside the house now, as though any time in the light would melt her. 'I don't feel like going to parties yet.'

'I'm sure you will be soon. You are the toast of every gathering.' He seized her hand and kissed it. She closed her eyes, sure he didn't even see her any more. Not really. 'I hate it when you feel ill.'

She sat down on the step beside him. 'Perhaps we could take a little holiday? A few weeks in the country? We could stay with Lily and Aidan. She's been inviting us for days.' Her sisters had visited so often, sitting beside her, talking incessantly, trying to hold her up. She didn't know what she would do without them, though they exhausted her, too. 'You could study there.' And they could talk there, really talk, be Rose and Jamie again.

But Jamie laughed and shook his head. 'Go off to the country now? It's hardly the time for that. I have too much work to do. And you should stay close to your doctors.'

'Why not?' she whispered, trying to hold

back tears. She felt hollow and cold again. 'I am so tired. Maybe I'll go alone to see Lily.'

He closed his eyes, as if already weary of this, of her. It was so very far from what she'd once imagined. 'Of course, if you like. You will be back before the end of the Season?'

Rose nodded, but she had the feeling she wouldn't be back, not to this house. She had to find herself again, she was so lost.

Jamie gave a soft snore and she glanced down to see he had fallen into sleep right there where he sat. He looked beautiful, almost peaceful, as if he had already floated out of their troubled lives. She leaned down and gently kissed his cheek one last time.

'I am sorry, my darling,' she whispered. 'You will certainly be better off without me.'

She rose to her feet and stepped over him, going back to her chamber and shutting the door softly behind her. It didn't even make a sound in that dark house that had never really been hers.

Rose came awake with a gasp, her throat closed, paralysed. She reached out in the shadows and grasped a handful of her sheets, her hand shaking. She realised the bedclothes were twisted around her, holding her bound as tightly as the past seemed to be tonight. She shoved them away and scrambled out of bed to fumble for her candle.

She seldom dreamed about her old life now. Keeping busy with parties and charities and visits and travel sometimes made her sleep a little deeper at night. Yet it seemed that seeing Jamie so much lately, talking about him with her sisters, had brought it all back. Would she ever be free of it?

She put on her dressing gown, wrapping the quilted satin folds around herself, and went to stir up the fire. Surely she was only chilled.

As the flames caught and flared in bright orange light, she saw the stack of invitations lying in piles on the mantel. Thick, creamy cards asking her to come to dances and teas and dinners and theatres. Asking her to laugh and forget. She did enjoy the parties very much. When she was there, with the lights and music and people, she couldn't think about much at all. But at night, like this—at night it was very different. In that darkness, there was nothing but memories. Those days with Jamie, the good and the bad. His kisses, the wondrous way it felt when he touched her, the sun of his smiles. It made her want to cry for what was lost.

When she had walked down the aisle, when she had said her vows, it had been the most true, most beautiful thing she'd ever experienced. She wanted only to be his wife. But nothing had turned out as she'd expected. And when their baby, their last hope, was gone...

She had seen they did not want the same things and she had been too young to realise that when she married him.

She dropped down on to a *chaise* and stared into the flames. She dared to let herself go back, back, into the past, for that moment. Jamie said he had changed and, in the glimpses she'd had of him at his house, at the ball, she did long to believe him. But she had once touched *those* flames and been singed. Her happiness had blown away on a cold wind. She'd once believed he was different from other men, so different from the man in Newport...

Lily and Violet dared to hope he'd changed, too. She had seen it in their eyes at the tea shop today. She trusted her sisters and knew they wanted only her happiness. If *they* thought he could, maybe she could, too?

Rose gave a choked sob and shook her head.

She wanted to believe it, oh, she did! If her own Jamie was still there, if there could be a new beginning for the two of them—yet she also feared.

It had to be on him now to show that they could rebuild their marriage, if that was what he truly wanted. She had tried and tried, until she had thought she would go mad. She had thought she *was* mad and couldn't trust herself any longer to tell truth from reality. She couldn't do that again now. She had to guard her heart, both from him and especially from herself.

Chapter Six

Rose sat back on the velvet carriage seat, smoothing her gloves, her skirts, and straightening her hat. She couldn't understand why she couldn't sit still, couldn't quiet her mind. Usually when she left for Pryde Abbey there was only excitement, anticipation, a happy feeling of release from the crowds of London, from being followed and speculated about the way she had been outside the tea shop. There were always so many artists at Pryde, of course, and sometimes they wanted to sketch her portrait, but it was never like in London. There, in those narrow old halls, it was all about the art, about the opportunity to just sit and be.

It was, in fact, exactly as she had once imagined her own house might be. Hers and Jamie's.

She took a deep breath and glanced out the

window. The sooty city had given way to the green of the countryside, hedges flashing past in a blur of celadon and emerald, the sky clearing overhead. Pryde was not far from London itself, in Middlesex, yet it felt like leaving her own life quite behind, heading into something like *A Midsummer Night's Dream*. She felt in need of the escape more than ever this time.

Surely it was seeing Jamie so much lately, when she'd spent months working so hard to forget him, that was nagging at her now. Of course it would snatch at old wounds, they had barely had time to heal as it was. Her dreams of him at night, the memories of their days together, good and bad, needed more time to fade, that was all. She just wished the forgetting would hurry up and happen.

'Enough,' she whispered.

The carriage turned through an open pair of gates, flanked by stone columns topped not with the usual lions or family crests but with marble statues of Apollo and Dionysus, the intellect *and* fun Pryde Abbey stood for. Rose smiled and felt her shoulders relax a tiny bit. She was only Rose here.

The drive to the old house was twisting and sharply winding, deliberately designed to reveal delightful little vistas of gleaming white statues and iron benches set in shadowy groves, little follies of domes and columns, a lake lined with docks and rope swings. There were already boaters dotting the shining waters, a few hardy swimmers diving into the chilly waters, artists with their easels set up to capture the late-summer scenes. The trees were beginning to shade from vivid green to gold at the edges, the flowers dropping their petaled heads under the breeze. The light was becoming amber, diffusing through the clouds, giving everything a jewel-like glow.

Rose, too, felt as if she was dropping into a new dimension, a place where everything shone and sparkled like a Byzantine mosaic. Where nothing was quite like it seemed, all was a painting, a poem. The Rose she had become, famous for her face, her gowns, her money, her marriage, but her heart and thoughts all unseen, didn't exist here.

She remembered how she'd once longed to bring Jamie here with her, when Violet had first introduced her to this artistic idyll. She had wanted Jamie to be free, too, to laugh. To help her find that happiness she'd once hoped they could share. That they could save each other with their love. If only…

'Such silly words,' she told herself. *If only.* Life was as it was. She could only control the tiny part she held in her own hands.

The carriage turned again and at last the house came into view. As always, Rose's breath caught a bit at the sight. Pryde had been an abbey centuries ago and the central part of the building retained its pillared walkways, its old stone walls and towers, its small, mullioned windows, but the wings to either side were newer, pale stone faced in red brick, festooned in swags of ivy. It was ramshackle, seemingly grown organically out of the landscape, not a place designed to appeal to Lily's royal circles. In fact, more modish people sometimes laughed and called it 'Downfall Abbey', but among more artistic types it was practically Valhalla.

Rose studied the gardens that spread around the house, expanses of rolling green perfect for lawn tennis and croquet, rambling flower beds spilling pink, white, red, yellow, purple blossoms on to the gravel walkways. Bending trees shaded white wicker furniture, bowers for quiet conversations and tea parties, all allowed to run a little wild. It gave her such a breath of fresh, green-scented air.

Rose also loved the people she saw gathered there: musicians playing their violins and cellos under those trees, artists, poets, even actors. It was all just a tiny bit outside respectability. Her mother would have hated it, which made Rose love it even more, and made her glad she would still have this sanctuary to come to whenever she needed it in the future, regardless of what happened between her and Jamie.

The carriage rolled to a stop in front of the portico, a shady stone canopy leading to shallow, pitted old marble steps and the half-open doors, painted red and hung with a worn brass knocker shaped like an ancient Venetian lion. As a footman helped Rose alight, Lady Madewell herself rushed out the door, a sea of spaniels around her feet.

'My darling Rose!' she cried, kissing Rose on both cheeks in a cloud of French vetiver perfume. 'Was it a hideous journey?'

Rose laughed. 'Not at all, though I always feel like I've come to a different universe in only a few miles.' Rose often thought that if she could have chosen a mother, Lady Madewell would be it. Unlike Stella Wilkins and her golden-groomed, Worth-clad, socially ambitious perfection, Lady Madewell exuded welcome, vivacity and sincere happiness. A tall, plump woman, a great beauty in her youth who had grown into handsomeness with dark, silver-threaded hair piled high in a haphazard knot, dimpled cheeks, sparkling sky-blue eyes and fluttering hands decorated with antique carnelian and topaz rings. She refused to wear corsets and bustles, as did so many of the artistic ladies who frequented her salons, but wore loose gowns in pale silks and muslins, Indian shawls and stacks of gold bangles that made music as she gestured.

Yes, Rose thought, she did wish Lady Madewell had been her mother. Or perhaps she wished she could be Lady Madewell herself, so free, so unconcerned, so loved, so firmly embedded in her own sense of self.

'Now, do come in, my dear, I know you'll want to rest a while before tea and then you'll be positively besieged by admirers, as usual! Our great celebrity beauty.' Lady Madewell laughed. She linked her arm in Rose's and led her through the doors, the cool shade of the house dazzling after the bright day. 'Monsieur

LeClerc is visiting from Paris, still so insistent he must paint your portrait.'

Ordinarily Rose would blush hotly at being called a 'celebrity beauty'. She would never have imagined such a thing a few years ago, nor would her family. Rose was merely Rose, small, thin, elfin. But after Violet had exhibited her photograph, it caught attention from other artists and her modelling services were in much demand, more and more as the months went on. She did sometimes still wonder at it all, but Lady Madewell's friends were so casual about it all, so sure she had a vital role to play as a 'muse' among them, that she didn't mind. If her husband was not able to admire her, then at least others could. 'I doubt he will have the time.'

'Oh, nonsense! A few quick sketches, a few *"Ma chère, tres jolie!"* comments and he will be happy as a lamb!' Lady Madewell led her through the haphazardly connected rooms, filled with uneven parquet floors, low, dark-beamed ceilings, brick fireplaces and Morris-papered walls, chatting about the guests and London gossip and new gallery exhibits she had seen, the dogs barking around them. A few people Rose knew called greetings from sagging old sofas and chairs beside overflowing bookcases, behind velvet-curtained window seats.

'Paul Adelman should be arriving this evening,' Lady Madewell said oh so casually as she led Rose up the winding old staircase, carved with elaborate flowers and vines and lined with dusty portraits. 'You two seemed to get along so well at our last dinner party! And then won every hand at bridge together, which was so unfair.'

Rose shook her head. 'He is very charming indeed.'

'Great beauties like you should never be alone, my dear, it is against nature,' Lady Madewell declared. They made their way along narrow, twisting corridors, hung with faded tapestries and new paintings from recent guests, including a photograph of the lake, shimmering with sunset light, by Violet. The dogs' paws clicked on the bare wooden floors.

'I am perfectly content as I am, Lady Madewell,' Rose assured her, smiling even as she tried to make herself believe that, too.

'Oh, my dear girl, believe me, I, too, have felt the sting of love's disappointment! But life is too short to live cloistered for long.'

'Lord Madewell seems very devoted to you,'

Rose protested, thinking of the way the man's eyes followed his wife wherever she went, the way they laughed and whispered together. She quite envied them.

Lady Madewell gave a silvery laugh. 'Oh, indeed! But we were not always so content, you know. I was young and romantic once, too, but alas never as lovely as you.'

They went past rows of closed doors, each with a printed card in its little gold slot proclaiming who was in that chamber. It was all very discreet, very proper, like all the other house parties Rose attended where certain people were placed carefully near the right other people. She had never participated in that little game herself, but maybe that day was approaching.

Rose's room was near the end of the corridor, the chamber she usually stayed in at Pryde. She noticed that the next door to hers bore no card.

Lady Madewell hurried around the room, opening the pink satin curtains to reveal a view of the back gardens and the lake beyond, letting the sunlight in on the white and gilt bed hung with more pink satin, the pretty mirrored dressing table, the flower paintings on the pink-striped walls.

'The Rose Room, of course, is all yours, my dear,' she said, nudging a pink slipper chair into place beside the white marble fireplace.

Rose unpinned her hat and took a deep breath. 'I do love it, thank you. It's the perfect room.'

'Well, do come down as soon as you're settled,' Lady Madewell said. She turned to leave, but then seemed to hesitate. 'My dear Rose, I feel I must confess something before you are taken quite by surprise. I have been rather naughty.'

Rose laughed. 'You, naughty? Never!'

Lady Madewell laughed, too, but it sounded rather embarrassed, her cheeks turning as pink as the curtains. 'Not an entirely new thing, of course, but this is—well, sometimes one must be polite, of course. I met the Duke a few days ago and he did look rather at a loose end, the poor lamb, so I asked him here for the weekend.'

Rose was stunned. 'The—the Duke? Which duke?'

Lady Madewell laughed again, nudging her toe along the flower-woven carpet. 'Byson, of course. It was most strange, as he has never been here before, but he seemed so eager to see the house. Yet I am sure it will be quite all right, my dear, we have so many guests coming you will hardly see him and you two *have* learned to get along, I'm sure.'

'I suppose we have,' Rose whispered. She and Jamie had never not 'got along', not really. In public, anyway. In private—oh, in private, there had been such happiness, until the quarrels came. Until the loneliness, the misunderstandings, the isolation. His absorbing studies, his brandy. Her parties. The silence. Her miscarriage. More silence. At least the people here liked her, really talked to her, despite her shyness and doubts.

But, yes, they got along now. In a fashion.

She flashed Lady Madewell one of her most brilliant smiles, the surface smile of photos and paintings. 'You must not worry on my account, Lady Madewell. Everyone enjoys your parties, and I'm glad to see Jamie might become one of them.' For whatever reason he chose to be there *now*. She had once tried so hard to get him to attend parties with her. Why now? Why, when it could no longer matter? Was he so serious about convincing her he'd changed that he'd throw himself into doing things he'd always hated? How would that make them any happier together if he was getting by on sufferance?

Lady Madewell clapped her hands happily. 'I'm so glad you don't mind, my dear! The more the merrier at Pryde, I always say. And if the Duke becomes a nuisance—though I could hardly imagine it of him, such a quiet young man—darling Paul, your parfit knight, shall be on hand.'

Jenny and a parade of footmen arrived, bearing Rose's trunks and hatboxes, and Lady Madewell gave a relieved smile. 'I shall let you freshen up, then, my dear, and then we'll see you at tea! Anon, anon.' She rushed out in a flurry of silk and barking spaniels.

Rose let her smile droop and turned to stare out the window as Jenny set about unpacking. The lawns were still green, the flowers still bright, the people gathered on their wicker chairs and on the croquet field still laughing. All was the same as before, but her sanctuary had the smallest rip in it now, letting in the cold from outside. Jamie was coming here.

She closed her eyes, and some of the old memories she'd fought against forced themselves back into her mind…

'What do you want, Rose? What will make you happy? You have everything here!'

Rose had felt the sharp tingle of tears be-

hind her eyes and she hadn't known what to do, where to turn.

'All I want is time together! All I want is—is my husband...'

How could he not know that? she'd asked herself. Did he not feel it, too? It had been so different when they'd first married, those long nights and mornings in bed, kissing, laughing, whispering, wrapped up together. Now he was gone all the time.

Jamie had given an exasperated sigh and run his fingers through his hair. 'I went to the Keatings' with you last night.'

'To a ball.'

A ball he hadn't wanted to attend, where they'd danced once and then he'd vanished into the library with his friends. She had dressed so carefully for the party, too, changed her hair three times, worried and fretted.

Surely a pretty wife, a charming wife, was important to a family like his. It was why he'd married her, after all. She'd tried so hard to be correct, to be English. To be what Jamie needed. It was all so confusing.

And they had not made love when they'd come home. Usually that was one thing she could count on, one thing to cling to. The two of them alone in the darkness, when he was only with her. That was their marriage; those were the things she had sought so fervently.

Yet it had slipped away and she hadn't known how to hold on to it...

There was a shout, a burst of muffled laughter, from the garden below her window, and Rose opened her eyes to find that the awful day of long ago was gone. She had to stay strong now to find her real path forward. She had nothing to fear from Jamie.

Nothing at all.

Jamie wasn't at all sure he should have come.

Pryde Abbey wasn't his usual sort of haunt. Everyone knew Lady Madewell, of course, and many of his writer friends moved in her milieu. She had been friends with George Eliot, her parents had known Dickens and she often invited writers and scholars to these parties, people Jamie would very much like to meet, but he had never been asked there before. Dukes generally weren't. Until Rose, until she'd burst out of her quiet shell and into a place Jamie couldn't fathom.

He reminded himself he was there for Rose. To show her he had changed. He would go anywhere, do anything for Rose. He had to show her that. Had to show himself, too, that he could be worthy of her again, at last and for ever.

He stepped down from the carriage. Dread and resolve and wild, passionate hope that he would soon see Rose again fought inside him, a crazy, roiling mixture. He had to laugh at himself—no wonder he had buried himself in his studies for so long. History long past had little power to unsettle him, to turn everyday life completely upside down as his beautiful wife did. As she had ever since the day he'd met her.

Pryde Abbey was completely unlike his proper London town house, and not much like his father's country seat, Greensted Castle, except in something of its old untidiness. He still thought of the castle as his father's house, his brother's, though it was now his in its unwieldy immensity. Pryde was also ramshackle, ivy-covered, sprawling in every direction as if it had sprung up there magically, a fairy-tale house where anything might happen.

Jamie had never envisaged himself in such a place, a spot of freedom, even chaos, yet he took heart from the sight of it now. Perhaps here, far from where he had long hidden from any emotions, something new would sparkle into being. If he could only break down his own damnable walls.

Lady Madewell hurried from the dim recesses of her enchanted house, smiling and holding out her hand, bangle bracelets jingling. Just as Pryde was different from London and Greensted, Lady Madewell was the opposite of what his mother had once been, the last of a long line of proper, shrinking, solemn duchesses drifting through dark halls. Lady Madewell was plump and rosy and smiling, vibrating with energy and welcoming kindness.

She was, Jamie realised with a shock, exactly what Rose might one day be if happy, contented years stretched behind her. If he could give her those years.

'My dear Duke! I'm so happy we could lure you to Pryde at last,' Lady Madewell said. 'I already told you I knew your mother when I was a girl, but I also knew your late uncle, a bit later on.'

Jamie laughed, thinking of his black sheep uncle. The one spot of laughter at Greensted when he was a boy, until he wisely ran off to India. 'Ah, yes, Uncle Eustis. I fear I didn't know him as well as I would have liked. He was rather—well, he did stand out at Greensted.'

Lady Madewell laughed, too, a tinkling sound like her bracelets. 'Ah, but we love black sheep here at Pryde! Not that it includes *you*, of course, Duke. Your work is so respected. I understand you are studying Goldoni now? *Servant of Two Masters* is a favourite play of mine.'

'I intend to write a monograph of his work soon, yes. A lively change from the ancients.' He had spoken to few people of his new studies; he wondered how she knew.

'My husband has an original copy of *The Fan* in his library. You must get him to show it to you. But beware, he can prose on for hours and hours about his precious collections.'

'It sounds delightful.' And so it did—Jamie all too often lost himself in libraries and bookstores, books were easy to decipher. Unlike life, which never yielded to study. Like Rose— every time he imagined he saw her, she slipped through his fingers like a sunbeam. Yet wasn't that one reason he ached for her so, one reason he loved her and perhaps one reason why it was so hard for them to be together?

Lady Madewell took his arm and led him into the house. The entrance hall was dim and cool, papered in Morris florals, lined with rough wooden benches that held outdoor boots and walking sticks and sheltered dog beds. 'The library is that way,' she said, gesturing to a half-open door. Jamie caught a glimpse of Lord Madewell at his desk, his bearded head bent over an open book. He waved without glancing up. 'We have only one rule at Pryde—well, two really. No, three! No guest shall ever be bored; they must do exactly as they please. No guest shall ever go hungry, thanks to Monsieur Moncler, my precious Parisian chef. Part of that rule is no poaching him, either, mind you. Too many houseguests have tried, though I know you and your Duchess will not, as you are both slim as reeds. Probably live off tea and toast, you poor things. And third, no guest shall go thirsty. My husband is as proud of his wine cellar as he is the library.'

Jamie laughed, utterly charmed by her. She did remind him of Rose; no wonder they were such great friends. 'Well, I only drink coffee these days, so I shan't be stealing your cellar or your chef.'

Lady Madewell gave him a surprised glance. 'Do you? How singular! But no doubt very wise. Coffee will keep you young. My friend Lady Polesworthy has sent for a special nurse from Switzerland to help her change her diet and such. I am sure we will all soon be doing that. Health will be the rage and we will all be as handsome as you and Rose. Now, would you like some tea, or I suppose coffee, while your trunks are taken to your room? We are very informal here. Everyone is already out on the lawn for now.'

'Am I the last to arrive, then, Lady Madewell?' he asked, wondering if he would soon see Rose. Wondering what on earth he would say to her.

'Oh, yes. The Duchess is out there as well, playing croquet, I think.' She laid her beringed hand gently on his arm, her smiling, dimpled expression hardening almost imperceptibly. 'My dear Duke, as an old friend of your uncle, I feel I may speak as—well, as an aunt might, I suppose.'

Jamie wondered how well she had known his eccentric uncle. 'I wish you would. I do hate how everyone feels they must tiptoe around dukes.'

'Oh, I don't tiptoe around anyone. It takes far too much energy.' Her hand drifted away to pat at her hair. 'Rose has become a good friend to us here and I am very fond of her.'

'As am I. Very fond indeed.'

She nodded solemnly. 'She has a kind heart. *Too* kind and therefore so easily bruised, I fear. Her beauty has brought her such attention lately and, if she continues to remain unprotected…'

'Lady Madewell,' Jamie said gently. 'I am very glad she has such a good friend as you. But Rose will never be unprotected as long as I am here. Never again, in fact.'

She studied him carefully, as if she wanted to read him, judge him. Finally, she nodded, but Jamie could tell he was under probation here at Pryde Abbey. 'Good. Now, Duke, do follow me. And remember the rules—everyone must do exactly as they like here!'

She led him through a pair of glass doors at the back of the house and on to a terrace that overlooked a rolling sea of green lawn. Old trees cast shadowy bowers over clusters of white-painted furniture, casual and haphazard. Tables were set up under blue-striped tent awnings, laden with silver tea services, tiered trays of cakes and sandwiches, silver buckets chilling champagne. A game of croquet went on along the grass, amid cries of dismay and shouts of 'You cheated!', pale dresses and flowered hats floating like their own flower beds. A lake lay at the foot of the slope, shining in the warming gold sunlight, dotted with rowboats.

It made Jamie feel even more strongly he had stepped into a fairy tale, a world beyond the real one where anything could happen. Even happy endings, where a troubled scholar could win back a beautiful princess.

Lady Madewell produced a cup of coffee from one of the silver urns and handed it to Jamie, pointing out the other guests around them. 'You know Mrs Keating, of course, and her daughter. And Mr Sykes, the artist, he was quite the sensation at the Royal Academy this summer. And Lord and Lady Trevelyan. He is a poet, so underappreciated at the moment, but his new work will be out in the autumn and will change that, I fancy. So evocative. Lady Heath, my oldest friend. She knows your mother-in-law, I think? And the Redfords. Miss Porter, the actress. Her dear friend Lord Wesley, the great scholar of ancient Assyria, I know you must know him! Maude Stanley, the opera singer, her husband, who is a playwright. You've seen *Call Me a Hansom Cab*? Too amusing.'

Jamie laughed, his head spinning. The Madewells did indeed seem to know everyone.

'Mama!' a voice cried. 'You have forgotten *me*.'

'My darling, I never forget you,' Lady Madewell said, taking the hand of a pretty, doll-like young lady in pink lace that co-ordinated with her bouncing golden curls. She was fashionable and possessed a peaches-and-cream beauty, unlike Rose's classical loveliness. 'This is my daughter Beatrice. She studies Restoration poetry. The Duke is interested in Goldoni now, darling.'

'Are you indeed?' Beatrice said, wide-eyed. 'I should love to hear about it all. His plays are so amusing as well as so sharp about the world. How I should have loved to go to university, if they allowed ladies as they should. So archaic.'

Jamie had a sudden memory of Rose, growing round with their child, smiling as she held his hand over the tiny wriggle.

If it's a girl, I'm sure you will single-handedly force them to let her into Oxford one day. She is bound to be a genius.

And so he would have, if their daughter had been able to draw her first breath. He swallowed hard and made himself smile at Beatrice Madewell. 'Archaic indeed. Some of the finest minds I have ever encountered belonged to women.'

A quick burst of laughter caught on the

breeze and turned his attention. *Rose.* He would recognise the sound of it anywhere, sweet and clear and like silvery bells. He glanced across the lawn to see her standing near the archery targets set up beyond the croquet lawn, her figure slim and graceful in white muslin and lace, a straw hat dangling down her back by blue ribbons. The light gleamed on her tousled curls and her face was tipped up as she aimed her arrow like the Diana she had been in her sister's photograph. She seemed to absorb the sun, radiated it, drew everything into her heat and light.

Had Rose really always been so very beautiful? He felt dazed, dazzled as he watched her, completely unable to turn away. Of course she had always been so beautiful. The loveliest woman he had ever seen. She'd pulled him in from the very first moment he saw her, with her large hazel eyes so full of wonder and sweetness, so much curiosity at life, the shining masses of dark red hair. So delicate and fairylike, yet filled with a quiet strength. He had wanted to lose himself in her, wrap himself in that hair, drown himself in her eyes, soar with her into the sunshine that she alone brought to his life.

He had never been tempted by a lady like

that before. Unlike his father and brother, he had too much respect for women, too much interest in their thoughts and wishes and ideas. But Rose was always his Diana, his goddess, and he wouldn't harm her. At least he had once thought that, until he'd let her down so badly. He had wanted her, not for a night or a Season, but for always—all the days and nights so he could discover everything about her.

But marriage had proved to be something neither of them had expected. Filled with problems neither of them could solve.

Jamie shook his head as he watched her bite her lip in concentration, her face solemn as she focused on her goal and let her arrow fly. It landed merely to the left of the bullseye. She let out a little dismayed cry and took another from her quiver, her head gracefully bent as she notched it to her bow.

Jamie took a gulp of his strong, cooling coffee. Yes—Rose had always been the most beautiful woman alive. Yet she had also been a bit fragile, trembling at the edge of life, and once he'd intended to banish all that and show her the strength that lay within her. She hadn't needed him for that, though. Here, now, she wasn't uncertain at all. She was famous, emulated, sought-after. Laughing and happy. Lady Madewell had said Rose needed protection, but did she? She was all glowing now. That was what he'd once wanted to give her, but he hadn't known how. He had never learned the tiniest part of how to find happiness with someone else from his own family.

He had a sudden, bright, flashing memory of carrying Rose across puddles after a quick rainstorm at Lily's summerhouse, the two of them laughing like she was right now. That sweet, sweet laughter only Rose could make, as she wrapped her arms around his neck and sent them both tumbling down on to a wrought-iron *chaise*. The taste of her skin under his lips, the softness of her sighs against him. There, all alone, so close nothing at all could come between them, he knew he could make her happy. That *they* were happy, perfectly so.

It was only when they left that sensual cloud, the solitary sanctuaries they made for each other, that he lost her. That he could never decipher what she truly wanted.

Jamie finished his coffee, forcing away the desire for something stronger. Giving in to temptation like that would lose Rose for certain, as it would no doubt send him spiralling down again. It would make him lose himself. He had to harden his resolve. He would find a way to prove himself to her, that was all. How he would do that, how he would win back his beautiful wife—well, he wasn't entirely sure about that just yet. His books had little to say on such subjects. But he was a quick study and Pryde seemed like a good place to start.

Rose turned her head, laughing again, her face flowering in the light, and a man stepped forward to help her with the arrow. He was tall and golden-haired, a god in his own right, and they seemed to know each other well as their heads bent close together and they whispered. He put his arms around Rose, his hand over hers as he guided the angle of her bow. She glanced up into his face and they giggled easily, intimately, as if they had often been together like that before.

Jamie frowned. Maybe this task was going to be even harder than he thought. Maybe there was more to her desire for a divorce than freedom from him.

Beatrice Madewell stepped up beside him and poured more coffee into his cup. 'That's Paul Adelman,' she said casually. 'He often visits here.'

Often? 'Is he an artist, then?'

'Oh, no. He's just funny, I guess. Amusing. Mama says she enjoys his silly stories. Lots of ladies do.'

Ladies like Rose? The one thing Jamie never could give her was 'silly stories'. Maybe she wanted, needed that now. 'Like you, Miss Madewell?'

Beatrice laughed. 'Me? Oh, no. He has no interesting conversation at all, I find. Merely gossip.' She glanced up at Jamie, searching, like her mother. 'I should think a lady like the Duchess would never pay him much attention, either. I don't know her terribly well—to be honest, I find her rather terrifying.'

Rose, terrifying? Jamie had to laugh, despite the damnable way Adelman had his arms around Jamie's wife. Jamie also found Rose terrifying, of course—she could shatter his heart as no one and nothing else ever could. 'Really? Why?'

'Well, she is so very beautiful, of course. *You* surely know that better than anyone. And she's always so quiet, so serene, so—so perfect. Who can measure up to her? Who can even tell what she's really thinking? Everyone who comes to Pryde is always talking, talking, talking. About the state of their souls, about beauty and truth, and the nature of anything at all. Maybe it's better to not jabber on and listen instead, as the Duchess does—as you do, too, Duke. You listen.'

'Am I equally terrifying, then?'

Beatrice frowned as she studied him. 'Yes, perhaps. To all these talkers, anyway. I think you have more important things to consider, as do I. But I think romance must require at least some talking. You should practice a bit, if you want to outdo men like Paul Adelman.'

He smiled at her. 'How could someone so young become so wise in romance?' He thought that once he and Rose had been like that, thinking they knew everything they needed to know to be happy. That they had to be together and, in doing so, all would be solved.

Beatrice shrugged. 'Oh, easy. Mama wants everyone to think she only reads poetry and philosophy, but she also secretly reads French novels. I borrow them sometimes. And I watch her guests. All those name cards on the doors. They move around so often. Whose room are *you* near, I wonder?'

Name cards on doors. Was Rose next door

to Adelman? 'I wouldn't know. I haven't been to my chamber yet.'

'You don't really look like the sneaking-about-at-night sort, anyway.'

Jamie feared his face was turning warm under her solemn regard. 'Do I not? Who does look like that?'

'Why, everyone, I suppose. It's all the Prince of Wales and his wicked ways. That's what my German tutor says. But I think the Prince must be bored. He isn't a thinker like you. Though even thinkers must get bored sometimes.' She studied the crowd, the canvases on easels, the croquet balls, the tea services. 'And I am not *that* young. I'm nearly eighteen. Isn't that how old the Duchess was when you got married?'

'Listen, Miss Madewell…'

'Oh, Beatrice, please. We are casual here… didn't my mother tell you?' She poured more coffee, watching Rose and Adelman as they tried another shot. 'You still love her, I think.' Jamie didn't answer, but she nodded as if he had. 'Like in a French novel. But I don't think the Duchess has a pert French maid to help your romance along. You should make her jealous. Nothing like jealousy to make a lady realise what she really wants. I'm not sure what happened between you and your pretty wife, but that always seems to work in novels.'

Jamie laughed. She really was very funny, Beatrice Madewell, but he wondered how a man like him could possibly make a lady like Rose the slightest bit jealous. 'Jealousy, eh? That is your prescription?'

'Yes. Aren't you jealous of Paul Adelman?' Before Jamie could answer, Rose and her arrow-wielding swain turned towards the terrace, his hand on her arm, and Jamie saw Rose suddenly notice him. Her eyes widened and her cheeks grew pink. Beatrice suddenly linked her arm in his and leaned close, laughing loudly and most charmingly, exactly like her mother. 'They're looking! Now you laugh, too, as if I said something extremely witty and you are very enthralled.'

Jamie felt as if he was indeed caught in some French play, or maybe *The Marriage of Figaro*, but he could hardly push Beatrice away. He laughed, though he feared it might not be very convincing—he was feeling rusty from not laughing for too long.

'There! See?' Beatrice said with a happy sigh. 'Oh, no, don't look! That would ruin it. Just watch me.'

Jamie carefully peered over his shoulder. Rose looked thunderstruck. Maybe there was something in this after all. 'You don't need to go up to Oxford, Miss Madewell. You need a stage.'

A stentorian boom echoed over the lawns from the open doors and Beatrice squeezed his arm. 'There's the first dressing gong. Let's go inside now, before you can talk to the Duchess and ruin my lovely stagecraft. You must think very carefully about what to say next.' She tugged on his arm and led him into the house.

'Must I really say something else?' he teased.

'Yes! It is quite vital, you know, but it must be the right thing.'

'You are very helpful, Miss M—Beatrice.'

'Oh, I know. The novels, you see, and also Lady Heath. She introduces couples all the time and she has such an instinct for who belongs where. Usually it has to do with money and estates, of course, but she knows a really successful partnership needs more. I quite adore her. If I can't study at college, I may become a professional matchmaker.' She bounded happily towards the stairs. 'And I do have a price.'

'Do you, now?'

'Indeed. I want to learn more about Goldoni.'

She sighed. 'You really do look like the kind of handsome tutor all us girls dream of getting, yet we never do. They're always old men with far too much hair in their noses…'

Chapter Seven

A Lady in Society Tells All

Who has been seen among the artists of Pryde Abbey? Why, none other than the Duke of B.! And among all the fair Duchess's admirers.

Shall he paint her portrait? Write her a sonnet? Or wave her off amid the wild Pryde gardens to find a new destiny?

We are agog to see...

'The blue silk for dinner, Your Grace?' Jenny asked as she put the finishing touches to Rose's hair. 'Or the pale green organza? I pressed them both.'

'Hmm?' Rose murmured, hardly hearing anything. Her mind was too full of Jamie, Jamie and Beatrice Madewell, laughing together in the sunshine. And what was he doing there, anyway? Could he be there to see her or for another reason entirely? 'Oh, the blue is fine, thank you, Jenny.'

She dabbed on a bit of rose perfume from the crystal bottle, tried on one pair of earrings and then another, but she couldn't seem to sit still. The party which she had thought would be an escape had turned strange, distracting. Seeing Jamie on the familiar lawns at Pryde, two things she would never have imagined could possibly match, had collided and she didn't quite know what to do. The careful mask she had constructed, Rose Byson, Society Beauty, seemed to be slipping away. She had to repair it, paste over the cracks, and quickly, before Jamie could see how his reappearance in her life had so deeply affected her.

She closed her eyes tightly and listened to the rustle of silk as Jenny prepared the gown, the rush of the evening wind past her window, laughter from somewhere down the crooked corridors. The summery smell of her open perfume bottle. Everything seemed brighter, louder, more intense, as the world had glowed into full colour when she first met Jamie, as if her life had been all grey before him. As if they were two lost halves coming together at last. Her brilliant new beginning.

She'd been foolish then, not knowing that beginnings always had endings, too.

She slammed her palm down flat on the dressing table, making the silver pots and crystal bottles, the engraved brushes, the framed photos of her sisters and their children, rattle and jump. It was all too late now.

'Your Grace?' Jenny asked, startled. 'Is everything well?'

Rose took a deep breath. 'Yes, yes, fine, Jenny. I dropped an earring.' She quickly pinned on a pair of pearl and diamond drops and went to let the maid fasten her into the Worth confection. Jenny was a good lady's maid and no gossip, but Rose knew how news could spread like a flood through servants' halls. She was too embarrassed to let anyone know that the serene American Beauty Rose was so unsettled by the appearance of her estranged husband.

She glanced in the mirror as Jenny finished looping together the layer of tiny pearl buttons and straightened the lace frills, the crystal-dusted white roses at the shoulders, the tulle loops of the elaborate train. It was one of Rose's favourite new gowns, a dress like the sea and sky, and one that made her look as if she floated on a cloud. A fabulous gown, she had found, was her best armour, the very best disguise she could don. Would it work tonight?

As Jenny went to find the pearl necklace and the kid gloves that completed her toilette, Rose drifted to the window. The Pryde garden was even more enchanted by night, with the greenish-silvery moon and blanket of stars just rising above it all. Lady Madewell had strung Chinese lanterns, red, blue, gold, through the trees and along the wild flower beds and overgrown walkways. Perfect for encouraging a giddy romance.

Rose traced her fingertips over the cool, thick, wavy old glass and a beam of lantern light caught on the diamond circle of her wedding ring. She curled her fingers around it, thinking of the instant Jamie slid it just there, held her hand to his lips and kissed it, and she had been so sure it was all for ever.

Laughter, real, present laughter, diverted her and she looked down into the garden. A couple strolled along one of the paths, already dressed for dinner. She recognised the lady as Beatrice Madewell, all gold and ivory in a stunning gown of peach-and-cream-striped organza, a simple, draped, almost Grecian creation that made Rose feel overdressed, overblown. Old, even. Beatrice turned to laugh at her companion, reaching out to touch his sleeve as he laughed, too, staring down into her flower-like face. He threw back his head.

It was Jamie. Jamie, laughing and carefree as she hadn't seen him in so very long.

And how very handsome he was, too, in his perfectly cut black-and-white evening suit, his hair shining in the moonlight like black satin. So tall against the more delicate Beatrice, his face bright, relaxed, younger.

Rose blinked hard against a sudden touch of prickly tears. It was silly, so very silly! She had thought of the divorce idea because Jamie, as a duke now, would need an heir. He would need an English lady who fully understood English ways and could give him that traditional life, as Rose never could. Beatrice Madewell was a lively girl, pretty, smart, pert. Yes, her family was an artistic one, but also an old one who knew how things worked. She would surely do well enough for Jamie.

Oh, it did ache.

'But this is exactly what you wanted,' she whispered.

'Did you say something, Your Grace?' Jenny asked.

Rose dashed her hand over her eyes and pasted on a smile. 'Not a thing, Jenny.' The gong sounded along the corridor. 'I should go down.'

Jenny handed Rose her gloves and carefully fastened the pearls around her neck. 'You do look pale suddenly, Your Grace. Are you sure you feel well? I could send for a tray…'

A tray in her room was tempting. To remain in the quiet of her room, with no one watching her, wondering how she would react to Jamie sitting right across from her. But Wilkinses were no cowards. She couldn't be the first. Jamie or not, she had come to Pryde to enjoy herself and, blast it all, she *would*. Jamie could flirt with Beatrice Madewell all night if he wanted! 'No, thank you, Jenny, I feel quite well. It was a— I think it's been a long day, that's all.'

Jenny nodded. She knew much, said little and was a very comforting presence with her freck-led face and kind eyes. 'Of course. You'll be the prettiest lady there, Your Grace. Remember that.'

Rose wasn't so sure about that. But she wouldn't let anyone else guess her doubts, not here. Especially not her husband.

* * *

'My dear Rose! How exquisite you look to-night, as always. Some sherry?' Lady Madewell called as Rose stepped into the drawing room. Luckily, she didn't see Jamie yet. Perhaps he was still exploring the garden with Beatrice. 'Dinner may be a touch late, the chef is so finicky about his sauce mousseline, and we are merely his abject slaves when it comes to cuisines.'

The drawing room was a cosy, warm space, like something out of a scene with the Shakespeare family. A group gathered around the pianoforte, singing madrigals, while Lord Madewell read in the shadowy corner. A portrait of Lady Madewell as a younger woman, hair loose, arms wrapped around little Beatrice, smiled beatifically at everyone and the butler handed Rose the promised sherry.

The garden door opened to a burst of giggles and Beatrice and Jamie appeared there, the two of them a little windblown. Lady Madewell hurried over to them, exclaiming they would catch a chill, wrapping her daughter in shawls, and Paul Adelman sneaked away to where Rose lingered by an open window.

He gave her a rueful grin and surreptitiously

lit up a Turkish cigarillo. 'I know my secret is safe with you, Rose,' he muttered, waving the curl of smoke out into the night. 'This is my last vice, I assure you.'

'Most of your secrets are safe with me.' Though she didn't often indulge, as Prince Bertie and his sister Princess Louise did, she took it from his fingers and gave it a quick inhale. It seemed to steady her, made her feel a bit like the deliciously naughty lady she sometimes wished she could be, but wasn't. She had been born with 'good girl' stamped on her brow.

Paul shook his head teasingly. 'So very odd, the Duke showing up like that. I wouldn't have thought him the Pryde Abbey type.'

'Jamie goes wherever other scholars can be found,' Rose said, gesturing towards a knot of Oxford sorts in the corner. They were arguing vigorously over philosophy.

'Yet he knows Lady Madewell is *your* friend,' Paul said. 'Is it some game he plays now?'

Rose wondered the same thing. It wasn't at all like Jamie to play cruel, deliberate games with someone; he was unlike many people in society in that way. He could hurt Rose so very easily without even trying.

Yet time could change people. It had certainly

changed her. It had hardened her shell and she didn't think she could bear it if he sought to play painful games with her now, on top of everything else.

If he wasn't being cruel, though, and not playing a mean game showing up at balls and at Pryde—could he then be serious about pursuing a lady like Beatrice Madewell? But hadn't he said he wanted a second chance to win back his wife?

Rose's head was spinning and she took another glass of sherry.

'Oh, my dear girl,' Paul said. 'Has he really touched a nerve with you? You must not let him bother you, not one tiny whit. If he realises now what he lost—and only a fool would not—it's just too bad for him.'

Rose made herself laugh. 'Indeed it is. He doesn't bother me at all. I merely…' She merely couldn't fathom what was happening now, after all these months apart. The feelings deep inside her, daring to peep up tentatively, fully, like daffodils after a snow. Jamie said he had changed. Could he? Could *she*?

'It's all such a bore,' she said.

Paul laughed. 'Well, we cannot have that.' He gestured towards Mrs Stanley, the famous opera singer, playing and singing at the piano, some melancholy German *lieder*. 'At least Lady Madewell found a real singer this time, not that dreadful lady who insisted on leading endless musical evenings last time. How she warbled and wobbled! What do you think, my dear Rose? Was poor Miss Smithson the worst singer in all of London?'

Rose smiled, half listening to Paul and his comfortable gossip. She never, ever had to work hard with him. 'I definitely prefer Mrs Stanley. But Miss Smithson had…something amusing, I think. At least she was a better singer than I could ever be.'

'Oh, *ma chère* Duchesse!' Monsieur Leclerc, the French artist, cried, peering at her through his monocle as he threaded his way through the crowd. 'How happy I am to see you here at last! We shall finish my series of sketches now, yes? I must have your portrait done for the Grand Prix in Paris! It will be the…how do you say? The sensation!'

'Of course, *monsieur*, I do look forward to it,' Rose said, holding out her gloved hand for his kiss.

She did so enjoy Leclerc's paintings; they always made her look far prettier than she was, with a plumper bosom and thicker hair, and a sweeter smile. She wondered if Jamie would like it when it was finished—or if he would even see it.

Several others soon joined their little circle and Rose found herself absorbed in the talk of paintings, or recent gallery exhibitions, of a rather new group of French artists who insisted on painting pure light of all things. She even forgot for a moment about Jamie, until he appeared, Beatrice on his arm, in the drawing room door with the playwright, the three of them deep in conversation about some no doubt very profound new play. Beatrice rested her cheek briefly on his shoulder and he smiled down at her.

Rose took a deep breath and made herself keep smiling, murmuring short answers to the conversation around her. Fortunately, artists seldom required lengthy replies; they needed praise for their work and always that smile.

But seeing Jamie again, here, in her own haven, almost made her long to run upstairs to her chamber and fling herself under her blankets. Which was quite ridiculous. Her parents had lived practically separate lives for as long as she could remember and they never caused public scenes. It was just the way of the world they lived in. She couldn't go on for ever never seeing Jamie again. She had to get used to it. Yet…she *had* imagined that after she saw him that first time, confronted him in his library, it would all be over. Her heart would no longer leap and pound at the sight of him, at the merest glimpse of his smile.

A foolish thought, for it pounded in her chest even now to watch him casually brush back a loose lock of hair from his brow.

'How shocking! The Duke of Byson venturing among us artists,' the singer, who had left the piano, exclaimed with a dramatic wave of her large feathered fan. 'Has he taken to publishing poetry now?'

Paul frowned as he studied Jamie. Lady Madewell had come to greet the Duke at the door, subtly drawing her daughter away. 'I wager he has another game in mind other than versifying,' Paul said, gently touching Rose's arm. She was glad of his quiet support.

The singer looked puzzled. 'Hunting and fishing? At Pryde? It hardly seems to be the place.'

Rose almost laughed to think of Jamie taking up such a bluff, hardy sporting life. Red faces and tweeds. Yet she, too, wondered what he was playing at here. A gamble on winning back their marriage? Or had he decided to let her go after all, and find a lady like Beatrice for his duchess, someone young and golden to give him heirs?

And why did that thought make her stomach ache so much!

Before she could reply, the butler announced dinner and the guests proceeded towards the open dining-room doors, linenfold panelling folded back to make the large drawing room into two spaces. Unlike more correct homes, no one was paired off according to rank, but made their way in all together, sitting where they would, moving their place cards to suit them. Paul automatically took Rose's arm. So Rose was quite surprised when Lady Madewell hurried to her side, Jamie and Beatrice behind her.

'Paul, darling, Bea has been quite longing to hear about your voyage to Cairo last year,' Lady Madewell said, though Beatrice looked quite doubtful. Paul, ever the perfectly polite guest, obligingly led Beatrice in, leaving Rose standing with Jamie.

He held out his arm with a crooked smile.

Did he, too, wonder what Lady Madewell was playing at? Or did he know perfectly well? Rose didn't like feeling quite so confused. 'Shall we, then, Rose?'

She glanced around the dining room. Most of the guests were already sitting down. Not wanting to make a scene, she nodded and took his arm. How familiar he felt under her touch! How many times had they walked thus, his sea salt and lemon smell around her, her cheek brushing his shoulder?

'You know I must,' she whispered as they trailed behind the others. 'I could hardly refuse, even here at Liberty Hall. Everyone does love to gossip about everything.'

Once she had cared so much, had wanted only to be the perfect English wife. Yet Jamie never seemed to notice her efforts, so she never even knew if they were right or not, and they were all futile in the end anyway. She still had to care, for her sisters, but for herself...

It had been so exhausting to be someone not herself.

'Do you care so much about gossip, then, Rose?' he said lightly. 'I shall have to remember that, if it makes you spend a little more time with me.'

'*Do* you want to spend time with me?' Once, those words, his time, his attention, had been all she'd wanted. Now it felt all so painfully late.

'What game do you play, Jamie?' she asked tightly.

They made their way deeper into the dining room, a fairy-tale space like all of Pryde. Once it had been a monks' refectory and it kept the beamed ceiling, the vast fireplace built for roasting an ox, the flagstone floor. There, austerity ended. The long table, draped in gold-embroidered damask, was covered with hundreds of candles in gilded and silver candelabra, creating a magical, flickering glow over the tapestry-draped walls. Gold chargers held blue-glazed plates, surrounded by green and blue Venetian glasses and gold-embossed flatware, low crystal bowls overflowing with white flowers and trailing greenery from the gardens. Footmen in old-fashioned green-and-gold livery waited behind each gold-cushioned chair and, instead of the usual calligraphy name cards, each place held a little poem to describe the guests.

*The American Beauty Rose has a world
that adores her*

*With a spouse bedazzled by the distant
past, we fear she sighs in boredom not for
long*

That was what Rose's said. Hardly Keats.
Her face turned warm and she crumpled it and
tossed it beneath the table as Jamie sat down
beside her. She didn't want to know what his
card might say.

As the clear soup was ladled into the gold-
edged bowl and golden hock poured into the
goblets, Jamie covered his glass with his hand
to indicate he wasn't drinking.

'Why do you think I play a game, Rose?' he
said gently. The rest of the party had launched
into an argument over a new production of *Mac-
beth* at the Lyceum and no one paid attention
to them.

Rose studied him in the candlelight. He
looked all golden there, all sincerity, all—all
Jamie with those solemn dark eyes. He hid nothing from her, not his curiosity, not his attention,
not even his trepidation about what she might
say. That was one of the things she'd once most
admired about Jamie. Loved, even. In a world
where all was secret, hidden, coded, he could
rarely dissemble. It was beyond him. Yet it also

meant the real world was a mystery to him, that she herself was a mystery. That it could sometimes be a struggle to really know each other.

'You say you have changed,' she murmured, taking a sip of the wine. 'How can I truly know that?'

'Rose.' He briefly touched her hand, light and enticing. 'I made you unhappy, made you feel alone—I never wanted that, not for a moment.' He swallowed hard and stirred his spoon around his untouched soup. 'You take my breath away just walking into a room. Just smiling. I can't play games when I feel like that. When you were gone, when I saw what I had done to you, to us—then I realised it all.'

'You realised—what?' Rose said, confused.

'That I had made the very greatest of mistakes. One I couldn't easily remedy.'

The soup was taken away, and fish, sole in lemon sauce, brought in, wine refreshed. Rose poked at it with her heavy fork, wondering if she had heard him right, if he regretted the past as much as she did. Around them, an argument was going on about the meaning of love as espoused by Shelley's poems.

'*Love's Philosophy* is quite clear!' Beatrice declared. 'They include love, sex and the interconnectivity of nature. The latter is used as an excuse for the speaker to plead with the listener for the first two. He is seeking out love and the sex he believes should come with it.'

'Is that what you think, Rose?' Paul, across the table next to Beatrice, asked her with a teasing smile.

Rose drained her wine glass. 'I think—everyone must follow their own hearts, of course. Their own instincts. The Romantics were right in that.'

'Yes!' Beatrice cried. 'It is the natural law. Love is all.'

'So you have turned Marlborough House set rules, then?' Jamie said to Rose with an unreadable smile. 'Do what one likes, as long as you don't get caught?'

Rose glanced at him over the platters of quail entrée being carried in, the champagne being poured and voices growing louder again. She doubted the old Abbey monks ever talked of this. 'I am not part of the royal set. And I think the poets looked at love and freedom rather differently than the Prince does. I have no interest in the Marlborough House set.' She had tried kissing a few men since Jamie, it was true, but it had always made her want to cry. To run away.

None of them had ever made her soar into the clouds as his kisses once had.

But what of Jamie? She had never really wondered if he'd sought other company, and the thought of such a thing now made her stomach ache. She gulped down her champagne.

'Indeed,' he said tonelessly. 'I have learned what a monk must feel like lately. I doubt Bertie ever has.'

Rose exhaled. 'If you *have* pursued others, none would blame you.' None would have blamed him even before they'd parted after her miscarriage had left her uninterested in the marriage bed and they'd drawn further and further apart.

'My dear Rose,' Lady Heath had once told her, *'a husband has needs, has restlessness, the poor thing, but it hardly matters.'*

Yet to Rose, and to her sisters and their husbands, such things had always been unthinkable. Bed games at house parties were as nothing compared to the happiness of already being in the right bed every night.

'I've never wanted anyone but you,' Jamie said simply. Beneath the cover of the tablecloth, he gently touched her hand. It felt so warm, so safe, yet so unsettling all at once.

Everything around Rose suddenly went very hazy and she closed her eyes.

Once she had imagined marriage would be easy and for ever, that she'd been so lucky to find love so young. Then she'd discovered it was not as simple as that. Yet she knew from her sisters that it could be something beautiful, a stunning summer flower that was always in bloom, yet in her case it had turned out to be one that dried and crumbled in her hand all too quickly when autumn came along. But was it, *could* it, be something else for her and Jamie? Something that changed like the seasons, different but still as beautiful in its own way?

She shook her head and slid her hand away. It was so dangerous to spend time with Jamie; it always wounded her in the end. Look at how he was already beginning to wonder if they could overcome their difficulties, but just because he'd turned up here didn't mean they could turn back the clock and forget everything that had happened. She needed proof that he had changed, as he claimed.

More champagne was poured, the entrée of lamb and mint sauce with garden peas served. Lady Madewell's table, with her grand French chef and perfect footmen, was renowned throughout London and tonight was no exception. The food was exquisite, the conversation and champagne-fuelled merriment like the lightest Strauss waltz, but Rose felt remote from it all. Watching it from a distance.

She pushed the lamb about on her plate and smiled and nodded at the playwright seated at her other side, listening to talk of his new work. She was acutely conscious of Jamie so close to her, his arm brushing hers, the scent of him.

'My dear Rose, you must eat a little more!' Lady Madewell declared, always motherly, always watching her guests. 'You have been looking rather pale lately, I fear. I shall send you some of my doctor's own excellent tonic, it does work wonders on the energy.'

Rose blushed as everyone looked at her. 'I am quite well, thank you, darling Lady Madewell. Just feeling the end of the Season.'

'And no wonder, all that dancing and gadding about,' Lady Madewell declared. 'Young people these days...'

'My sister has invited me to Baden,' Rose said. 'I may go. A change of scene might be interesting.' She glanced at Jamie out of the corner of her eye and saw that he watched her intently.

'Ach, these German watering holes, so dull,'

someone opposite the table declared. 'No culture at all. What you need is the South of France! I was so enamoured of Nice last year.'

'In my day, Malvern or Tunbridge was the place,' Lord Madewell, who seldom spoke in his own home but always seemed content to smile at his wife, nodded emphatically. 'You'd be right as rain there in no time, Duchess. Ladies do eat such spicy food nowadays, it's no wonder everyone is ill.'

'And the tight lacing…' Lady Madewell clucked. 'I so much prefer these new fashions, don't you, Lady Heath?'

To Rose's relief, the talk turned from her own health to fashions and travel in general and the claret and pudding and cheese were served on gleaming antique silver platters. There was no time to talk more with Jamie, either.

After the meal, also unlike other fashionable houses, the gentleman and ladies did not separate but went together back to the drawing room for coffee.

Lady Madewell clapped her hands. 'Who shall play for us first? Or maybe charades, or piquet?'

'Oh, no,' Paul said. 'I have learned the most

amusing game at Houghton. Character Sketches, it's called. One learns the most fascinating things about one's friends.'

'Oh, yes, I have heard of that one,' Beatrice said. 'Imagine if you were writing a book and you must create a whole new person in only words. From their childhood to now, their likes and dislikes, families and sense of humour and everything.' She smiled across the table. 'Different for you painters, I think.'

'Not at all,' one of the painters refuted. 'Before we can truthfully portray a person on canvas, we must know something deeper about them. Not merely the shape of the nose, but the personality that shines through in the eyes.'

'Exactly,' Paul said. 'So—what does the character you are creating desire? What do they fear? What are their surroundings, and how do they affect them? For instance, I would say...' He glanced around the room and smiled at Rose. 'That someone can be the most beautiful of all on the outside, seem as though they have everything they could desire—but an artist would see sadness in their fine eyes. Uncertainty. They wish to do what is right, but they yearn for so much more. They yearn to...'

'To be themselves,' Rose whispered.

'Yes. That is all anyone should want,' Beatrice said.

'But in this world, that is a rare privilege indeed,' Rose said shortly, feeling suddenly tired. Tired of hiding, or wondering what *was* right, what she should do next. Who she really was. What was her character sketch? 'Excuse me, I have a headache, I fear, and will retire early. Thank you for a lovely dinner, Lady Madewell.'

She hurried out of the room, leaving the others to outline their characters. She was halfway up the stairs when she heard Jamie call, 'Rose? Are you unwell?'

She glanced over the balustrade to see him below, his handsome face tilted up to her, his eyes filled with concern. Like her old Jamie, the one she still mourned. The one she still longed for. 'I am well, thank you, Jamie. Only tired.'

'Is there anything I can do to help?'

She smiled at him sadly. He was the only one who could have done anything, but she feared that it was too late now. 'Nothing, thank you. Goodnight.'

She turned away, only to gasp as she heard swift footsteps behind her and then felt his hand on her arm, turning her gently to face him. He put a finger under her chin and looked intently into her eyes, searching for who knew what, before lowering his head and just brushing his mouth against hers.

As though she'd been struck by lightning, she jerked back, her hand flying to her lips. It had only been the briefest of touches, barely a proper kiss at all, and yet it had stoked something inside her that she hadn't felt for far too long.

He began to say something, but she turned and fled up the stairs as though the very devil was after her, leaving him standing there, watching her.

Chapter Eight

Rose stretched her stockinged feet out before her on the striped blanket, beyond the shade cast by her parasol, to let the sun warm her toes during the afternoon picnic by the lake. Her satin shoes were cast to one side. It felt naughty, delicious, and for a moment she let herself merely *be* in the day. The moment. She had had a surprisingly deep sleep after their dinner last night, deeper than she had enjoyed for a long time. Now that all the cold ham and chicken salad, the cakes and lemonade and champagne, had been consumed, the day had turned lazy and somnolent all around them.

She closed her eyes and for a moment she was sitting by another river, with Jamie holding her hand for the very first time, and she dared trust, for the first but not last time in her life. How sweet it was, how perfect.

How had it all gone so wrong?

Rose opened her eyes and studied Jamie now, carefully tilting her parasol so her interest wouldn't be noticed. He sat with Beatrice under the shade of a tree, Bea chatting merrily as he smiled up at her, lounging on his elbow beside her. It was not the way he usually smiled at Rose, intent and questioning, but filled with amused light, at ease, careless.

He turned his face up to the sun, his smile widening with delight as if he was greedy for that warmth. The light behind him, the shadows cast around the sharply carved angles of his face, made him look like a god or a saint, gilded and unearthly beautiful, and her heart ached and yearned for him as it once had, when she had feared she would burst if he did not smile at her.

Lady Madewell sat down next to her, her large straw hat concealing her face. 'The sun does agree with you, Rose dear. You look very *content*.'

Rose wondered wryly if she often looked *dis*-content these days and smiled and wriggled her toes. 'I always feel happy at Pryde.'

'And you are always most welcome here. But

I meant what I said—perhaps some time away could do you some good. I always feel invigorated by travel. The London Season is most wearying, to even the most hardy souls among us, and city air is so unhealthy.'

'I will certainly consider it. But I enjoy the distractions of London.' And so she did; at a party, the theatre, a gallery, she had no time to think. But travel was sounding more tempting all the time.

'Yes, my dear, do. I should not recommend Baden with the royals. Your sister is truly worthy, of course, but it all sounds so *dull.*'

They were silent for a moment, listening to the breeze rustle through the trees like whispers, the laughter of the others, the splash of oars in the waters of the lake drifting lazily past. Paul claimed Beatrice for a game of boules, leaving Jamie alone.

'Oh, Byson, why don't you take your wife for a row on the lake?' Lady Madewell called. 'I'm sure the water breezes would do her good, it's become such a warm day.'

Rose, shocked by Lady Madewell's suggestion and wondering if she had turned to matchmaking like Lady Heath, glanced at Jamie, sure he would protest. After their brief kiss last night when she'd run away like a schoolgirl instead of an experienced married woman, surely he would not want to be alone with her in a tiny boat, adrift in the middle of the lake, only the two of them? What would they say? What would she *do*? Encourage him to kiss her again?

But he just shrugged and kept smiling. 'Of course, I should enjoy that very much, if Rose agrees.'

'I don't think...' Rose said. She looked at the lake, the shiver of the breeze on the water, the couples laughing together in the boats...

She swallowed as a memory suddenly invaded her mind, of a time in their summer house, of another kiss that had led to desperate lovemaking against the wall...

'Yes, of course, that would be pleasant,' she said hoarsely, surreptitiously reaching for her shoes.

Jamie rose lazily, gracefully, to his feet in one fluid movement, cat-like in his graceful strength, and offered her his hand. She slid her fingers into his, curling into his touch as she once did all the time, and let him lead her to the dock. She could feel the gazes watching them, but she knew nothing but him in that moment. Felt nothing but the nervous butterflies deep inside of her. He helped her on to the narrow, velvet-cushioned seat and she fussed with her parasol to avoid looking directly at him.

'Rose,' he said quietly, climbing in across from her, his knees brushing hers through her dotted muslin skirts. 'If you would rather not…'

'Oh, pooh,' she said with a laughing insouciance she was far from feeling. 'It's too fine a day to waste sitting about. And Lady Madewell, dear as she is, seems to want to insist I am wasting away of ennui or some undisclosed illness, like a heroine in an Italian novel. If I take some exercise, I can persuade her that is hardly true.'

He laughed and shrugged out of his coat, leaving him in his shirtsleeves, the light shimmering through the sheer fabric to reveal his muscled shoulders and arms. Rose glanced away. 'No, you are hardly wasting away.' He loosed the oars and pushed them off into that gold-dappled water.

Rose leaned back on the soft cushions and admired the view for a moment. The water and the boats, the ladies in their pretty white dresses, the little domed summer house on the shore. They flowed smoothly, swiftly past it all. Everyone called Jamie 'the scholar Duke', but she had always known he was so much more besides—including an excellent waterman. His arms pulled strongly at the oars and he took off his straw hat and drew his forearm over his damp brow, disarranging his dark hair.

She tilted her parasol and watched the line of the shore rather than ogle her husband's powerful arms, the light on his glossy hair. No matter how much she wanted to stare and stare, remember and remember.

'Rose...' he said roughly, as if he read her thoughts, as if he remembered, too. 'Rose, I...'

She felt a sudden pang of understanding. Just because he was 'the scholar Duke', read poetry of all ages, knew so many beautiful words and thoughts, that did not mean he always had his own poetic words to explain his emotions. Just like her. She'd often felt so lost with him. So filled with a longing she hadn't quite known how to express.

'Oh, Jamie. Are you going to apologise for kissing me last night? Kissing your own wife?' she said, trying to laugh, but not quite succeeding.

'I can if you want me to.'

'Certainly not. A kiss is hardly a graven sin, especially considering what we've done together before.'

Rose suppressed a gasp at a sudden vision of a bedroom, a tangle of sheets, Jamie's dark head between her legs, pleasure like fire blazing through her...

He seemed to remember that, too, for a dull red flush touched the cut-glass ridge of his cheekbones and she shifted as the tension rose until she could almost choke on it.

They reached the edge of the lake and found themselves in a quiet, wooden glade. A rope swing swayed gently from an oak branch and a few stone benches were scattered about, but it was quiet there. So quiet they could almost be the only two people anywhere in the world.

'Shall we walk for a while?' Jamie asked.

'Oh, yes, please. Lady Madewell has promised a game of Epigrams later and I would rather escape that. They make me feel so very dull-witted,' Rose said. 'The longer we can stay away the better.'

He laughed and sounded like the old Jamie again, to her relief. He rowed them to a small inlet and jumped out to tie the boat to a low-hanging branch. He lifted her out of her seat and to the loamy shore, his arms around her as she suddenly swayed on the solid land. She leaned against him for a moment, smelling the sea salt cologne and lemony sunshine of him, feeling his tall body pressed against hers. A wave of disappointment touched her when he let go and she turned away to shake out her skirts, straighten her hat. She backed away and furled her parasol, suddenly so very aware they were all alone, far away from anyone else.

She sat down on one of the low branches and gazed out over the lake. He came to stand beside her, his booted foot propped beside her, his arms crossed on his knee, also looking out over the water. They were quiet, but for once there was no tension in it, no fear. There was only—*them*.

'I do love this place,' she said. 'The peace just seems to get inside one, doesn't it? Like nothing bad could ever happen here.' Nothing like Newport, glittering, false, dangerous.

'Very different from your London parties, eh, Rose?' he said lightly.

She shook her head. 'I have to keep myself busy somehow. I have to...' She had to forget.

'Rose, I never thought—' he said, breaking off to shake his head.

She glanced up at him. How sad he looked! She curled her lace-gloved hand into a fist to keep from reaching for him. 'What is it, Jamie? Despite everything, you can talk to me.'

'I know you're not wasting away, but Lady Madewell seems to think you are—not as healthy as you should be,' he said carefully. 'I worry about you.'

'Is it my consumption-like pallor?' she said, trying to laugh. 'I am quite well enough, I assure you. A bit tired, yes. I have never been as strong as my sisters, I fear.' And less so since she'd lost the baby. All that blood. All that sadness.

'Do you really think a time away, a real rest, could help you?'

Rose shrugged. 'That is always welcome. New sights, new people, new parties…'

'Not that kind of rest, Rose. I'm no doctor, but even I can think more parties wouldn't be helpful.' He reached for her wrist in its lace glove and held it as carefully and tenderly as a piece of rare glass.

Rose gulped. 'Then what would you prescribe, Dr Jamie?'

'Why not come to Greensted Castle for a few days?'

Rose was shocked. She'd never been to his ducal seat, not once. When they'd first married, it was the domain of his father and brother, and it was said to be rather gloomy and vast. 'With you?'

He gave her a careful smile. 'Am I such an ogre, then? I'm not proposing locking you in a dungeon to feed on bread and water. A few days of country quiet. Doing whatever you like. I know you enjoy riding and there are some excellent pathways there.'

'With you?' she said again.

'You need seldom see me, if you wish. I could even take my meals in the library.' Just as he had in the last days of their marriage. He sat down beside her, his shoulders stiff, and she realised he really did want this for some reason. 'I confess I could use a lady's stylish advice. The place is rather a mess. Not at all ducal. I know I have no right to ask you for anything…'

'Oh, Jamie. You do know me well. Nothing will persuade me faster than asking me for fashion advice.' She sighed. She suddenly longed to be there with him, to have him to herself no matter how late it might be to save their marriage. To see his home, picture his future. Maybe it would help her to move forward, too.

'And it would give us a chance to talk. Truly talk. Divorce is such an enormous step,' he said.

'And we must be sure. Yes.' She thought of

him laughing with Beatrice Madewell, of all the young and highly fertile ladies out there who would happily snatch up a duke, divorced or not, and bear him an heir. 'I will consider it.'

'That is all I can ask.' He peered up at the sky, all cloudless azure, the sun glowing amber. 'It's turned quite warm. I think I'll take a swim.'

Rose stared at him, her memory bombarded with enticing images of Jamie plunging after her into the bath on their halcyon honeymoon, his lean, gorgeous body completely bare, his arms seizing her in a passionate embrace as they laughed and kissed. She turned away to fuss with the handle of her parasol. 'Now?'

'When better? A lake, a warm day...'

Rose had to laugh, despite herself. 'Oh, Jamie. You do still surprise me, you insane man.'

He laughed, too, lighter than she had heard him in so long, and cast off his boots and stockings to climb on to the rope swing. He stood up on the wooden seat, his fist wrapped around the knotted cord. How free he looked then, so far away from the cares of their London life, the dukedom he hadn't wanted to inherit, her young, lovely Jamie again. He set the swing flying, faster and faster, out over the water.

'Jamie!' Rose cried, jumping up from the bench, half laughing, half baffled. Who *was* this man? So full of fun. 'Whatever are you doing?'

He grinned at her. 'You should try it, Rose! It's like flying.'

She remembered the tale he had once told her from one of his ancient books about a man who flew too close to the sun and crashed to earth. 'Oh, Jamie...'

With one last, great, joyful whoop, he let go of the rope and dived into the lake with a plume of splashing water.

'Jamie!' she screamed, when he vanished under the shining waves that closed over him, glass-like, and didn't come back up again. She kicked off her heeled shoes and dived into the water, kicking past her muslin skirts towards where he had disappeared, glad she hadn't worn one of her heavy silk frocks and thankful for those long-ago swimming lessons at Bailey's Beach. She gasped at the chilly water and could see only green-blue waves. No Jamie.

Then hard, strong hands caught her around her waist and lifted her high. Jamie laughed up at her and she beat at his shoulders, furious, then giggling, until she nearly toppled down again and had to hold on to him even tighter.

He moved them to where the water was not very deep and they stood there together, sun-splashed, entwined.

Rose shook back her wet hair, her hat lost, and it tumbled like skeins of seaweed from its pins. She was sure she had never looked so bedraggled—the American Beauty Rose looking like a pond frog.

Yet she couldn't stop laughing, giggling until she snorted lake water, holding on to Jamie as if they were two naughty children afraid of being caught by a strict nanny.

'Are you all right, Rose?' he asked. 'I never meant for you to come in after me.' He lifted her into his arms and carried her towards the shore, as he once had over the doorway of their honeymoon chamber.

'What else could I do when I thought you were drowning, you ridiculous man?' she gasped. 'If I had my bathing costume, I could best you in a swimming race all the way across the lake! I learned at Newport as a child, you know, although my mother was horrified. But my father took my sisters and me to Bailey Beach whenever he was there.'

'I'm not sure you *could* best me, you smug minx. I'm not such a bad swimmer myself.'

Rose was surprised. She'd never seen him swim, not really. But then, when had she had the opportunity? They hadn't travelled together much; in fact, they'd never spent enough time together, the two of them, for one reason or another. 'Are you really?'

'Of course. My life isn't all about books. I learned in freezing Scottish lochs that would put your Bailey's Beach to shame. My parents sent my brother and me there every year, to get us out of sight for a while, I suppose.'

Rose realised then that she knew very little about his family, either. His father and brother had been distant figures, having not much in common with Jamie and no interest at all in his wife, and he never spoke of his mother, who'd died long ago. But Jamie didn't seem to want to talk about his family any more, as they had reached the shore. He handed her his discarded coat, left draped over the bench, and she wrapped it close over her sodden dress. She wrung out her hair, trying to not laugh about how unhappy poor Jenny would be that it would never fully dry before dinner.

They strolled back towards the party, squelching ridiculously all the way until she giggled again, as they sounded more like Lady

Madewell's spaniels after a paddle than a duke and duchess should. Yet Rose couldn't remember when she last felt quite so wonderfully carefree.

'So sweet, don't you think?' Lady Madewell said, gesturing from under her parasol at Rose and her husband as they made their sodden way towards the house. 'People who can laugh together like that after all those poor children have been through? Like a romantic novel!'

'Do you think so?' Lady Heath murmured, and took a sip of her lemonade. 'Rose *is* a sweet girl who deserved better out of life, but they have been through so much…'

'Oh, yes, I forgot you were such a friend to her family,' Lady Madewell said. 'You must have known her before she married?'

'Yes. I knew her mother when we were girls and she was sent to England for finishing school.' Lady Heath remembered those days, beautiful Stella who'd married so wisely—when she herself was so foolish. But it all seemed to have turned out well enough. Unlike for poor Rose.

'I remember you arranged for her sister Lily

to meet her Duke. Did you happen to have a wee hand in Rose's match?'

Lady Heath laughed. For all Rose's sweet shyness, she had been the most independent of the Wilkins girls when it came to romance. 'None at all. It was young love at work when Cupid saw *her*. And I merely seated Lily next to Aidan at a little dinner party I gave—they did the rest themselves.'

'Indeed,' Lady Madewell murmured. Everyone in society knew what Lady Heath did to pay for her bread, introducing suitable young and not so young couples who might benefit from each other. She specialised in American ladies of means and English gentlemen of breeding, but she knew very well more was needed to make a successful match than dollars and titles. And tender hearts were often a hindrance rather than a help. But one could only wish for the 'romantic novel' when it came to a lady like Rose Wilkins.

Lady Madewell went on, 'I could hope Cupid was a bit more pragmatic about where he aims his arrows sometimes. I admit I am quite fond of Rose—she is almost like another daughter to me. I would love it if she could find real happiness.'

'She is a very kind soul, I agree. And so lovely,' Lady Heath agreed. She glanced at Paul Adelman, who watched Rose so wistfully. But was he right for her? Lady Heath had her doubts. 'Do you think there could indeed be some hope for Rose and the Duke? Or better to risk scandal at this point and let them part?'

Lady Madewell laughed. 'My dear, what is scandal next to true happiness? I would not have all I possess now if I hadn't been willing to take risks. Discovering where our happiness truly lies—*that* is the challenge. To know ourselves... like in the character sketches. I would like to help Rose find her happily ever after, but I am not sure enough of her desires to be of much use. You have so much more experience helping people with that sort of thing than I have.'

Lady Heath was not so certain of that. It was true she had found a knack for helping couples 'find their happiness', or at least find suitable partners in life, and it helped her set a fine table indeed. But Lady Madewell made matches as often and swiftly in the merry corridors of Pryde Abbey. It was just that her matches, unlike Lady Heath's, were usually not of the 'orange blossoms down the church aisle' sort. In Lady Heath's opinion, that was the sort of match one needed *after* marriage and it satisfied many, many people. But could it satisfy Rose? She had her doubts.

'I think we could give them a little more opportunity to be together, as they have here thus far,' Lady Heath suggested. 'They're not spending much time alone very often, not when they have to seek it out for themselves. They have been through too much, I fear, to risk more hurt, especially Rose. It was inspired of you to invite him.'

Lady Madewell smiled happily. 'Yes, I thought so, too. He looked so lost and unhappy there in the bookshop. But I confess, I am not entirely sure what to do with them while they're here. I am not used to encouraging *married* couples. Should I lock them in the boathouse together?'

Lady Heath laughed. 'Oh, you *have* been reading romantic novels! Nothing so drastic is needed, I think. Merely a few after-dinner games, like we have been doing. Ones that encourage a bit of frivolity?'

'You are so clever. Of course. I shall ask Bea to arrange some hide-and-seek, or maybe blindman's bluff, to help bring people closer together.' Lady Madewell frowned at some footmen setting up tables under the trees. 'No, no, the tea things don't go there! Here, let me show you…'

Lady Heath smiled as she watched the footmen quickly rearrange the tables. She had not been so sure she should come to Pryde for this party; she'd had a rare few days free when she could read and think. But it was proving quite amusing, as well as very useful.

She reached for her portable desk and opened the lid to take out a few scribbled pages.

> *My dear Readers, you will not believe the merriments this Author has seen today! So very much to tell you…*

Chapter Nine

As Jamie changed for dinner that night, going through the familiar motions of fastening his brocade waistcoat, choosing cufflinks, smoothing the hair that would always wave in an unruly fashion no matter what pomade he used, especially when Rose had once run her fingers through the locks and laughed at its wildness, he couldn't quite stop thinking about that afternoon. Couldn't stop smiling, even laughing out loud once, startling his valet.

It had been such an amazing day. Rose sitting so close to him, the two of them alone in the middle of the lake as they hadn't been alone in so very long. As he had begun to think they would never be alone again. Rose laughing, so alive, so happy, her hazel eyes sparkling almost golden, so easy and comfortable with him again, that white strain around her eyes vanishing into a smile. To hold her so close, to feel her skin, her warmth—he had thought his heart would burst, that he would almost die from the happiness.

Maybe it was this magical place, this house unlike any other he had ever seen, that gave Rose that laughing, warming, glorious life in her eyes—here she seemed to belong. If only he could give her that, too, the happiness that came with that sense of belonging. If only he could always make her smile.

He let his valet help him into his evening coat, brushing at the shoulders, his thoughts so far away. Back and back into what might have been if he hadn't ruined it all.

The way his foolish actions, his carelessness, his ignorance, his neglect had once stolen her smile and ruined her happiness haunted him every day. How could he have been so blind? How had she borne it for so long?

Most importantly—how would he ever make her see he had truly changed? Prove they could have a life together, a different sort of life?

He'd felt so absurdly alive as he'd spun her around in the water and the sunlight. His life had been empty of laughter after her departure and before he'd met her, too, lacking in silliness and fun and intimacy; even a tumble into a cold lake had felt wondrous because she was with him. How he had longed to kiss her again, to taste her lips until she forgot, too, and they were only Rose and Jamie again.

'Will that be all, Your Grace?' the valet asked and Jamie dragged himself back into the present moment to glance into the mirror.

He had never cared much how he looked. Books couldn't see him, after all. His mother had been a great beauty, his father a bluff hunting-fishing-and-shooting countryman who only wanted his sons to join him in his interests. Jamie had been a disappointment to both of them as the son of a duke, yet that had never really mattered to him once he grew up—until he met Rose and had to have her. His beautiful, beautiful wife.

But now he hoped he at least looked respectable, so he could appear a plausible match for her. He smoothed his hair, tugging his waistcoat into place.

'Yes, very good, thank you,' he said and turned to make his way downstairs.

He heard the party long before he reached the drawing room. Rose sat in the corner, her head tipped up, smiling as a bearded old Frenchman sketched her portrait. Her gown, coral-coloured silk trimmed with shimmering gold lace, glowed in the old-fashioned lamplight. Her smile widened a bit when she saw him, until the artist clucked at her and she went back to her pose.

'Oh, Byson, I do apologise,' Lady Madewell cried, gesturing to the butler to hand him a sherry. 'Dinner will be too, too late, as it seems my dear chef has seen his asparagus hollandaise quite ruined and is making a terrible fuss about it all, even though my husband quite despises asparagus. So we must be patient for the moment. At least Paul is so amusing at the piano.'

Paul Adelman—the man who was much too handsome, much too friendly with Rose. Jamie was absurdly relieved he was occupied at the piano.

'Oh, Mama, we should dance,' Beatrice said.

'The mazurka,' another lady said. 'It's so lively, such fun!'

'Oh, yes,' Beatrice agreed. She gave Jamie an expectant glance, but another young man quickly claimed her hand and whirled her on to the floor. Jamie turned to Lady Heath. Though she had once known his mother, she looked much younger in her eau-de-nil gown and jade tiara, her smile rueful as she nodded to him.

'Would you do me the honour, Lady Heath? It's been too long since we've been able to hear each other's news,' he said. In fact, he wasn't sure he had seen her since his own wedding.

She laughed. 'Oh, my dear Duke, I am so old and my dancing days are quite behind me.' That was clearly false, for she was as slim and quick as Beatrice Madewell, but her goal was made clear as she took Rose's hand and drew her from her chair, over the artist's vociferous protests. 'But I am sure the Duchess knows all the latest dance steps. Pryde is so unconventional that no one cares if husband and wife dance together all night if they wish!'

Rose looked startled, but she took his hand willingly enough and let him draw her closer, closer than he would have dared if they hadn't been even closer in the lake. Closer than they had been in much too long.

'I do hope you've recovered from our, ah, rather unexpected little swim,' he said and felt thrilled when she laughed. They twirled in a circle, close and quick.

'I am very well, thank you,' she said. 'Only my dignity was injured.'

That beautiful laugh still echoed in his mind, sustaining him, making his feet as light as if they had Mercury's wings attached as he spun her again. 'I don't think you could ever be less than perfectly dignified and graceful. Less than…perfectly perfect.'

She glanced away. 'I was hardly the perfect Duchess, was I? Not like Lily.'

You were perfect for me, he thought, *until I ruined it all.*

Rose rested her hand on his shoulder as they turned and twisted around the other couples, chatting about the music, the other guests, anything but what he was actually thinking. What, perhaps, they were both thinking. 'I do believe Lady Madewell and Lady Heath are conspiring about something,' she whispered, nodding towards the two ladies chatting confidentially in the corner. They did seem intent on watching Jamie and Rose.

Jamie wondered if they were 'conspiring' a romance and, if so, how he could persuade them to help him in his efforts to win Rose.

The piano song changed to a march and Beatrice clapped her hands. 'Follow-my-leader, now, everyone. This way!'

There was a great scramble of confusion and

giggles as everyone fell in behind Beatrice and her dance partner, following them on a meandering path through the drawing room, around and over the sofas and chairs, making a circle around her scowling father. They trailed through the dining room, all set with silver and crystal for the ruined dinner, an empty breakfast room, Lord Madewell's library, up the stairs, then down and back up again.

Jamie held on to Rose's hand, keeping her with him as long as he dared. The line broke into chaos at the top landing of the staircase, some of them going down again, some to the right into a darkened corridor.

Jamie and Rose waltzed to the left and through a doorway and found themselves alone in a small, dark, silent, dusty attic.

Rose laughed nervously, her stomach fluttering at being so near him again, feeling his heat, smelling the scent of—of *Jamie*. 'These games here at Pryde—you must think them so silly.'

'Not silly at all, if they bring us together like this,' he said huskily and his arms reached out for her in the darkness, drawing her closer. She rested her forehead against his shoulder, the soft wool of his coat warm on her skin. She closed her eyes and let herself be present in that one moment, alone with him.

She felt his kiss on the top of her head, and she tilted her face up to his. His eyes glowed like dark stars. His lips touched her brow, the pulse that beat at her temple, her cheek, tiny touches that made her tingle all the way to her toes. All the loneliness, the icy coldness, of those months on her own disappeared then, just for this moment.

She stretched up to meet him and at last his lips met hers. A small, questing, sweet kiss, but it made that flame burn even brighter. She moaned against him and he dragged her so very close there was nothing between them at all. Their kiss deepened and he pressed her back against the wall.

'Rose, I—I've missed you so much,' he whispered roughly.

'I've missed you, too, Jamie. But...'

'But I have much still to prove to you. Amends to make. I know.' He stepped away from her, his breath ragged. From somewhere beyond their hidey-hole, there was muffled laughter. 'Rose, I know I have no right to ask a favour of you...'

Rose stiffened, suddenly wary. 'A favour?'

'I asked you before. Come with me to Greensted. Please. For a few days. A time for us to talk, for me to show you the house. It's a bit of a mess, I'm afraid, but we would hardly be alone. There are dozens of servants.'

'Go with you to the country?'

'For a few days only. You could do as you like, walk, ride, read. Tell me how to improve the house, which it urgently needs. Bring one of your sisters, too, if you like.'

Rose had to laugh as she imagined being stuck in the country with Violet. But she couldn't laugh to think of being alone with Jamie. Look what happened whenever she saw him! Kisses, those drugging, sweet kisses that always addled her.

But they *were* sweet indeed...

'I—I still need a little more time to think about it,' she said quickly, as footsteps rushed along the corridor outside. Before she could change her mind, could kiss him again and forget all their past pain, she slipped out of the dark attic and back into the light of the party.

Chapter Ten

Why, oh, *why* had she agreed to this? It must have been a moment of madness in that attic at Pryde Abbey, the insanity Jamie's kisses always brought over her.

Rose stared out the carriage window as town turned to countryside, hedgerows and stone walls, the distant smoke of farmhouse chimneys. She'd only seen Greensted Castle once, from a distance, on their way to a honeymoon cottage on the estate, long before Jamie had so unexpectedly inherited the dukedom. It had seemed quite forbidding and she was glad then it would never be her home.

Now—well, now it *still* wasn't her home. She was a duchess who wasn't really a duchess. And Jamie would be there.

She would be all alone with Jamie.

Rose sat back on the tufted velvet seat with a sigh. It was true she longed to get away from London for a while. Her latest visit from the doctor had left her with the same advice from him—she needed fresh air, a change of scene, a rest. And places like Pryde, wonderful as they were, always proved as noisy as town. As filled with people following, watching. Talking. And Baden would be filled with royal etiquette, even if her dear Lily was there. A time of quiet was prescribed. And Greensted had a vast park where no one could trespass.

Yet what peace would she find with her husband? What would happen between them? After their kisses at Pryde…

She closed her eyes, thinking of being in his arms, laughing together in the lake, the silence and temptation of being with him in the quiet attic. He had been her old, wonderful Jamie then, the man who she had once thought understood her so well, who'd tempted her to every wickedness. Maybe that was really why she had agreed to visit Greensted.

The carriage jolted and slowed. She opened her eyes to see that they had turned into the imposing gates of the ducal estate, the ancient crest high above the stone and iron, the rows of trees darkening the drive.

Rose sighed as the house came into view. It hadn't improved much from her memory. All cold grey stone, vast and lonely, set in a rolling park, not softened by any bright flowers. A medieval tower loomed at one end, the remnants of the original house, and she wondered if an unruly princess had once been imprisoned there.

But maybe, even in the short time she would be there, she could do something with it. Make it all a bit less gloomy, a bit less duke-ish, a bit more like Pryde. And maybe, maybe, beyond that, she could help Jamie, too. Help them both move into the future, even if it was, in the end, apart.

The carriage rolled to a stop and two footmen hurried to open the door and lower the steps. As Rose climbed down to the gravelled driveway, peering up from beneath the brim of her hat to examine the acres of staring windows and towering chimneys, Jamie himself rushed down the curving stone steps to greet her. His hair was waving wildly as usual, his spectacles glinting in the grey light, his smile tentative, beautiful, tempting. He reached for her hand, his own fingers ink-stained as usual and he kissed her cheek, his lips warm on her skin.

'Welcome to Greensted, Rose,' he said. 'I know it's not quite as comfortable as what you're used to, but I hope you'll find it interesting none the less.'

Comfortable? She couldn't really remember the last time she had felt that way with Jamie. Maybe in the lake at Pryde, when all fear and caution had fled. Unsettled, passionate, sad, longing—yes, all those things, but comfortable? She remembered days when they were first married, sitting by the fire reading together, smiling at each other, holding hands, falling down to the carpet in kisses and laughter and blurry, heated passion...

'I am sure I will, Jamie, thank you.'

He took her arm and led her up the stone steps, through the open front doors. The entrance hall seemed larger than many entire houses, all pale, icy blue and white plasterwork in whorls and swirls, a white marble floor cold even through her kid boots, the only furniture large, blue satin benches she couldn't imagine anyone sitting on and blue and white porcelain vases taller than she was. A staircase curved to the floors above, more blue and white and gilt.

To her surprise, two long lines of servants, headed by a very elderly butler and stern-looking housekeeper, waited. Everyone bowed and curtsied as a young maid shyly presented her with a bouquet of white roses, everyone's curious, cautious eyes fixed on Rose. As if she was a proper duchess or something. The lady of the house.

Rose was startled and blushingly embarrassed, but she tried to think of what Lily would do right now, her perfect, composed older sister, so beloved by everyone who resided on her estate. Rose smiled gently at the maid, and said, 'How very lovely, thank you.'

'Welcome to Greensted, Your Grace,' the butler said ponderously. 'I am Johnston and this is Mrs Smith, the housekeeper.'

'We are very glad to meet you, Your Grace,' Mrs Smith said, her austere tone seeming to add the tacit words 'at last'. 'I shall be most happy to meet with you at any time convenient to Your Grace to go over the household accounts. I hope you will find everything at Greensted to your liking.'

'I am quite sure I will. I can see how very well run everything is.' And so it was, the chilly hall immaculate, the rows of servants perfectly straight. She simply had not expected to have to play hostess. She glanced at Jamie and saw he looked as bemused as she was. He gave her a rueful smile and squeezed her arm.

'Your lady's maid has arrived, and been shown to the Duchess's Suite,' Johnston said, 'and tea is laid out in the Blue Drawing Room.'

'Thank you, that sounds most pleasant,' Rose said.

'Shall I introduce the staff?' the butler said and Rose nodded, making her way along the long line with Jamie. She tried very hard to remember everyone's name, everyone's position; it would never do to always be 'the scandalous one who did not care one jot'.

'I am sorry about all that ceremony,' Jamie said quietly in her ear as he led her up the soaring staircase towards the state rooms, the eyes of centuries of Bysons staring down at them from faded portraits, judging them. Judging her. Rose peeped over the balustrade to see the servants still watched, too, as still as soldiers in formation in their two lines. 'I did tell Johnston it was merely a brief, private visit, but those words don't seem to be in the household's vocabulary.'

'I would imagine not, in such a place as this,'

Rose said. 'It is a ducal seat, after all. I worry about—well, about what expectations might be disappointed later.' Later, when they parted for good and a new duchess arrived.

'I'm sure they will manage well enough,' he said vaguely. 'They have seen worse.'

'Worse?' she said sharply, wondering what awful things could possibly have happened within these silent halls. What Jamie had seen that he never spoke of to her.

He just shook his head and ushered her into what was obviously the Blue Drawing Room. It was papered in blue French silk, the carved chairs upholstered in darker blue, worn velvet, the windows covered in blue satin. The ceiling soared above them, painted with a scene of classical gods and goddesses peering down from a cerulean sky. But to her relief, it was not nearly as vast and cold as the hall, with a cheerful fire laid in the white marble fireplace and daylight streaming in from the tall windows. A woman's portrait hung over the mantel, a dark-haired beauty in white and gold silk and pearls, a half-smile on her lips, a beringed hand reaching out to a small dog. Greensted rose behind her, the gardens summer-green, but her dark eyes, Jamie's eyes, were filled with sadness.

'Is that your mother?' she asked, curious. Jamie seldom mentioned her, though others said she had been a famous beauty. From the little Rose had seen of Jamie's father, she imagined the lady's lot had not been a cheerful one.

'Yes,' was all Jamie said. He offered her a chair at the round, marble-topped table near the bow window, laid out with silver and fine Meissen china, as well as stacks of sketches.

'What are these?' Rose asked as she took off her gloves and hat and poured out the tea, studying the colourful images. They seemed to be rooms, bright with fashionable chintz and flowered Morris papers like at Pryde Abbey, carpets and over-mantels and sofas.

'Some ideas for the renovations here at Greensted,' he said. 'Here, have a raspberry tart. Your favourite, yes? Our cook made them especially. I wanted your opinion on some of these plans; your taste in such things is so much better than mine. I see clearly how fusty and uncomfortable this old place has become, especially compared with houses like the Madewells', but I simply have no idea how to improve it all.'

Rose took a nibble of the raspberry tart, which he had indeed remembered was her favourite, and sifted through the sketches. She laid some aside, commenting on details she especially liked, a few improvements that could be added, ideas for 'American comforts' like bathrooms, which Lily had installed at her homes. New artists whose works would look well in the drawing room.

'I assume you have arranged the library at least to your liking.' She laughed. Libraries were the one room Jamie always did notice.

'Actually, I've carved out a little corner for my work, but most of it is still too much my father's space. All those mounted fox heads staring at me.'

Rose found a few drawings of more suitable spaces for reading and work, not merely for waiting for the hunting season to begin, and reached for a pencil to add a few more details. She grew quite absorbed in the task, in the artistry of bringing a home, a real home, into being, and when she glanced up she was surprised to find Jamie watching her closely. His eyes were filled with wonder, a small smile on his handsome lips.

'I— Well…' she said, her throat tight, and turned away, feeling that dreadful blush creeping into her cheeks again. It was so long since he looked at her like that, completely absorbed only in her, as if he was trying to read her very thoughts. As if he *saw* her. It reminded her too much of the old Jamie, the one she'd loved so much, the one she'd married. She feared she couldn't bear that now, couldn't bear to find that man again just to see it all vanish once more like so much mist. How could she trust herself? How could she trust him?

She tidied the sketches into a stack again and set them aside. Perhaps she had made a mistake coming to Greensted after all. She had only recently begun to consider finding a new life for herself, to mull over new paths. Now Jamie sat right beside her, with his beautiful night-star eyes, with the warmth and the delicious smell of him, reminding her of all she'd once longed for. Maybe all she might still long for, deep down inside, despite everything that had happened.

He seemed to sense some of her confusion, for he gently touched her hand, the feeling of his skin against hers making her shiver. 'Rose. Please. I meant nothing—nothing *pushing* about asking you here. I had no idea how to be a proper husband to you. But if you'll let me, I'd like to be your friend. I'd like to try to gain your trust.' He tapped at the sketches. 'And I very much value your artistic opinion on this house.

I want it to be something you would think elegant, comfortable. A place where a duke could be proud to live, I suppose.' He smiled ruefully, that crooked grin she had always found so hard to resist. 'I'm afraid I have as little idea how to be a proper duke as I did a husband.'

Rose swallowed hard. 'I would like to be friends, too, Jamie. I truly would. And I can see that this house could be lovely indeed, with a bit of bringing into the nineteenth century.' A home they might once have shared, if things had turned out differently. 'I think I should probably rest for a while before dinner.'

'Of course. I've kept you here too long.' He rose to his feet and bowed as she hurried out of the room, but she could feel him watching her the whole way.

Chapter Eleven

~~~~~~~~~~~

A Lady in Society Tells All

London is desolate this week, my darlings, as the Duchess of B. has gone off to the countryside. And not merely the country— to the ancestral pile of the Dukes of B.!

Shall she ever emerge from those ancient halls at all?

This Author is on tenterhooks to find out, as I am sure are all the eligible gentlemen of town...

Rose was very glad when Johnston informed her that dinner was to be served in a small breakfast chamber instead of the grand dining room. She'd peeped into that magisterial space and was quite sure she and Jamie would be lost in there, with its mahogany table that surely could seat a hundred, its dark red walls and hangings, its Venetian glass chandeliers and buffets lined with silver. She already felt uncertain enough about what she was doing in that grand house, where everyone treated her like a duchess when she felt like anything *but*. To preside over a multiple-course dinner at the foot of that massive table might feel as if she was slowly being crushed by velvet and mahogany.

Yet when she saw the breakfast room, she wondered if the state dining room wouldn't have been better after all. She would have been so far away from Jamie they would have been shouting to be heard if they spoke at all. She would not have felt the danger of his nearness, the temptation to move even closer to him.

Here, in this pretty little octagonal space with tall windows looking out on to a moon-dappled garden, everything seemed so intimate and romantic. The round table, draped in white damask and laid with white and yellow china, the yellow striped cushions and yellow silk curtains, spoke of sunniness and newness.

Jamie stood waiting to hold her chair, looking strangely nervous and far too adorably handsome. 'I hope this room will do, Rose. We can go to the dining room if you like, but it always feels cold in there to me. I thought you might prefer it here.'

She nodded, daring to wonder if she could have this one night with her old Jamie. With her old self. 'It is very pretty, thank you.' She sat down and carefully smoothed her leaf-green silk skirts around her as Jamie seated himself across from her. She'd dressed with particular care that evening, in one of her favourite new Worth gowns, foaming with white lace and tulle, and her wedding gift pearls. Jenny had pinned up her hair in one of the latest styles, a loose, low knot made stylish by Princess Alexandra, twined with pearls and fastened with a diamond crescent moon Jamie once gave her. She hadn't worn it since they parted and she wondered if he would notice.

All of England called her 'beautiful' now, though she was never entirely sure if that were true. She'd really only ever wanted one person to think her beautiful and once upon a time he had. Once he had looked at her as though she was the very moon and stars and sun. Maybe she still longed for him to look at her like that.

She pushed aside such daydreams and concentrated on what was before her, the here and now. They had agreed to be friends. That was no small thing.

But it was no easy thing, either. Not when she looked at him now in the moonlight, saw her husband again. Not when memories crowded so closely around her she could barely swallow.

Footmen in the blue-and-gold Byson livery served the soup and poured ruby-red wine into her Venetian glass goblet, but none for Jamie. He had only that coffee again. Perhaps he really had changed. No drink, no distractions, no quarrels, his attention only on her and this moment they had together. Yet there was such sadness in his eyes, too, even as he smiled his old, beautiful smile at her. Had *she* done that to him?

'Tell me more of your new project. Goldoni, yes?' she said as she took a sip of the soup. She wasn't even quite sure what it was. Cream of asparagus? It was quite salty and she almost laughed to think a grand house like Greensted needed someone to take the menus in hand as well as the decorating.

'Yes,' Jamie answered. 'I am travelling to Venice soon to consult some of their archives.'

Venice. He still planned on that. So he would soon be gone and even this fragile friendship, these little moments together, would end. Rose stared down at her bowl, trying to hide her thoughts, her feelings. 'I've always wanted to see Venice. When Mother took us to Italy, she didn't consider it educational enough. Too crumbling and decadent. It sounded so marvellous.'

He smiled, that old, bright, flashing smile she loved so much. 'It would suit you. It's an old soul, like you. Elegant.'

'Am I? I always feel like a young, foolish soul,' she said with a laugh. The fish course, something pale and flabby and as unrecognisable as the soup, appeared.

'Of course you are not foolish. You know art and true beauty better than anyone I have ever known. And you understand people. You're kind to them. Even to undeserving ones like myself, of course.'

Rose was flustered by the compliments and terribly moved. 'Well, I do envy your travels, Jamie. Your purpose in life. I shall probably only end up taking the waters at Baden with my sister, curtsying to ancient princesses and playing bridge all evening.'

He laughed. 'I have heard the waters there are quite…soothing.'

'My curtsy is anything but. I always think

I will fall over when I must perform one. And the last time I went to a watering spot—' She broke off and looked away, poking her heavy silver fork at that fish. It had been to Tunbridge, after she'd lost their child. Her doctor had thought it would revive her 'low spirits', bring her strength back, but all she had wanted to do was lie alone in her darkened room. Fall down, down, down, and be with her lost little girl. And Jamie hadn't been there to persuade her otherwise. Too immersed in his work, his colleagues, his friends...

She gestured for more wine. 'Tell me more about your work, then.'

As the entrée, overcooked lamb, and the once again unrecognisable savoury were served, they talked more of Goldoni and his plays and Venice, the latest plays in London, her sisters and their work and her nieces and nephews, Lily's royal service and Violet's photography. Anything but the two of them, Rose and Jamie. But Rose actually started to *enjoy* herself.

She laughed as Jamie told her a tale about an unfortunate man who'd knocked over a whole shelf of medieval manuscripts at the British Museum. How nice it felt to sit and chat with him, to be at ease. She couldn't remember when she last felt that way. She told him of parties she had attended, a garden she was planning at her little London house, silly, small things she feared might bore him. But he laughed when she described funny details of tea parties and breakfast regattas on the Thames, and she felt such a golden glow of happiness to hear that sound. It was almost like meeting a congenial new stranger, yet someone she'd also known so well. This new/old Jamie.

She felt herself being enticed by him once more as she had so long ago, when they'd first danced, first kissed, first whispered secrets to each other. And she had thought herself beyond such things, that old Rose walled up behind a hard shell.

Jamie toyed with his silver fork with those long, elegant fingers touched with ink and she had to glance away. Once those hands had done such magical things to her…

She pushed away the plate of pudding, a mushy charlotte russe, and Jamie smiled and shook his head. 'The cuisine is quite appalling, isn't it? I fear I hardly notice it here any more. It's been so terrible for so long. My mother would have been mortified. This was a real ducal seat when she was alive.'

Rose realised he seldom talked of his family, especially not his mother, the beautiful, sad woman in the portrait. And her brief impression of his father and brother was only that they were very different indeed from Jamie. 'The lady in the painting? She was certainly as pretty as they say.'

'She was indeed.'

'You never talk about her, or your childhood.'

He frowned, pushing his fork across his plate. 'She died a long time ago. And my childhood— well, you have seen this house, can you imagine being a child in it? It was quite dull, to say the least.'

Rose wondered if *their* child, if the baby had lived, would have had a 'dull childhood', too, here in this vast palace. But she knew no child of hers would—she wouldn't let it. She thought of her own childhood, running through the nursery with her sisters, laughing and arguing, swimming at Newport, sledding in Central Park in the snow. 'I doubt *dull* is exactly the word I would think of.'

He shoved away his plate, not looking at her. 'Oh, no, it was very dull indeed most of the time. When my mother was alive, she would sometimes take us out on excursions, riding or to historic castles and churches, or just walking in the woods, and I enjoyed my lessons with the tutors, before we were sent off to school. They were men who appreciated learning, who appreciated—well, being appreciated, I suppose. Having a pupil who liked languages and history and philosophy. My brother only liked his ponies and his guns, as did my father. And, of course, they both liked their brandy a great deal. As did my grandfather, they say. His drunken exploits were legendary.'

Rose ached to think of it all, a lonely boy marooned in a house of drink and silence. No wonder he'd turned out as he had with only that example to follow. 'Your father was a countryman through and through, I suppose.'

'Oh, yes, through and through. He had little use for a city son, you see. Luckily I seldom saw him, just heard his drunken shouting and there wasn't even that when I went to school. It was blessedly quiet there. And when I was a little older and forced to spend time here, there was always brandy to take the edge off the misery...' He looked lost in thought for a long moment, in painful memories, and Rose longed to go to him, take him in her arms. But then he gave a careless smile. 'That's all hardly unusual, though, here in England. I suppose your child-hood must have been very different.'

Rose was startled to realise that, as she knew little about Jamie's past, he knew little about hers. America always felt so very long ago and far away now, a different life altogether. A life that had little to do with *her*. And yet she felt as though she had just glimpsed a long-hidden secret in only a few words, a hint of the demons inside Jamie, and she didn't want him to see her own secrets.

'Yes, it was, I suppose. But we were girls as well as Americans,' she said. 'We didn't often see our father, either. He was always working so hard. When we did, though, it was like a merry holiday. He would bring us sweets and dolls, take us out in his carriage, even show us off at his club to all his friends. Mother was much more strict. She came from an old South-ern family, you see, and we were meant to be fine ladies, even if our father was 'Old King Coal', newest of the new money. We had gov-ernesses, no schools, and she took us travelling when were older to get some culture. Florence and Rome and Paris. There was Newport in the summer, once she was finally accepted there.

It took her years. Then Papa built her that fine cottage she longed for...'

And there was that terrible summer there in Newport, in her family's beautiful summer chateau. Her first big mistake in romance. But she never wanted to think of that again.

'Never mind about trying to choke down this pudding,' Jamie said. 'We can go out for a ride tomorrow, have luncheon at the Queen's Head in Greensted Village. They do a very nice lamb stew, I hear, and a bread and butter pudding.'

Rose laughed. 'Have you been talking to my sisters, then?'

Jamie shook his head. 'I doubt they would speak to me these days. But what would they say?'

'You sound rather like them, that's all. They're always trying to get me to eat.'

'Well, I don't blame you one jot for not eating this,' he said, but he did look rather worried.

'Dinner has been lovely, truly. This is such a pretty room. And being able to talk to you. I've—I've missed you,' she admitted.

He smiled again, shyly, her old Jamie. 'And I have missed you, Rose. So much.' He pushed back his chair and held out his hand to her. 'Walk with me?'

She stared at his hand, that tempting touch he offered for a moment before she took it, sliding her fingers over his as she had a million times before, and yet now it all felt brand new. He felt so warm, so strong and steady and safe under her touch, so familiar and so foreign all at the same time. How quickly they'd fallen back into their old intimacy.

He led her through a glass door into the garden beyond. The night had grown cloudy, lit only by faint, chalky pale rays of moonlight and the lamps that glowed in the windows, making her vividly aware of Jamie beside her in the dimness. The silence. They seemed to be the only two people in all the world.

'Do you remember the night of the Gregsons' ball?' he asked.

Rose smiled. 'How could I forget? That was when you first kissed me. When you asked me to marry you. I was shocked out of my wits. So were you, I think.' She looked up at the sky and remembered it had been just like this, the night, the lit house behind them, Jamie's hand in hers, and yet then her heart had been bursting with hope.

'I was rather shocked, yes. I never meant to blurt out those words to you like that, with no skill or charm or poetry. But once I'd said them, I knew it was right.'

Rose had known it was right then, too. She had been so dizzy with the knowledge that everything she'd wanted had come true, that she had found love and belonging at last. But they were not those people now. Surely he had thought he was getting something, someone else with her. They really hadn't known each other well enough at all. They had met and married in such quick, dizzying succession. But that night at the ball had been pure magic. So perfect that even now she felt the memory of it like a fragile, bruised beauty all around her.

'I thought it was right, too. When you kissed me, I knew where I should be, was sure we would never be parted again. But life can't always be like that, can it?'

'I wanted to make everything perfect for you, Rose. To make you smile every day. Instead, I only made your life so much more difficult than I'd ever intended.'

Rose was astonished at his words, so stark and simple and filled with sadness. She thought of what he'd told her about his family, their distance, their fundamental differences from him, his mother's sadness and his father's drinking.

Jamie had surely needed to smile more, just like Rose needed to.

'I couldn't give you anything you wanted, needed,' he continued brokenly. 'Not even a child.'

Rose was seized with a sharp, physical pain deep in her stomach. The one thing they had most longed for above all others—the child, a new family, a new start. The thing that could not be.

'Please, no, Jamie,' she whispered. She closed her eyes against the tears she couldn't cry any more. He held on to her as she tried to turn away, held her close against him, and she laid her cheek against the beat of his heart. Let his warmth seep into her.

'I am so very sorry we lost her, Rose,' he said simply.

'Oh, Jamie. Once those few words were all I wanted to hear from you. But now…'

'Now it is too late?' he said, such a terrible finality in his voice.

'I—I don't know,' she murmured and held on to him with all her strength.

Chapter Twelve

The day was cool but bright when they set off from the Greensted stables the next morning. To Rose's surprise, she had slept well after they'd parted last night, Jamie kissing her cheek as they left the dark garden, things still uncertain but somewhat peaceful between them again. It felt like a new day, one where the possibility of something very delicate and as yet unknown could begin to grow again. Maybe they could really be friends.

She laughed as her horse frisked into a gallop, carrying her into the wind, blowing away the strange night. They rode out through the gates and on to the rutted lane beyond. It felt like bursting free from a prison into light and air again, a holiday like when her father would carry her and her sisters out of the schoolroom and off to the park merry-go-round.

And Jamie escaped beside her. Despite his protests of being a 'city son' he was a very good rider, his seat in the saddle easy and graceful. He had taken off his hat and let the breeze ruffle his hair, laughing with her.

They let the horses have their heads across an empty field, leaping over ha-has and ditches and boulders, flying across meadows.

'What pretty country this is,' she said, studying the way the pale blue sky met the late summer fields, the white dots of sheep in the distance, the low grey walls.

'So it is. I always liked exploring it when I was a boy. There's a nice wood over that way.'

'Perhaps there was some of the country lad in you, after all?'

Jamie laughed. 'I doubt it. I always had a book with me. Hedgerows and shady meadows are the perfect reading spots.'

'And yet you harbour secret talents. You're an excellent rider. And I remember you were a dab hand with a phaeton in the park when we were courting.'

'You had to be a good rider in my family. And you aren't so bad yourself.'

'Oh, my mother heard that all English ladies were excellent horsewomen, so we had to learn, too.' She patted her horse's sleek neck. 'I was terrified at first, I admit, but then I found I rather enjoyed it. Much easier exercise than lawn tennis and I liked the clothes. So elegant.' She reached up to straighten her veiled black silk top hat.

Jamie laughed again, and Rose realised he, too, seemed to feel much more relaxed today, as if their confidences in the night garden had loosened something inside of them. 'And you do look most elegant, as you always do.'

'Come, then, let's race. I can tell my horse is feeling her oats!'

She swiftly spurred her horse forward. She'd almost forgotten what it felt like to ride like that, focused only on the speed, the freedom. They raced along, neck and neck, laughing uproariously until they pulled up at the end of a drive.

'I declare a draw,' Jamie said.

'A draw?' Rose cried in protest. 'I am quite sure I won! But I will not demand a forfeit.'

'If *I'd* won, I would demand you visit some tenants with me as my prize,' he said, gesturing up the drive.

'Visit your tenants? Really?' Rose thought

of the servants at Greensted, the unspoken yet heavy expectation of being the Duchess, and she felt her old shyness wash over her. What would these tenants of Jamie's think of her?

'Yes, the Hammonds. They are very nice people, I promise. I used to sneak here to their farm to eat seed cake when I was a child.' He sounded quite wistful, as if he had indeed been so lonely as a child.

Rose felt a pang at the thought of his emotionally barren childhood. 'Then I would enjoy meeting them.'

She followed him up the drive to a two-storey farmhouse, neatly thatched and whitewashed, flower boxes at the windows and a vegetable garden hemmed in by a stone wall. Rose could see how well Jamie was making sure his tenants lived.

The green-painted door swung open and a broad-shouldered, sun-browned farmer stood there, a little girl with long, golden plaits holding his hand. They waved and the girl jumped up and down in excitement. Rose remembered her own lost little girl then, who might once have been this child's playmate. Growing up on this estate, as Jamie had.

'Your Grace!' the man said. 'We didn't expect you today.' He gave Rose a curious glance.

'I heard you were having a problem with your roof, Mr Hammond,' Jamie said as he swung down from his horse, reaching up to help Rose. 'And that your mother has been ill. I trust she has recovered?'

'Aye, thanks to the doctor you sent over. Just as bossy as ever, she is.'

Rose looked up at Jamie, realising again how kind he was to those who relied on him.

'Duke! Duke!' the little girl cried. 'I have a new doll! It looks like this lady.'

Jamie laughed and swung the child up into his arms, twirling her around as she giggled. 'Then it must be a very pretty doll indeed. This is the Duchess of Byson. Rose, this is Mr Reginald Hammond and Daisy. His mother, Mrs Jane Hammond, used to feed me seed cake.'

The girl's cornflower-blue eyes widened, and she wobbled a curtsy after Jamie carefully put her down. Mr Hammond bowed, his expression puzzled but friendly. 'You are very welcome, Duchess. Please, do come inside. I only wish we had a grander reception to offer! My wife has gone to visit her sister in the village.'

'You are so kind, Mr Hammond, and I am

honoured to be here,' Rose said. She took Jamie's offered arm and stepped through the doorway into a well-scrubbed small hall, flagstone-floored, where sweet-scented dried herbs hung from the darkened ceiling beams. Doorways to either side seemed to lead to a sitting room and dining space.

'For heaven's sake, Reggie, offer Her Grace some tea!' a querulous old lady called from the sitting room. 'Show the manners I taught you.'

Mr Hammond flushed dark red. 'Yes, yes, of course, Mother. Tea.'

'And there are cakes!' Daisy said. 'I helped bake them.'

'Then I am sure they are quite delicious,' Rose answered with a smile.

'Daisy, dear, why don't you take Her Grace in to your grandmother and then fetch the tea, while I show the Duke the roof?' Mr Hammond said.

Daisy unselfconsciously took Rose's hand and led her through to the sitting room. It was small and very warm from the fire blazing in the scrubbed grate, but as impeccable as the hall, with bright rugs on the old wooden floors and cushions scattered on the chairs. A tiny, white-haired lady wrapped in shawls sat by the fire.

'Ah, so *you* are the famous Duchess,' the old lady said, examining Rose until she could feel herself blushing. 'As pretty as they say. Daisy, dear, do go and fetch the tea things, there's a good girl.'

As Daisy rushed off on her errand, Rose sat down on the stool next to old Mrs Hammond.

'We are glad to see Lord James, as he was, back again. His agent is excellent, but there's nothing like the interest of the Duke himself to make things happen,' Mrs Hammond said, taking out some knitting from her bag. 'His father and brother had no time for the house or the estate, but Lord James was always such a good lad. Always interested in what was happening here. He loved my seed cakes.'

'Yes,' Rose murmured. 'A good lad indeed.'

Mrs Hammond gave her a searching glance. 'But every fine house needs a mistress, I say. Someone sensible and good. And being pretty, too, is never a bad thing for a duchess, is it? Lord James's mother was a beauty, but she's been gone so long. Greensted isn't what it used to be.'

Rose had no idea how to tell Mrs Hammond

the truth—that she and Jamie were not truly married, not any longer. Luckily, Daisy returned, carefully balancing a tray of tea things and cakes, her doll under her arm, and there was nothing else to say. Not yet.

The Queen's Head did indeed serve a fine lamb stew and, to Rose's surprise, she found she had a good appetite after their ride. The public house was not very busy at that hour and no one really talked to them, but Rose noticed the few customers casting curious glances in their direction.

'Do you know those men, Jamie?' she asked. She took a nibble of her parsley butter potatoes and gestured with her fork towards a knot of old men sitting in the corner with their pints, staring at her. Her mother would have been appalled at her manners, which made Rose feel even happier about the day.

Jamie shook his head. 'I'm sorry to say I don't really. The one in the green tweed seems rather familiar. I fear I don't yet know the Greensted neighbourhood as well as I should. I shall have much to learn.'

She remembered the cosy tenants' cottage,

the warm welcome. 'The Hammonds seemed to know you well.'

He laughed. 'They are different. I used to follow Mr Hammond's father on his work round sometimes. He liked to study the local flora and would always have such interesting botanical facts to tell me. He was very patient with a pestilential little boy. And as I believe I've already mentioned, Mrs Hammond shared her seed cake with me, which has always been the best in the neighbourhood. But I never had the chance to meet most of the people here. It never felt like—' He broke off with a frown.

She remembered what he'd said of his lonely childhood. 'Not like home?'

'Not really. I was isolated as a child and then was sent away to school so young. My brother was going to be the Duke, responsible for everything here. As the "spare", I was never given much reason to return. Now, I have to learn to see it as my place. The people my duty to help, if I can.'

Rose nodded. She could understand duty, certainly; her sisters were devoted to each other. Lily had first married Aidan to take care of them all and Rose would have done the same if it were necessary. She even envied such a sense of real purpose. She sought such a thing all the time, a purpose, a reason. But she did ache to think of Jamie as a child, so lonely, so lacking in a real home. At least she'd had her sisters, always, and they were her real home. She had once tried to give Jamie a family like that, too, but they both knew how she'd failed.

'Can you make it feel like your place now?' she said, scooping up the last of her stew.

He looked thoughtful. 'Perhaps so, yes. The people here are good-hearted, as you've seen, and I can use some of my ideas and interests to make a few changes. There are vast resources here that could be used for the benefit of many, not just for shooting parties as my father did. And the house can be made bright and welcoming again.'

'Like a new school, maybe,' Rose said, thinking of little Miss Hammond.

'Yes, for a start. And there are some interesting agricultural experiments being done on nearby estates with similar soils. I think Greensted's farms would be well suited to such things, to increase our yields. Perhaps we could even expand the stables.' He smiled self-deprecatingly. 'But I shouldn't bore you with that.'

'I don't mind at all,' Rose said, and she didn't.

She enjoyed listening to Jamie, enjoyed his enthusiasm for such a wide range of subjects, how interested he was, how he made things come to life before her eyes. It was what had first fascinated her about him, that interest, that enthusiasm, that intelligence that had no snobbery about it. That, and his beautiful dark eyes. His lips on hers, so gentle but so filled with hunger, so enticing it had made her forget all about what had happened in Newport. Erased her fear. The touch of his graceful hands on her skin...

Stop it right now, Rose, she thought fiercely, and reached for her glass of cider. She and Jamie were to be friends now.

'I do like hearing you talk,' she said. 'I always have. And I agree with you. Greensted has marvellous potential. And you have seen what Lily and Aidan have achieved with their estates in such a short time. So much can be done.'

'No, no, I refuse to bore you, we have so little time together,' he said. 'I would rather hear more of *you*, of your life now. Who would have imagined I would be married to a famous beauty? My brother would never have believed it. And my father was sure no lady would ever have me at all.'

Rose shook her head. 'No one could be more

astonished than me that a stranger might want to buy my photograph in a stationers' shop. I'm not at all sure how that happened. Violet took my image at a fancy-dress ball one night and the next thing I knew everyone was buying it.'

'I absolutely know how it happened. I knew you were the most beautiful woman in all the world the first time I saw you at that garden party.' He smiled at her, a smile so full of wistful memory, of admiration. Rose stared back at him, wishing, longing.

She was very grateful when the maidservant came to their table, interrupting whatever emotion was roiling in her heart. The girl, apple-cheeked, friendly, gave them a quick smile.

'Can I get you anything else, Lord Ja—that is, Your Grace?' She gave a hasty curtsy, seemingly flustered.

Jamie laughed reassuringly. 'I've been telling the Duchess all about your delicious bread and butter pudding, Janet.'

'Indeed he has and I have to admit it was quite my favourite when I was a child,' Rose said. She'd thought she was full from the stew and potatoes, but to her amazement she was still hungry for the sweet. That ever-present knot in her stomach had vanished. 'I do hope it's on your menu today.'

Janet beamed. 'Oh, aye, my auntie has baked some fresh, Your Grace. She'll be glad to bring it out herself. Was the stew to your liking?'

Rose glanced down at her plate, amazed to see it was empty. She would be as round as a lamb herself soon. 'I would be happy to eat it every day,' she said honestly.

Janet beamed again and removed the empty plates. 'You're welcome here any time at all, Your Grace. We're all so excited to see a duchess at Greensted again and I don't mind saying so. It's been ever so long.'

Rose smiled, but she couldn't help but feel a guilty pang. She would be gone soon enough and Janet and the Hammonds would have to wait a little longer for a duchess to appear again.

'How is your father, Janet?' Jamie asked her. 'Is his rheumatism better?'

'Oh, aye, it comes and goes. He has trouble managing the stairs some days, but he's still able to keep his eye on everything. He'll be wanting to know all about you when you leave!'

'Rheumatism?' Rose asked, thinking of a nanny she and her sisters had when they were children, who would sit with her feet up most of the time, but would read them hair-raising ghost stories that had delighted them with terror. 'My old nanny used to suffer from it and she used this special salve she taught my sisters and me to help her mix up. I'm not sure how well it works, but it's quite simple and smells rather nice, if you would like to me to give you the recipe.'

Janet beamed. 'How kind, Your Grace! He'd welcome a bit of relief and I'd like to smell something besides ale all the time.' She bobbed a curtsy again. 'I'll fetch your pudding, then, shall I?'

As she left, Rose leaned closer to Jamie and said, 'And you claim you know nothing of your neighbours! You seem to have met almost everyone *and* know their stories.'

'Only the Hammonds, and Janet and her father and auntie,' he said with a bashful smile. 'And you claim you would make a terrible duchess, but everyone loves you already.'

'If handing out salve recipes is all it takes to make a duchess, I would be darling at it,' she said with a laugh. 'It's all the other things I would be terrible at. Not like Lily, who seems born to it all.'

'Oh, Rose.' He took her hand in his, raising

it to his lips for a quick kiss that made her toes tingle. 'We do seem to underestimate ourselves, you and I.'

Rose stared at their joined hands, the flash of her wedding ring. 'Perhaps that has been our problem all along.' She let go of him when Daisy and her equally beaming aunt brought out the pudding.

As they left, the staring men in the corner gave them respectful nods and Rose felt for a moment as if she was really part of something. This village, this neighbourhood, this spot where everyone could play their parts and everyone knew everyone else. It was…a little strange. And rather nice.

'Shall we walk for a while?' she said as they untied their horses. 'I haven't eaten so much in ages!'

'Yes, of course. It is a lovely day.'

As they led their horses along the lane, Rose spied a millinery shop, a dressmaker, a lawyer's office, a lovely ancient church with a square Norman tower and leaning old headstones dotting the peaceful churchyard, and a tea shop. Everything a village needed, really. Jamie pointed out places where he hoped new businesses could be installed, a ramshackle building he said had once been the village school before it closed.

'Rose,' Jamie said as they passed a half-timbered inn. He sounded tentative, and the contentment of their luncheon suddenly vanished. 'Are you certain you have been feeling quite well lately?'

Rose frowned. 'Oh, Jamie. You've mentioned this before. Do I not look well enough to you?'

'You look as beautiful as the moon, as you always do. I was just—well, yes, concerned, I suppose.

Rose nodded reluctantly. She didn't want to tell him that the doctor had advised her to have a break from London life. 'I have just been a little tired lately, I admit. But I am already feeling better. Did I not just eat the most enormous meal?'

They turned down a narrow pathway and found themselves in a grove of trees, shady and green, like some place a circle of fairies might dance in.

'This was one of my favourite spots when I was a child,' he said. 'I could hide here and read, it was so pretty, so...so like a fairy tale, I suppose.'

'I can see why. It's lovely.' She gently touched the tree, the bark rough through her glove, and smiled up at the leafy canopy. She glanced over her shoulder to find him watching her tenderly. 'What are you thinking about so deeply, Jamie?'

He smiled at her, brushing back a lock of windblown hair from his brow. 'Perhaps I am only thinking something very, very shallow?'

'Oh, no. I know that expression.'

'I was thinking, if you needed a little more rest, a place entirely new and different, why don't you come to Venice with me? I know you would love to see it.'

Rose was shocked—and, she had to admit, a bit intrigued. She stopped short in the middle of the street. 'Venice?'

He took a step nearer, his expression very earnest. She did know that look: he used it when he wanted so much to persuade her to do something—like when he'd asked her to marry him. 'Yes. It's not the season of parties there, so it should be peaceful. I have my work to do, but you could wander around the museums and churches, take naps, read, eat gelato, whatever you like.' His smile turned more coaxing, more irresistible. 'We would have separate suites, of course. The palazzo I rented is much too large only for me.'

Rose was terribly tempted. Venice! She *had* longed to see it, ever since she'd looked at pictures of it in a book as a child. So ancient, so romantic, so wonderfully eerie. And with Jamie beside her…

Once, she had dreamed of seeing such places with him. Bridges and ancient palaces and art so beautiful it would make her cry. Those dreams, like all the others, had collapsed into dust around her. But the romance and mystery of a place like Venice—would she really be sorry if she went? Or more sorry if she stayed?

She stared up into his eyes for a long, silent, tense moment. He looked back, earnest, waiting, unreadable. He touched her hand. Even through their riding gloves she could feel the familiar warmth of him, the way his fingers fit so perfectly around hers. That old tenderness.

'Let me show you how I've changed, Rose,' he said quietly. 'I couldn't bear to know you were going about your life thinking poorly of me. Just—stay with me for a little while in a place we don't know together. No expectations at all; you make all the decisions. I don't want you to remember our marriage as all terrible. Or remember me as an ogre.'

'Oh, Jamie.' She reached up and ran her fingers over his cheek. 'I have never thought if you as an ogre. You are much too handsome for that.' Other things she had thought, yes. She had thought she'd disappointed him so much as his Duchess that he couldn't bear to be with her; that he'd hated their lives together, that his demons would always chase him. But an ogre— no. Only a man. A man she'd held most dear.

He laughed and took her arm, strolling along the street again, her head brushing his shoulder. 'Maybe you thought I was a mere bridge troll, then. If you don't like it in Venice, you can return to England and I will start proceedings for a divorce, if you are sure that is what you want. I will even be the guilty party. Let me have Venice first.'

'Is this journey a requirement, then, if that is what we decide is best?'

In answer, he took her hand and raised it to his lips, kissing each fingertip as if it was a precious jewel before he held her palm tenderly to his cheek.

'Not a requirement,' he said hoarsely. 'A plea.

Spend some more time with me, Rose. Let me show you…'

Show her—what? That he had changed, that he was really her Jamie again? He had vowed to change before, to give up drink as apparently his father and brother never could, to spend more time with her and less with his work and his cronies. They would reunite then, in a storm of kisses, passionate promises, only for it all to vanish again into the ether.

Yet—yet she could already see that some things had really changed. There was no drink now and when he talked with her she could see his mind was nowhere else but on her, on them. Her darling old Jamie, the man she had adored so much.

He seemed to sense her wavering and his smile widened. 'It wasn't all bad after all, was it, Rose? We did have happy times, too.'

'No. It wasn't all bad.' There had been their wedding, that vision of tulle and orange blossoms, the honeymoon of wild, delightful discovery, the rooms filled with flowers, the dances and laughter and kisses.

She shook her head, trying to push the misty tendrils of the past far away from her. 'I was silly and so young. I thought it would always be just that way, the same way it was on our honeymoon, and I know that's totally unrealistic.'

'Surely we can at least talk now and I can start to make you see things as they once were. As I want to see them, too. The real me. The real *us*.' He looked so young then, so serious. 'No one but you has ever seen me like that.'

Rose suddenly wanted to burst into tears, to throw her arms around him and never let him go. 'I will consider it, Jamie. That's all I can promise right now.'

He nodded. 'Then I can at least hope. That's something, anyway.'

Jamie found he couldn't sleep that night, the moments he had spent with Rose turning over and over in his mind. Rose walking along the lane, smiling in the sun, laughing over her bread and butter pudding, mesmerising everyone she talked to. The feel of her hand in his.

And more than that, times even further back, lost moments. The garden party where he first saw her, the glowing white of their incandescent wedding day, her hopeful face as she told him she thought she was pregnant. Then the lost baby, her empty eyes, his hopelessness. His failure in caring for her properly. Everything, everything.

He felt the tug of that inexorable old craving deep inside, the craving for a gulp of wine or brandy or whisky, the warm forgetfulness it would bring. That craving did not come upon him often now, but when it did it was sharp and insistent. Finally, he gave up even trying to sleep, tossing on his dressing gown and heading to the library in the dark silence to try to lose himself in his books instead of a bottle.

But he found he wasn't alone after all. The library door was half-open, a golden light shining out into the Greensted gloom. He pushed the door all the way open and peered cautiously inside.

Rose sat at the desk, frowning in concentration as she peered down at the papers in front of her. She wore a velvet-collared robe, pale yellow, and her hair fell down her back in heavy waves, as deep red as a sunset in the lamplight. She was so deeply focused that she didn't notice him there and he stood staring at her, just letting himself know, believe, for a moment that she was really there. Not another dream, not another occasion that he'd just imagined her.

He must have made some sound, and she

glanced up, startled. The pen fell from her fingers with a clatter and her eyes were wide.

'Jamie! I thought everyone was asleep,' she said. She self-consciously smoothed her loose hair. 'Did I wake you?'

He moved cautiously into the room, towards that enticing circle of light beyond all the gloom of the old house. Towards her. 'Not at all. I just couldn't sleep. I thought I would—well...' His gaze flickered involuntarily towards the cabinet holding an array of dusty bottles. Rose's attention turned there, too, and she frowned. 'No, I didn't come down for that,' he explained. 'I thought I would read for a while.'

'I couldn't sleep, either. I kept thinking about everything we saw today in the village.'

'So what are you working on? Letters?' He sat down in the chair next to the desk.

'I was just sketching a little idea for that girls' school. Lily built just such a thing at Roderick Castle, you know, and it has been a great success.' She showed him the paper, the sketch of clean lines and scribbled directions for desks and shelves and cupboards. 'See, it's that empty building you showed me, that was once the school? I think if you made just these changes, you could fit in at least twenty girls. If you put the teacher's desk here and perhaps a small dais behind so that—' She suddenly broke off on a laugh. 'I am quite interfering, aren't I?'

He thought she was marvellous. 'Not at all. It is a truly excellent idea. I can think of several girls, including Daisy Hammond, who would greatly benefit.'

'Yes, Lily's school has already placed several girls as lady's maids, even teachers. She has one pupil she thinks shows great promise in art. Girls do deserve a good start in life, the chance to find their talent. They...' She suddenly dashed away a shimmer of tears in her eyes. 'They deserve people to care about them, a chance to be happy...'

She turned away, the tumble of words broken on a soft sob. 'They deserve as much care as we can give them. The care I couldn't give...'

Couldn't give their own tiny girl. Jamie's heart ached. 'Oh, my dear. My Rose.' He knelt down beside her chair, reaching for her trembling hands. She didn't draw away from him and he wrapped his arms around her tightly, trying to keep her safe. Wishing so much he had always kept her safe. 'I know, I know. I miss her, too.'

Rose looked down at him, her eyes wide as

if she suddenly realised it had been his loss as well. His hopes of a family gone. 'Do you—do you think about her, too? Of what might have happened if she had lived?'

'Of course I do. My tiny Oxford scholar, my little beauty. It was all my fault, Rose. If I'd been there for you more...'

'No, no! How can you say that! I was her mother. I should have...'

'Shh, my love. No, never your fault. Never, never.' He leaned closer and his lips touched hers, no passion, no seduction, just the warm, clinging touch of their kiss, the comfort they each craved so much. The comfort they had denied themselves for too long.

The comfort that eluded them still.

Chapter Thirteen

'You're going where? To *Venice*?' Lily cried.

'With Jamie?' Violet added indignantly.

Rose tightened her lips and nodded. She had to brace herself when her sisters sounded like that; it had always been the hardest thing for her to stand up to them. Yet she knew going to Venice was something she had to do. The right thing to do. It was the only way she could move forward with no doubts.

'You both said I should have a holiday,' she said. 'And that maybe Jamie needed a second chance. Remember?'

'Raise your arm a bit—like so,' Violet said, frowning in concentration as she showed Rose how to pose. Even arguing about an estranged husband could not quite distract Violet when she was taking a photograph. 'No, that's not quite right, either. Try to the left, a teensy bit. And we thought you needed to *rest*, not worry about James again!'

'You needed to forget about everything,' Lily said. 'Not plunge right back into old troubles! He needs to be the one to work for his chance.'

'It's not like that,' Rose said, posing as Violet directed. She felt rather stiff, posed as an ancient sibyl in a draped yellow silk gown and sheer veil, her arms raised and face beatific as if she could see the future. She wished so much she *could* see it. But she was glad at least one of her sisters had something else to focus on for a moment. If they were all facing each other across a tea table, she wouldn't know what to say, how to keep that wretched blush from her cheeks. 'He has work to do on his new Goldoni project and I've always wanted to see Venice. He's rented a huge palazzo. I'm sure we will rarely even meet at all. He says…'

'He says what?' Lily asked suspiciously.

'Says he wants me not to remember him as— as an ogre. That he's changed.' She shifted again at Violet's gesture. 'Not that I've ever thought him an ogre.'

'Of course he wasn't *that*,' Lily conceded.

'He's too quiet and scholarly to be a real ogre. But he did make you unhappy.'

'And I made myself unhappy, too. He's not the only one who has changed. Who has got older. Who has learnt difficult lessons.' She realised suddenly that was true. She had seen so much, learned so much, in the years since she met Jamie. She'd seen more of the world, discovered more about herself. She remembered their kiss as they'd finally mourned their baby, the moment binding them together where once it had torn them apart. 'Perhaps I need to see it for myself. To really close this chapter and make the correct decision going forward.'

Lily and Violet exchanged a long glance before Violet turned back to her camera. 'Stand—like—that. Don't move an inch!'

Rose froze, her arm raised, gazing off into an imagined landscape of Grecian hills. She could feel Lily looking at her, too wise, too motherly, too all-seeing.

'You must do whatever you deem right, Rose darling,' Lily said. 'And we are here for you, no matter what. What exactly happened when you were at Greensted? They say it's quite the old Gothic pile.'

Rose sighed. Of course they wanted to hear

all about her visit to Jamie's ducal home. She'd put them off long enough since she'd returned, running to the theatre and dances, anywhere there couldn't be quiet conversation. 'I looked at sketches for redecoration. It *is* quite a dusty old pile. We went riding, met a few of his tenants…' Kissed, held hands. Started hoping again. But she couldn't tell them *that*.

'Quite the travelogue,' Lily said as Violet fussed with her plates and Rose lowered her arm, shaking out her shoulder. 'And you do look quite well since you returned. You haven't really been Rose without the roses in your cheeks!'

Violet grinned. 'Country air agrees with you, does it not?'

'My lungs hardly know what to do without London soot any more,' Rose protested.

Lily frowned. 'But this Venice visit…'

'It won't be for long. And I've never been to Venice! I need a little more time away from all of…this. Just like we've talked about.' She sat down across from Lily, stretching out her legs.

'You needed time away from Jamie,' Violet said.

'I know, I know. But now I must make certain the next step I take is the right one for us both.'

'Of course you must be sure,' Lily said, handing her a cup of tea. 'Now, shall we send for some cream cakes? Violet, dear, are you going to mess about with that photographic plate all day long?'

'You know she will,' Rose said.

'This will be my best image all year, I am sure of it,' Violet said, but she did sit down with them, wiping her stained hands on a towel. 'It's bound to win a prize at the Photographic Exhibition. Now, Rose, if you do want to go to Venice, won't you let me give you a teensy lesson in photography? The new cameras out of Germany are so lightweight and simple, and there will be so many gorgeous vistas you'll want to capture while you're there...'

Rose took off her gloves and unpinned her hat, leaving them on the table of her little hall. The afternoon post waited there, mostly invitation cards, but she couldn't quite face them all yet. She adored her sisters and every hour she spent with them, but they did sometimes leave her feeling a bit limp with exhaustion. Of all the masks she wore in her life—heiress, society beauty, separated wife, duchess—she held on to none more tightly than the one she put on for Lily and Violet so they wouldn't worry about her. But they seemed to worry quite enough, anyway.

Rose reached for one of the bouquets that waited, all the tokens from admirers that arrived every day, and absently stroked the soft, deep red petals. Were her sisters right, then? Was she making a mistake going abroad with Jamie? It had seemed like an easy, strangely natural thing to do when she was actually with him. When she looked into his eyes, felt his touch on her skin, it was easy to let hope carry her away like a warm ocean wave, even when it had once dropped her suddenly on to a lonely beach.

And yet—the days at Greensted had been so lovely. Talking, riding, walking. It felt as though she'd found her husband again, but also saw a new man at the same time, one older, more confident, more sure of himself and what he wanted. She had caught a glimpse of a life that could be wonderful if she only dared reach out for it.

She turned and hurried through the open door to her drawing room. The lamps hadn't been lit yet, but she liked the shadows—they gave her some space for thinking before the hectic social evenings started. So much of her life now was filled with brightness and speed,

moving so quickly from portrait sittings to teas
to balls to theatres that she had no time to think.
Perhaps she had made her days that way deliberately, so she couldn't think too much. Far
too much. But she needed to really think very
carefully now. She couldn't afford to make any
more mistakes.

She went to the window and stared down
at the street below, quiet now while everyone
was getting ready for their evening parties. The
windows all glowed gold. She'd loved this little
house when she first found it, the only place
that had ever been hers alone, her very own
refuge. Tall and narrow, decorated in feminine
pastel colours and pretty floral paintings, piles
of books, baskets of her embroidery. Compared
to vast Greensted, it was a mere bird's nest, and
she suddenly wished Jamie sat there with her,
that she could see him in one of her cosy velvet
chairs drawn close to the fireplace, across from
her at her little walnut table in the dining room.

It would be just the two of them in Venice.
Alone in a place where they had never been, a
place that belonged to neither or both of them.
Wonderful things might happen—or truly terrible things.

Rose never thought of herself as a risk-taker.

Not like Violet, forging her own artistic career, or Lily, the first of them to chase an English life so very different from their American childhoods. Rose even sometimes thought of herself as ridiculously frightened of so much. What had happened in Newport had made her wary for so long. Yet when she first met Jamie, she hadn't been frightened. She'd known she loved him so soon, that a life with him was surely what she wanted, and she was still rather proud of that bold step, even though it had turned out not to be anything like she'd expected. She felt as though Venice could be the right step now.

Was she wrong again?

'It's only Italy,' she whispered to herself. If all went badly, she could leave in an instant and return to London, alone. Being the child of Old King Coal Wilkins brought with it rare advantages, financial advantages that she had never taken for granted. She wasn't tied to Jamie for the roof over her head and the food she ate, as far too many women were with their husbands. She was tied to him by the love she'd felt for him—and that was the flimsiest of gauzy ribbons.

But, oh, what if she really did still love him? Rose clenched her fist in the fine satin of her curtains, her vision suddenly blurred by a film of tears.

The door opened, and her butler appeared with a bow. 'Oh, Your Grace, I apologise the lamps haven't been lit yet. You should have rung.'

Rose surreptitiously wiped the tears away from her eyes and smiled. 'It's quite all right, I was about to ring the bell, in fact.'

'You have a caller, Your Grace.'

'A caller?' Surprised, Rose glanced at the gilt French clock on the mantel. It seemed rather late for visitors and she wondered with a surge of hope if it was Jamie.

'Indeed, Your Grace. It is Lord Paul Adelman.'

'Oh. Only Paul.' She laughed, relieved and disappointed. At least Paul would be amusing, distracting for a few moments. 'Please send him in.'

He frowned. 'Will Lord Paul be staying long? Dinner…'

'I shouldn't think so. I will take a tray in my room after he leaves. There's no reason to worry about a large dinner.'

'Very good, Your Grace.'

Rose quickly dashed away the last of her

tears and glanced in the silver-framed mirror to smooth her hair and pinch a little pink into her cheeks.

Paul swept in and kissed her cheek. Unlike her windblown appearance after the photographic session, he looked impeccable in his evening suit, his golden hair like guineas. 'Rose, my darling! How lovely you look. You've been missed.'

'And how ridiculous you are. I just got home from a long afternoon at Violet's studio and I am a rumpled mess. But it's good to see you, too. Are you off to Scotland soon?' She waved him towards one of the velvet chairs where she had pictured Jamie sitting. 'Some brandy?'

He sat down and propped his feet up on a tapestried stool, comfortable as always when he visited with her. 'Oh, yes, please. Scotland is set for next week. I shudder to think of it, all those damp treks along hills and lochs, freezing and catching no fish at all. But one must keep in well with one's relatives.'

'Indeed one must.' The butler brought in the drinks tray, and Rose poured out two brandies.

'You are lucky that your relations are sensible enough to either stay in London or go to their large, comfortable estates.'

Rose laughed. She *did* like Paul; he was comfortable and uncomplicated and sophisticated. It had often seemed to her that it might be a good and sensible idea to marry him; he would never disappoint her, but neither would he make her feel too much for him. 'Oh, I don't know. Lily is soon off to Baden with the Princess. My sisters never do seem to yearn for chilly Scotland, though.'

'What of you, then, American Beauty Rose? Where are you off to next? It will be dull here in London soon.'

She took a long drink. 'I am not sure. Lily did want me to go with her, but it doesn't sound like fun, really.'

Paul shuddered. 'No, indeed. Princess Alexandra, while a darling and so beautiful, is so very *demanding*. Paris might suit you better.'

Or maybe Venice. 'I am quite sure it would.'

'But what of something sooner, like tonight? Come to dinner with me.'

Rose shook her head. 'I'm a little weary, I'm afraid. Violet will do that to a person. I think I'll have a quiet night at home.'

He looked astonished. 'You? Weary? Do you feel quite well, my dear?'

'I feel very well indeed.' And she found,

rather to her surprise, that she *did* feel well. Better than she had in a long time. 'A little tired, that is all. I'll see you at Lady Hamilton's card party before you're off to the lochs, though.'

'Yes, of course, I wouldn't miss it. Lord Hamilton owes me after I lost so much to him last time.' He finished his drink and put down his glass to reach for her hand. His touch was pleasant, sweet, and it didn't make her feel as though lightning had struck as Jamie's touch did. 'Rose, my dear, I know I sound ridiculous when I try to be serious, but I have to say—I want you to know...'

Rose worried that she knew what he was going to say next. But she had no answers for him yet. Not to anything. 'Paul...'

He drew her closer, so slowly, so gently, so practised, and Rose felt a nervous flutter. She let him kiss her briefly, wondering and perhaps hoping it might make her feel like Jamie's kisses did. That all her doubts about reuniting with her husband could be swept away just like that.

It was a very nice kiss, soft and sweet. Yet it was still nothing like Jamie's kiss. There were no sunbursts, no urgent longings. In fact, she felt nothing at all.

She drew back and smiled at Paul. They

could have a nice life together. She knew that so well. They would own society together. He would never, could never, hurt her as Jamie had. Yet neither did he make her soar. *You are the only one I want*, Jamie had told her, when she was foolishly jealous of Beatrice Madewell. Maybe there was only one for her, too. And it wasn't the man standing in front of her right now.

'After Scotland, perhaps we could talk, yes?' he asked, smiling, bemused perhaps at her lack of response.

Rose could only nod. 'Perhaps, yes.'

Once Paul was gone, Rose sat back down to pour another brandy. Yes, she *would* go to Venice. It was the best way, the only way, to be completely sure what to do next.

Chapter Fourteen

Rose was rather weary by the time she stepped on to the boat that would carry them into Venice at last, on a cold and misty afternoon where she couldn't see anything. It had been a long journey by carriage, boat and train, with lost luggage being found at last by Jenny's ingenuity, and seasickness. Most of all, she had felt uneasy simply because of all the time spent with Jamie, after all their months apart. They had rarely travelled together even before the separation, being mostly based in London. Their country honeymoon had been a lovely time away from the city, but brief, and even then he had spent much time working while she went on walks and wrote to her sisters.

Going to Italy together was very different. She'd seen *her* Jamie again, the good and the not so good. The patience and good humour, the distraction. The time alone with him in small train compartments, the moments when she was sick on the boat, the smiles and laughter over tiny, swaying dinner tables—it had shown her so much. Reminded her of so much.

And the temptation to kiss him, to touch him, was always there. She didn't know what to do, where they stood with each other. But surely that was the purpose of this visit, to see how they felt about one another, how they might move forward. She had to rein in her impatience, her fears. No matter how hard it was.

She'd begun to think her sisters were right, that she hadn't completely considered what it would really mean to go all the way to Venice with Jamie. Then there were moments she was certain she was right to be there. That for the first time she had to be *sure* of decisions she made about her life.

Now there were no decisions to be made, because they were actually here. Alone. She sat beside Jamie in the boat, wrapping the collar of her coat closer against the chilly wind off the lagoon, and leaned on Jamie's shoulder. He felt so strong and warm, an anchor in the fog that surrounded her, was inside of her. He flashed her a smile and touched her gloved hand.

Then, suddenly, a mirage appeared before her, rising through the mist. A floating place of domes and bell towers, fairylike. The light on the water didn't seem to come from above, but out and up, shining on the water and the buildings, pearly pink.

As they drew closer, she glimpsed the gleam of some gilt angel atop a church dome, seeming to beckon them. She felt Jamie's hand squeeze hers and she held on to it tightly, knowing he felt this, too. This magic all around them. The boat crept to a bumping crawl as it entered a narrow canal, and they were actually *in* that dream city. Part of it all. Together.

They glided past close-packed, tall houses, pale yellow and blue and cream and pink, their lower storeys peeling with damp decay, lacy balconies overhead. Through open windows she caught glimpses of frescoes, the shine of glass chandeliers, blurred figures. She heard a different kind of sound than London clamour— muffled bits of music and conversation, the splashing backwash from boats against moss-soft steps, feet crossing bridges.

She looked up at Jamie, filled with wonder

and astonishment. He looked captured by it all, too, his handsome face enraptured, and they watched each other, sharing it all. Bound together in the experience.

'Is this real?' she whispered.

'I don't know,' he answered simply. 'But if it is a dream, this place, here with you, I never want to wake up.'

'Nor do I.'

Their boat turned from the narrow waterway to the Grand Canal, laced with arching bridges, crowded with vessels. Rose stared around, wide-eyed, at pale palaces, merry cafes, gondolas gliding past. It all seemed to undulate around them.

A narrow vessel slid past, grander than the others, the *felza* decorated with wreaths of flowers and fluttering ribbons, a couple sitting on gold-and-white velvet cushions. The young man, looking so proud and nervous, wore a fine, dark suit, while his companion was dressed in a white lace gown and veil, clutching a bunch of roses as she waved to the vessels behind them, which carried more finely clad passengers, laughing and brandishing champagne bottles.

'A wedding party,' their boatman said. 'Soon

they will be like you! On their—what is the English word?—their honeymoon.'

Rose felt her cheeks turn warm and she glanced away as Jamie laughed. 'You think we are on our honeymoon, *signor*?'

'Of course! The holding of the hands, the shy glances—I row many new couples around Venice.'

Rose had to laugh, too. She thought of her own wedding as she watched the Venetian bridal party glide past. The satin and lace, the hazy, happy feeling as she walked with her father down the aisle past hundreds of curious eyes, her own gaze intent only on Jamie at the altar. The cake and champagne and jokes and dances. It had been wonderful, but it felt so far away now.

And she remembered the wedding *night*, such a glorious revelation. She had never felt closer to anyone, happier, more certain the future held such delights in store for her—until the days that followed, the loneliness, the realisation that life might not work out as she hoped. She could see now that she and Jamie had never really learned how to be together as a happily married couple. But they had this, right now, and she was going to make the most of it.

Their boat eased up to a small landing, between striped poles. Rose tilted her head back to study the house, their home for now. How very different it was to staid Greensted, to London! It was all lacy, creamy stucco work, scrolls and crests, a loggia high above looking out on to the canal. Exuberant, romantic and elegant all at once, sighing with history.

Jamie helped her up from the boat and held her hand as they made their way through a pair of carved gates, a family crest mounted high over their heads, surmounted by lions and cupids. Rose held on to him closely, fearing she might float away in the face of such a delightful dream.

There was no army of servants waiting for them as there had been at Greensted, expecting her to act the Duchess. There was only one woman, tall, austere, dark-haired, clad in black silk with a bunch of keys at her waist, and a footman who hurried to deal with the baggage.

'*Buena sera*, Signora la Duchessa. I am Signora Pollatini,' the woman said, studying Rose with narrowed eyes as if to make sure she was worthy. 'Welcome to Palazzo Verini. If you would follow me? I'm sure you must be weary from your journey.'

Rose and Jamie followed the clink of her keys through a small dark courtyard and up a flight of rough stone steps that led to a long central corridor, the *portego* that ran along the length of the *piano nobile*. Rose had read about the palazzo on their journey, about how the oldest part of it was sixteenth century, built by an ancient family that boasted of two doges and a princess of Malta, as well as a few cardinals and a saint. She could envisage them there, those dignified old Verinis in their velvets and pearls, gliding along in this old, shadowed space.

The wall to their left, lined with closed doors, was hung with faded tapestries, portraits framed in peeling, elaborate plasterwork. There were a few satin-cushioned chairs, a carved chest, a sculpted lion. To the right, large windows looked out over the Grand Canal, turning ink-blue with the twilight. The waves cast shadows on the walls, like a moving presence.

'This is the newer part of the palazzo,' Signora Pollatini said as she turned and led them through a long enfilade of doors. 'The small drawing room…'

Rose almost laughed aloud to imagine such a room as 'small'. One whole wall of windows opened on to a terrace, lit now with tall candelabra. There was a glorious view of the canal from there, the white-and-gold wedding cake dome of the Salute church across the way. Red damask walls glowed, while faded sofas and chairs of pale green were grouped on the flowered carpet. Marble-topped tables held commedia figurines and vases of fresh flowers, while a small desk in the corner was perfect for writing letters.

'Contessa Verini likes to use this room for her reading and embroidery when they are home, with limoncello on the loggia before dinner,' Signora Pollatini said.

'It's exactly as I would have imagined it myself,' Rose said, and it was. The next room seemed perfect for Jamie, as if the palace was absolutely made for them: a little library, lined with shelves of old leather-bound books, with a carved desk, a globe, a fireplace flanked by more marble lions. She glanced back at Jamie with a happy smile, finding him watching her, looking worried she might not like the house. But how could she not? It was perfect. Perfect for *them*.

'The dining room,' Signora Pollatini said, guiding them along the enfilade. Rose glimpsed old portraits staring down at them, a mosaic floor, a cloth of cobweb-fine Burano lace on a silver-laden table. 'And the *salone*, the ballroom. You will have parties there, yes?'

Rose peeped into the darkened chamber and thought she had never seen anything quite so grand, not even in Newport, where fake Venetian style abounded, along with fake Versailles and fake Tudor manors. Not even when she was presented at Buckingham Palace. The whole space was a lavish rococo spectacle of white plasterwork wreaths, garlands and cupids on pale green walls, framing huge paintings of Venetian views. The ceiling was a domed scene of a classical revel, gods holding aloft jewelled goblets while more cupids flew around them, against a perfect blue sky and fluffy white clouds. Pink brocade chairs lined a parquet floor and she could envisage the Murano glass chandelier lit, music and dancers. She would indeed love to have parties there.

She glanced up at Jamie, and he looked rather less enthralled at the idea of parties. 'I—I'm not sure,' she told Signora Pollatini. 'The Duke has much work to do while we're here.'

The housekeeper looked disappointed and rather disapproving. 'But all Venice will wish to meet you, La Duchessa. I would be most happy to help you with arrangements in any way.'

'Yes, Rose, of course,' Jamie said. 'You must have whatever gatherings you would like in this house.'

Rose nodded, sure he did not mean that, and went to the last door.

'Your chamber is here, Duchessa,' Signora Pollatini said. 'And Signor il Duca's is over there. I will see about your luggage and have some dinner sent up.' She gave a stiff curtsy and rustled away.

Rose looked uncertainly around the room. It wasn't large, but it was very grand, with a tall, heavily carved bed draped in blue satin, a lacy dressing table near the tall window, a white marble fireplace with a mantel decorated with a gilded clock and frolicking shepherdesses. All very pretty, all suited to an eighteenth-century princess. But she was much too aware that she and Jamie were alone in the fading light—with a bed next to them. He smelled of lemon and sea salt soap, of *Jamie*, and his warmth seemed to reach out and wrap all around her. She longed to reach out and touch him, feel his cheek under her fingers, take his hand again, but that old shyness held her still. Shy—with her own husband! How silly she was, she thought, but there it was.

She peeped up at him and found him frowning as he studied the bed. 'Jamie...'

'I'll leave you to settle in, shall I?' he said quickly. He kissed her hand and left her, the door clicking shut between them.

Feeling quite alone, Rose went to peer out the window. There was a courtyard garden below, green and shaded, lit with windows from the palazzo across the way. The moon was starting to rise on the horizon, pale gold and as stunning as everything else in the city.

'Andare all deriva,' she whispered. It was one of the Italian phrases that had struck in her memory. *To be adrift.* She certainly felt that now. Unmoored, floating like Venice itself, not knowing where to alight. She glanced at Jamie's closed door and wished so very much that she could alight with *him*. Yet in that moment she felt lonelier than ever before.

Chapter Fifteen

Rose studied herself carefully in the mirror, making sure every curl was in place, every lace frill of her rose-pink dress perfect. For some reason, she felt sure she must look her very best that night; nervous butterflies tingled in her stomach and she felt like a silly, shy schoolgirl again. As she had when they'd first come to England and all she had cared about was whether Jamie would be at that night's ball, that day's tea party. All she'd wanted was to see him again.

'You look lovely, Your Grace,' Jenny said, smoothing the cap sleeve of the gown.

'Do you really think so, Jenny? Should I not have worn the blue instead? This dress is so old…' She had, in fact, worn it on one of the last nights she'd danced with Jamie, when they were still truly married. That was probably why she had kept it, to look at the pretty, full, rosy folds and remember a beautiful night when its train swirled over a dance floor and she had thought her worries were over.

'Oh, no!' Jenny said. 'This seems right for Venice. It is the colour of the sunset.'

Rose nodded. 'Yes, exactly so.' All that day, while Jamie worked in the palazzo library, she had wandered the city. She saw the great Titian altarpiece at the Frari church, the Bellini at San Zaccaria, so transcendent and serene she sobbed, the Veronese at San Sebastiano. And everything, everywhere, seemed to glow that beautiful pink.

'I'll find the matching shawl, Your Grace.'

As Jenny dug through one of the trunks, Rose wandered to her window and stared down at that hidden little courtyard garden. It was like her own hidden treasure, a tiny oasis of green silence in the city of water, crawling with white flowers that scented the evening air, sweeter than any perfume, lined with towering cypress trees and dotted with stone benches and fountains. She pressed her palm to the glass and closed her eyes, and suddenly she felt as if she was in another garden completely, another time...

In that moment, she was no longer in Venice, no longer Rose the Duchess, but Rose Wilkins in Newport, at her very first ball. A different garden was laid out before her, the grand structure of the Beechwood mansion rising behind her.

Her mother had worked so hard for years to be accepted in Newport, and now here they were, at the largest Astor cottage of all. Not a dinner or tea for Mrs Astor's true intimates, but a large ball, yet Stella Wilkins knew it was a grand start.

Rose was excited, shy, hopeful, terrified.

So she'd wandered out to the gardens, sloping down to the night-dark sea. The house was all alight behind her, shining on her pale yellow silk and tulle gown. It was so quiet there after the music, the laughter; the salty-fresh air was clear after the profusion of lilies and roses in the Versailles-like rooms.

Rose had wandered towards a lantern-lit pergola that looked out at the sea, thinking she would sit there for a moment until her mother might look for her.

But she had not been alone there after all. Gerald Mayhew, known as the eligible bach-

elor of the summer, had been standing there at the railing, smoking a cheroot. Golden-haired, Apollo-like in his evening clothes. She had dared to talk to him twice before, to try to flirt as the girls did in novels, hoping he might look at her. She had even laughed with him in front of others, trying so hard to catch his attention, overwhelmed with joy when he'd smiled at her. Talked to her.

Rose, flustered, shy, infatuated with Mr May-hew, had started to back away.

'Oh—I am sorry,' she'd stuttered. 'I thought no one was out here.'

He had smiled at her, a gorgeous, gleaming white grin, and ground out his cheroot. 'No, not at all. It's Miss Wilkins, yes? It was quite delightful making your charming acquaintance earlier. Please don't run away. It's rather noisy at Mrs Astor's parties, you know, and I was seeking a bit of peace. Yet it's become rather lonely. I'd love such beautiful company.'

Beautiful.

Rose had felt her cheeks turn warm under his smile, his attentive gaze. He was actually talking to her! 'Yes, it—is rather loud in there.'

'You're the one with the twin, aren't you? The

*redhead who dares to swim at Bailey's Beach
with no stockings.'*

*Rose had laughed. That had been only one of
Violet's exploits, to the horror of their mother.
Everyone did always remember Violet, always
tsked at her wild ways. Violet never cared. Rose
sometimes wished she could be more like her.
That was why she'd tried to flirt with Mr Mayhew.*

*'Yes. Violet. My older sister is Lily. She is the
beautiful one.'*

*His smile had widened. 'I wouldn't say that
at all. You are quite lovely yourself, Miss Rose
Wilkins.'*

*Rose had swallowed hard, suddenly feeling
the flutter of something cold, almost foreboding
in the pit of her stomach. 'I should go back...'*

*'Please, don't. Sit with me for a while. It's so
rare to meet someone new here in boring old
Newport. Especially one with such an interesting father. They say his fortune is even grander
than Mr Astor's!'*

*Rose had slowly sat down on one of the cush-
ioned benches, startled when he took her hand
and leaned close to her. He'd smelled of smoke
and champagne and expensive cologne, but she
had suddenly longed to flee. Her pleasure in*

flirting with him earlier had faded and she'd felt silly and fearful.

'I must go,' she'd gasped and started to stand up.

His hand had tightened on hers, hard and bruising, and pulled her back down again.

'Beautiful Rose Wilkins,' he'd muttered and kissed her, his teeth clashing on hers, his hand tearing at her sleeve.

Through the haze of her terror, her claustrophobia, Rose had suddenly remembered something Violet had told her once. 'If a man tries to get fresh,' Violet had said, 'stab him with your hatpin. That's what Hattie Smith told me and she used to ride the streetcars.'

Rose had had no hatpin, but she'd had her pearl headpiece. She'd wrestled one hand free, snatched it out of her curls, and stabbed him in the side of the neck.

He'd let her go, cursing, and she'd run as fast as she could away from the pergola. The brilliant lights of the house had blurred through her tears, but she'd kept on running, running.

His mocking laughter had followed her. 'They'll never believe you if you tell,' he'd shouted. 'A girl like you! You led me on right in front of everyone.'

Fortunately, the first person she'd seen was Lily, wandering the pathway, obviously looking for Rose. When Lily had seen her, her hair falling down, dress torn, tears on her cheeks, she'd gasped and rushed to take Rose into her arms. Lily hadn't asked questions, hadn't done anything but hold her close, letting Rose sob on the sleeve of her new satin Worth gown.

'Oh, my darling Rose,' she'd whispered. 'I'm here, I'm here. You don't need to be frightened any more. Men are such brutes!'

And Rose had never felt so frightened, so alone, so foolish again, not until she'd lost her baby and Jamie had been nowhere to comfort her. Yet even that dark thought felt so far away here in Venice.

'Your Grace? Are you ill?' Jenny said, her tone alarmed.

Rose opened her eyes, startled to find herself not in Newport, young and alone and afraid, but in an old Venetian palazzo. She glanced at Jenny, who watched her wide-eyed, poised to run for help if Rose should faint once more.

'I am sorry, Jenny,' she said with a smile. 'I just—felt a bit dizzy.'

'You should sit down. Let me find you some water,' Jenny said, pushing one of the satin-cushioned chairs towards Rose, and looking for the water pitcher and vinaigrette. She always knew what to do now.

'I am quite well now, Jenny dear, I promise. I only…' Rose sat down heavily, pushing those old memories away, away, as she always did. They were gone now, so long ago. Nothing to do with her present life. Surely.

Signora Pollatini knocked at the chamber door, given away by the clink of her keys. 'The gondola has arrived, la Duchessa. Il Duca waits at the *portego*.'

'*Grazie, signora*, I will be there momentarily.' She took one more deep breath and stood up, letting Jenny wrap the lacy shawl around her and hand her the kid gloves. She patted at her hair, making sure the elaborate curled coiffure, pinned with diamond stars, was still in place. Newport was gone; Venice was the reality now. Venice and Jamie.

She hurried down to the *portego*, where Jamie waited by the gates leading to the water landing. How handsome he looked, she thought, her breath catching a bit at the sight of him. So tall and elegant in his dark evening clothes, his cloak tossed carelessly over his shoulders, his dark hair gleaming in the torchlight. No matter what, he was here with her now and she was safe with him. Her husband. Newport was finished. She had only *now*.

He turned to her, his eyes widening for an instant. 'Rose,' he whispered. 'How beautiful you look.'

She laughed. 'And so do you. Look beautiful, that is. I shall be the envy of all the Venetian ladies tonight.'

She took a deep breath and reached for his hand, letting the night and the city and her husband catch her up until she forgot all else. He helped her on to the narrow velvet cushion and tucked the warm blanket around her before he sat next to her, so close, his shoulder and knee pressed against hers as the boat slid out into the water with a soft splash. Venice at night had an even more dreamlike quality, of mist and shadows, footsteps pattering across bridges, the murmur of laughter echoing from far away, the smell of roses and canal water and wine in the air. Church bells rang out their melancholy songs. Rose held tight to Jamie's hand, as if trusting he could lead her through this strange land.

Impulsively, she leaned against him and pressed her lips lightly to his cheek, inhaling deeply the scent of him, feeling the tickle of his evening whiskers on her lips. She remembered that lonely feeling last night, the melancholy of that ancient city, but at that moment it was gone. She was—happy. For the first time in so very long.

Jamie looked at her with a surprised, pleased smile and squeezed her hand in return. 'What was that for?'

'Kisses seem to belong in Venice, don't you think?' She sat back on the cushions, still holding on to his hand as she watched a couple dash over a bridge overhead, laughing together. 'It's glorious here.'

They landed at St Mark's Square, and Jamie helped her from the boat into a festival of music and dancing. Moonlight gleamed on the angels and gilded domes of the church, turned the lacy stuccowork of the doge's palace to spun sugar. The waters of the lagoon beyond were inky, while bright torches made the piazza seem almost like daytime. A band played under the arches of a loggia, and couples swirled around the flagstones of the piazza, a whirl of colour and lace and ribbons and laughter.

'How beautiful.' Rose sighed, holding tightly to Jamie's hand as she took in the glorious scene.

'Beautiful,' he murmured, watching only her as she watched the dancers. 'Will you do me the honour of this dance?'

She glanced out at the piazza again. The music was as intoxicating, spiralling higher and higher, carrying happiness up and up like a wave to the sky. She *did* want to dance, to whirl in Jamie's arms over the Venetian stones. To be part of this night together, so deep and dark and filled with secret possibilities. She found she didn't need parties and distractions here, as she did in London. She needed Jamie, their new world of bridges and churches and walks and laughter. And this moment.

She nodded and took his hand, letting him spin her into the dance. They twirled under the moonlight, giddy, dizzy, until they waltzed together into an alleyway off the square, holding on to each other.

The walkway was quiet, tucked away from the party. She could still hear the music, the laughter, but it was only an echo. She and Jamie were alone, except for a stray cat and a woman singing hidden on a balcony overhead.

'Oh, Rose. How beautiful you are,' he said, and she heard so much in those simple words.

Others had told her that, but she'd found it never meant anything unless Jamie said it.

She trailed her fingertips over his cheek, his skin so warm and alive. That heat, that old passion flaring up again, seemed to flow over her, into her. Coaxing her frozen, frightened heart into beating again.

His head tilted towards hers and she went up on tiptoe to meet his kiss. She twined her arms around his neck to hold him to her and felt his touch at her waist, pulling her even closer.

They fit so perfectly together now, after all this time, their lips, their hands, as if she had been just waiting for this moment. She parted her lips and felt the tip of his tongue touch hers, felt the kiss slide down into frantic, blurry *need*. She wanted to forget the past and begin all over again.

Jamie pressed her back against the wall, his touch hard and hungry as his hands slid up her back, tracing the curve of her breasts through the silk and lace of her gown. She moaned softly at the sensations, all fire and ice at once.

Her head fell back against the wall as his kiss slid to her neck, the soft spot of her bare shoulder above the lace frill. The tip of his tongue traced a circle on her skin and she buried her fingers in the waves of his hair. *This* was what she missed so much—the way only he could make her feel. She almost sobbed at the intensity of those feelings, the overwhelming joy of being in his arms again.

He rested his cheek on her shoulder, holding her. Their rough, warm breath mingled, their heartbeats pounding together. Rose caressed the tumble of his hair, her hand shaking.

'Oh, Rose,' he whispered. 'What you do to me...'

Rose laughed. What *she* did to *him*? He upended her whole world and had done ever since they'd first met. She pressed one soft, lingering kiss to his temple, to the life pulse that beat there, holding tight for a moment before she let go.

He stepped back as she adjusted her dress, her hair, as the real night settled around them again. How wondrous his kisses still were to her; she had been a fool to think they wouldn't affect her any more. Jamie always made her feel so safe *and* passionate, so different from anyone else had or could. But a lingering doubt remained, making her shiver suddenly as if in warning. It had all proved false in the past— should she trust it now?

He held out his hand to her, his fingers trembling a bit, and they walked together back to the party, her head near his shoulder. They didn't speak; they didn't have to. Once they had read each other without even trying. They'd lost that somewhere along the way, but now she could feel herself slipping into the habit of it again. Strange, yet so very wonderfully familiar.

Perhaps she *would* regret it, once the magic of the Venetian moonlight faded into ordinary light again. But she couldn't bear to think of that and couldn't think of anything except this moment with him, her Jamie. Her husband again, for this precious evening.

Chapter Sixteen

'Shall I go out with you today?'

Rose glanced up from reading *A Lady in Society* to see Jamie across the breakfast table laid out on the loggia. At first the morning had seemed quiet; she had barely slept last night, after their kiss and now she was too daydreamy to do more than pick at her plate, sip her chocolate, stare out at the Salute dome across the way, feeling the breeze pluck at the silk ruffle of her morning gown. She didn't dare watch Jamie, stare at him as she longed to.

'Of course, if you like,' she said, setting down her chocolate cup. 'I would enjoy that.'

He smiled, as if relieved she would welcome him. 'What are your plans?'

'I thought I would look at a few more churches. Perhaps the Miracoli? I'm told it's very beautiful, like a little jewel box. But then that's all I've really seen in Venice so far—churches. They are all so exquisite, so filled with unexpected art treasures. I've never had so much fun playing tourist!' But her favourite part of the day was being at the palazzo with Jamie, sitting by the fire, watching him read, as she had when they were first married. She tried to store up the quiet contentment of those moments to keep with her, no matter what happened next. 'Then maybe we could just wander? Or visit a gallery, or the Accademia. Every corner has something unexpected to look at.'

'I've found that, too. Statues and fountains, houses that have been loved for generations. Nothing is lost here,' he said almost wistfully.

She glanced out over the marble balustrade to the day beyond. It was a glorious morning, the light all blue and gold, bouncing off the waves on to the walls and the church domes, as if it was all made of water. Of illusions. Women with their market baskets over their arms crossed the bridges, calling out to each other, laughing, while children skipped ahead and dogs barked. 'I never want to leave here,' she said impulsively. Yet real life, in her sisters' letters, followed here even to the breakfast table.

'We can stay as long as you like,' Jamie said, pouring more coffee into his cup.

'But Greensted…'

'Ah, yes. All that duking that must be done,' he said with a rueful laugh. 'But not for a while. The Verini family have said we can extend the lease on the palace if we like, as they have much business on the mainland.'

Rose laughed. 'Of course I would like!' She thought of London, of Paul and her sisters and divorce, and suddenly had such a powerful desire to let those things hover in the past for as long as she could.

'Are those letters from your sisters?' Jamie asked, gesturing with his fork towards the post next to her barely touched plate.

'Hmm, yes,' Rose said, opening the one from Violet. Those were always the shortest. 'Vi is getting ready for another photographic exhibition, so that's most of her news. She has a new image of our niece as a woodland elf and a photo she took of me as a Grecian sibyl, and she has high hopes for both of them. Lily is getting ready to leave with the Princess and is blooming with health with another soon-to-be arrival. I'd suspected as much.' Rose smiled and then suddenly a pang struck her heart as she thought of her own lost baby. She carefully laid the letter down. 'And they worry about my health in a damp place like Venice. Lily says I should seek out a doctor while we're here.'

Jamie frowned in concern, immediately distracted from Lily's news as she'd intended. 'Should we look for one?'

'No, no,' Rose insisted. 'I feel very well, better than I have in a long time. My sisters do like to fuss, I believe they still think I am a child, even though Vi and I are twins. You must not worry, too. Now, what would you like to see today, Jamie?'

It was indeed a beautiful day when they stepped out of the palazzo gates, the morning mists entirely cleared, the sunlight sparkling on the waters, the bowl of azure sky overhead. Rose took Jamie's arm as they set off towards the Miracoli, walking rather than rowing to take it all in, every stone and balcony and water step. Rose smiled to be with him, to match her steps to his and hold on to his lean muscled arm, sharing every inch of the day with him. It was to be savoured.

They chatted easily about art and Jamie's work, of her sisters' news, the galleries they passed. They stopped at the arc of a bridge to study the canal, filled with vessels, the air sweet with smells from the market of meat and baking bread and fruit. Rose opened her blue-striped parasol against the sun and tilted a smile up at her husband.

Under the cover of the parasol, he drew her closer to him and that laughter, that joy, sparkled into something as shimmering and irresistible as that sunlight on the water. His lips met hers, sweet, perfect, like sunshine itself.

A boatman passing beneath the bridge saw them and called out, 'Ah, *amore*!', making Rose and Jamie jump and then laugh.

'Kissing your wife on a public bridge,' she teased him. 'So shockingly un-duke-like!'

They strolled on, hand in hand, Rose smiling at everything around them. 'It's all so delightful,' she gasped as a handsome Venetian boy tossed her a flower from a balcony, shouting, *'Bella, bella!'*

'They do have the finest taste here,' Jamie said.

Rose paused to gaze through the window of an art gallery, enthralled by a display of boxes. One was especially lovely, pale wood inlaid with gold and mother-of-pearl, depicting a courtly scene of a Renaissance dance.

'It's a wedding chest...a *cassetina*,' Jamie said. 'That box in the middle.'

Rose tilted her head, studying the gorgeous thing. 'Is it really?'

'Yes. It could hold the bride's dowry jewels, gold combs or silver perfume flasks, or even baby linen blessed by the pope. If you opened it, you would see it's lined with silk, inlaid with mirrors for the bride to admire herself.' He laughed. 'I saw one mentioned in a play I was studying. It sounded fascinating, so of course I had to seek out and examine some real examples. The perils of research, it's a winding road.'

'It's so beautiful. I wonder who it was made for. What they put into it.' She imagined some Renaissance couple, probably an arranged marriage, of course, but still full of wistful hope for happiness, perhaps. A lady in a velvet gown sewn with pearls, her long golden hair tumbling over her shoulders as she tucked lace and flowers and jewels and spices into this very box, praying for a good husband. A bright future. Such a delicate thing to have to nurture and so easily damaged.

'Why don't we go in and look at it? You

might buy it, if it speaks to you. Put your own hopes into it.'

'I...' Rose didn't know if she dared have any hopes left. She was counting them out every day now. 'It looks frightfully expensive.'

Jamie laughed again, soft, teasing, and touched the sleeve of her velvet, blue and black passementerie walking jacket from Doucet. 'I think you would be fine if you wanted to treat yourself. You have thousands sitting in Threadneedle Street alone.'

She glanced up at him curiously. 'Do I? How?'

'That money your father gave me when we married and the railroad and steel shares he signed over to me, I invested it in the five per cents, and the profits go into an account in your name. The Byson estate is meant to send you regular statements.'

Rose was dizzy with the thought. Jamie took money that was his, her dowry from her father, and just—gave it back? To her? 'That isn't right. Surely my father meant it to be for your use, as with Aidan? But then, I am only a woman and my father always said I couldn't fathom such things.'

Jamie frowned in chagrin. 'That is absolute

rubbish! And I should have made sure you saw those statements every month. You are much too intelligent to be kept in the dark about such things. I'll have the paperwork sent on immediately. In the meantime, you can buy as many wedding chests as you like.'

Rose glanced at the beautiful box again. No—she could not afford to hope too much, not just yet. But she couldn't help a tiny, bright spark of feeling learning that Jamie was making sure she had her own money. Her own real freedom. 'Not today. We should go and see the church.'

He studied her closely for a moment in that disconcerting way he had, the way that made her sure he could see her, all of her, deep down. He held out his arm. 'Of course. Now, see that palazzo there? Contessa Montadini lives there, such an ancient family, so many scandalous stories…'

She took his arm and let him lead her onward, listening to his tales of the houses they passed, laughing, fascinated. That was one of the things she'd missed so much about Jamie, along with his distractingly passionate kisses—his knowledge and the humorous, interesting ways he talked about it. Sharing it, not showing it off. How he made her feel a part of it all, not too silly and weak to understand anything.

And now, he'd even casually handed her a future all of her very own. How many men would do such a thing? Only Jamie, she thought.

'Here we are,' he said, gesturing to the church that suddenly rose up before them, all white and pastel pink and green, shining in the daylight. A beautiful teacake of a structure, elaborate and sweet, somehow so perfect in Venice.

Rose tilted back her head, studying the inlaid facade from beneath her hat, the dome that rose above them. 'It's not nearly as large as the Frari, is it? But so very pretty. Look at that mischievous little angel there!'

They went up the gleaming white steps and through the doors, into the cool, shadowed interior. The smell she now thought of as so Venetian—roses, lemon polish, dust, the tang of the waters—wafted over her and she smiled. She wished she could bottle it and take it home, inhale it on lonely days to remember this grand time. She drifted along the aisle, her half-boots clicking lightly on the marble mosaic, drawn in by one lovely sight after another. Pale saints, smiling angels, carvings, pale pink memorials, the altar draped in shimmering gold, rising to heaven with gilded cupids. Light filtered from the skylights high above, pale and diffuse. Heavenly.

'How lovely it all is,' she whispered. 'Like being inside a glass of champagne!'

'Or inside a rose, all pink and white,' Jamie said with a smile. 'It suits you perfectly.'

Rose blushed at the compliment and fussed with her parasol.

'It is the favourite wedding church of Venice! Fifteenth century,' a moustachioed, exuberant tour guide exclaimed, hurrying towards them from the altar. 'You see the image of the Madonna over the altar? She brought a drowned man back to life once and blesses unions with long life and many children. Some visitors to our city also like to marry here, for the good fortune of it. Perhaps you are here to elope, *signor* and *signorina*? You have that romantic look!'

Rose laughed and feared she was blushing yet again. She ducked her head to hide under the brim of her hat. 'Oh, no. But I do—that is, I do love this church. I could envisage the most beautiful weddings here.' Weddings—they did follow her around so much lately. The gondola procession when they'd first arrived, the inlaid box in the gallery window. Now this perfect jewel of a church, made for lace and orange blossoms and kisses.

She glanced at Jamie, who had wandered away to study a memorial tablet. He looked so thoughtful, so distant.

'*Signorina?*' the guide said. 'You would like to see the altar closer, maybe?'

'Yes, *grazie.*'

She strolled further into the church, amid the pastel marbles, the gleam of silver. At the golden altar, a father held up his little daughter, showing her the miracle-making Madonna. They giggled together, affectionate, easy, adorable. The girl curled her hand around his, trustingly, her tiny face framed in golden ringlets staring up at him in adoration.

The church suddenly seemed to swim around Rose, a blur of green and pink, going dark at the edges. She swayed and was falling, falling...

'*Signorina!*' she heard the guide cry, as if from a very long way away, or as if she'd floated underwater. Drowning.

'Papa!' the little girl sobbed. 'The pretty lady is ill!'

'No, no, don't worry, little one,' Rose whispered, before it all faded away.

* * *

'Rose! Rose, my darling, can you hear me?'

Rose tried to open her eyes, to answer Jamie, to look at him, but everything felt so cold, so far away still. *I'm fine*, she tried to say, but her head ached so much.

She pried her gritty eyes open and blinked up at him. Amber light from one of the windows outlined him, turning him into one of those gilded Venetian warrior saints, and she wondered woozily if she had tumbled down into some other world or time. Then she remembered—she had fainted, right in front of a guide and a clutch of other tourists. She groaned in embarrassed chagrin.

'I'm—awake,' she murmured and squeezed Jamie's hand.

'Thank heavens,' he said fervently. 'Can you sit up?'

'Perhaps I can help,' an English voice said. 'I'm a doctor.'

Rose carefully turned her aching head to see the man who had been showing his daughter the art. He was a tall, kind-eyed man, with greying dark hair, a concerned frown. His anxious-looking wife stood behind him, holding their wide-eyed daughter's hand.

'No, thank you, I—I'm all right now,' Rose said.

'I'd rather he took a quick look at you, darling,' Jamie said. 'Otherwise I fear to move you.'

He'd just called her darling! And she thought he'd said it before, too. Was it because it was what would be expected of any caring husband… or had he perhaps not even noticed he'd uttered it…twice?

'I probably did not eat enough breakfast,' she said, but she did let the doctor move closer. He knelt beside her, taking her wrist to check her pulse. 'I am Rose Wilkins, Doctor. Well, Rose Byson.'

'And I am Dr Foster, from Brighton. You gave us rather a fright, Mrs Byson.' He gently checked her eyes and examined her head for a bump, his movements gentle and soft. She rather liked him and wished she had such a physician at home. Someone competent and concerned.

'Oh, I am so sorry to have frightened your little girl,' she said.

Dr Foster laughed and examined the back of her neck. 'I am sure you have quite made her day. She's only seven, but most enthralled with my medical cases, the more elaborate the better. She will be more knowledgeable than me any day now.'

'Does the lady have concussion, Papa?' the girl called.

'Follow my finger, Mrs Byson,' the doctor said, and then smiled in satisfaction. 'It doesn't appear so. Nothing broken, either. But you must be vigilant. I would call your doctor as soon as you return to your lodgings.'

'I'm afraid we have no doctor here, we've only been in Venice a few days,' Rose said.

'Then feel free to call on me if you have any concerns at all. We're staying at the Lamperello Hotel.' He handed Jamie a card.

'I wouldn't want to interrupt your holiday. You've been so kind...' Rose protested.

Mrs Foster laughed. 'You would be helping me no end, Mrs Byson. He cannot bear not to work for two days in a row. He gets grumpy as a bear.'

'I do understand,' Rose murmured, thinking of Jamie and his studies. She gave the little girl a nod and a smile. 'I do feel quite well now, my dear, no concussion. You and your father have rescued me.'

The girl giggled and Dr Foster said, 'I would

suggest resting for the next few days, Mrs Byson, and a good meal right away.'

'Yes, certainly. Thank you all so much.' Rose smiled as the doctor bowed and left, holding his daughter's hand and his wife's arm. Jamie knelt down beside her, his face creased in concern.

'We should get you home,' he said, gently helping her up and leading her down the aisle, as careful as if she was a Murano glass ornament. She had the urge to laugh at how much like a wedding recessional it felt.

She thought of their lovely palazzo, her lonely, lush bedroom, and realised she didn't want to shut herself away in there quite yet. Jamie was sure to go back to work in his library again and she didn't want to give up this day with him.

'I'm quite well, I promise,' she said as they emerged into the bright blue day. 'It was as that kind doctor said—I should eat something. That's all.'

'Then let us find a cafe. Some nice limoncello, yes? And pasta, a meat *and* a sweet.'

Rose laughed. 'Yes, Nanny, of course.' She held on to him, her head still a bit light, and let him lead her to a welcoming little restaurant with bright yellow awnings and a display of sweets in the window to satisfy any nanny.

She seated herself happily in a curtained alcove, breathing deeply of the lovely scent of garlic, spices and wine. She smiled up at Jamie, who still looked at her with deep concern in his eyes. She took his hand and kissed it, giving it a reassuring squeeze. 'I do feel fine, I promise.'

'You will say if you start to feel ill again, Rose?' he said. 'And I do think it would be good to have Dr Foster call at the palazzo for a proper visit. He seemed kind.'

'Oh, yes, very kind. I wouldn't want to mar his holiday, as he seems to be the sort of man who refuses to take them very often. But, yes, I shall send for him if I feel worse. I am quite well enough now.' She smiled down at the soup that had arrived, a lovely shrimp bisque. Greensted needed cuisine like this. 'You won't ever tell my sisters about this, will you, Jamie? I feel positively silly right now, fainting like that. They'll fuss about their delicate little sister again. I wouldn't even be surprised if they showed up in Venice! I am *not* as breakable as everyone thinks. I just need to remember to eat a little more.'

'You know I wouldn't tell them. And I never think of you as delicate and breakable.'

Rose tilted her head to study him. 'You don't?'

'No. You're the strongest, bravest person I have ever known. You put up with me, didn't you? And you walked away when you were not treated as you deserved to be.'

She was astonished. 'I didn't know you thought I was brave.'

He looked surprised at her surprise, his coffee cup half raised. 'I've always known that about you. Admired that about you.'

'But I don't think a strong person would just faint like that.'

'It gets so stuffy in these churches sometimes, no matter how beautiful they are. I'm surprised I didn't faint myself. And I should have made sure you ate a decent breakfast before we left. Look, here's the pasta now. I want you to eat every bite.'

Rose smiled and dipped her fork into the seafood ravioli that had been delivered. 'It was rather warm in the church. And then I saw...'

He tilted his head curiously. 'Saw what?'

'It's very silly. I saw Dr Foster lift his adorable little daughter up to show her the art and they were so very sweet that I—' She broke off, staring hard at her plate.

'Oh, my darling.' Jamie reached out to gently touch her hand. 'My Rose. I am so sorry.'

She couldn't help a little thrill run down her spine at his use of that word for a third time. Deliberately, this time? 'I don't think of it much now.' Only every *other* day, not every day. 'But sometimes, there is something that catches me out…'

'I should have been with you when it happened and afterwards. In town and ever since. But I am here now. I want to share anything you want to tell me, anything at all. I will do anything to win you back, Rose, I swear it. The drinking is gone for good, I promise you, and there is only you. No matter how long it takes.'

She nodded and dared to peep up at him. She saw, deep in his agonised eyes, that those simple words were true. He *was* there for her now. He was truly sorry. They did have the chance to be together again, if they could be brave enough to reach for it.

She swallowed hard. She desperately wanted to be, but the truth was that she wasn't sure she was quite brave enough, no matter what Jamie said. Not yet.

'Shall we order the veal blanquettes in lemon sauce?' she said. 'I find I have an appetite after all.'

...
...might revenge... the wall, there dazzled...
broad smile: he said, 'And I have done...
your share at...

Chapter Seventeen

'*Viva Amina, la-la-la,*' Rose sang, her fingers dancing over the keys of the piano in the palazzo's music room. The night fairly shimmered outside the windows, all gold and green against the deep blue sky, the fuzzy reflections off the jewelled domes. The magic of a Venetian night, unlike any other place she had ever seen. She had drifted to the music room after dinner, drawn to sing again, while Jamie sat with his books at a nearby table. He didn't seem to work much, though, spending all his time watching her, smiling that half-smile she never could quite read.

The last notes of the aria slowly died away, leaving the soft splash of water from the canal outside, the muted echoes of voices beyond the half-open windows.

Rose smiled as she glanced at Jamie. His chin was propped on his palm, his papers forgotten, as he watched her with rapt attention. 'I'm afraid I'm a bit out of practice,' she said.

'You were wonderful,' he said. 'It's been far too long since we had such an evening.'

'Yes, it has,' she said quietly. Even before they'd separated, such evenings, so common and cherished when they'd first married, had become increasingly rare. And therefore treasured by her. But she always smiled to think of those newlywed nights, her playing or sewing, him reading or reciting beautiful poetry to her that made her soul soar high above with the beauty of it. Then they would touch, kiss and…

She blushed and pushed away *those* memories. Those long, warm, perfect nights of absolute joy. She went to sit next to him beside the open window and gazed down at the passing boats filled with revellers, the church towers floating in the misty night air. She peeped over to see what he was reading. *'Orpheus and Eurydice,'* she said. How she had felt like poor Eurydice, in the shadows when she'd fainted at the Miracoli! Drawn up from the darkness by her husband. 'I remember when you would tell me those ancient tales.' When they were first married, enthralled with each other, and would spend their evenings sitting close, like this, talking and silent and holding each other.

Caught by the memories, she leaned closer to him and pressed her lips to his in a long kiss, then another and another, as if she had been storing them up for too long. Much too long.

He groaned and drew her against him, seeking the taste of her lips, and she was completely wrapped up only in him. Lost in the pleasure that only Jamie had ever given her. Once, she had thought he could be the one true thing she'd always wanted, but always feared she'd never have.

Now—now those things seemed possible again, like that elusive opalescent light of Venice she wanted to hold in her hand, but which always slipped away. Maybe she could grasp it now at last.

Rose settled herself in her satin-cushioned seat in the gilded box, studying the Teatro Goldoni through her opera glasses. It was a beautiful little jewel box of a place, all pale pink marble and gilded trim. The curtain on the stage looped and spun in pale blue satin and gold fringe, and her eye could barely focus on one gorgeous thing before it rushed to another.

'How very exciting!' she said merrily to Jamie as he sat beside her. 'It feels like going to the theatre a hundred years ago. Look at those frescoes! There is nothing so beautiful in London. The Lyceum is like a coal heap beside it.'

Jamie laughed. 'The Vendramin family first owned it in the 1620s, but it was rebuilt in 1720 and then 1818, so not that old.'

'Oh, I refuse to believe it! I must keep picturing it all as it *should* have been. Ladies in ruffled and jewelled satins, men in knee breeches and powdered hair, the candles and laughter and decadence.'

'What have you been reading lately? Naughty rococo novels, I think.'

'I have been reading through your library at the palazzo, if you must know, and the Verinis seem to have had some shocking tastes through the generations. I read a biography of a woman named Caterina Dolfin—she sounds astonishing. A divorced woman in the 1770s! A writer and *saloniste*, her life filled with scandal and intrigue. Perhaps I shall start writing a series of historical monographs myself. Lost loves of fascinating ladies.'

She meant it as a joke, but he looked at her seriously, consideringly. 'You really should. Your interest in women's lives and history—it would be the perfect project. It could rescue lost history for posterity, which is so important.'

'Really?' she whispered uncertainly. None of her London admirers who painted her portrait or wrote poems about her eyes ever complimented her intelligence. Told her she was capable of so much more than being a scandalous Professional Beauty. It made her feel warm all over that Jamie had done so. 'Perhaps I shall. It could be a way to hold on to Venice a little longer, even after we must return home.'

If only she could hold on to Jamie a little longer, too. Especially as he was last night, wrapped casually in a brocade dressing robe, his shirt open to reveal his strong throat, a hint of hair at his chest. His hair was rumpled above his spectacles, his bare feet tucked up on a stool. So casual, so sensual, so easy to be with. Her Jamie. Even here, in his formal evening suit, his hair glossy, he was still the most handsome man she had ever seen.

She turned away, studying the theatre through the Fabergé opera glasses Vi had given her after she'd attended the royal wedding in St

Petersburg a few years ago. She glimpsed several Venetian aristocrats she had read about in the newspapers and a couple of people she knew from London.

In one box, there sat a man with golden hair, shining in the gaslights, laughing with a lady in a scandalously low-cut bright green gown. There was something familiar about him, about that laugh...

She quickly swung her glass away, her breath caught in her white satin and tulle bodice until she gasped.

That Newport garden, hands reaching for her, panic, helplessness. You led me on in front of everyone!

'Rose!' Jamie said, concern in his voice.

Rose made herself smile. It couldn't really be him, could it? Gerald Mayhew. He was thousands of miles away. She was simply being fanciful. She made herself smile. 'Oh, look,' she exclaimed brightly. 'There is Dr and Mrs Foster, in the box opposite.' She waved until she got their attention and they waved happily back. Their daughter wasn't with them, but they sat with a formidable older lady clad in beaded purple and sable, her grey hair dressed high, amethysts and diamonds gleaming. 'I do hope we can find them at the interval, so I can thank them properly for their great kindness.'

'I'm sure they'll be glad to see their patient looking so glowing again.'

She smiled happily. Her health *was* better, despite the damp of Venice. She was surprised at how well she felt, how she jumped out of bed every morning excited about what the hours might hold, her body feeling light for the first time in ages. She'd even been eating more, sleeping better. Perhaps it had been the sooty London air all along. She couldn't let old memories of Newport ruin all of that now. The cream satin curtain, heavily tasselled with gold, swished up, and the orchestra launched into the prelude of *The Fan*.

As the curtain dropped for the interval, Rose blinked, surprised to find herself back in the real 1870s world again. The humorous play had quite transported her, making her sure she truly *was* there. She had barely heard or seen anything else except the actors.

She adjusted her lace shawl over her shoulders, reached for her fan—and suddenly remembered seeing the man before the curtain rose, the man who looked so much like Gerald

Mayhew. She stiffened and quickly scanned the theatre, but whoever he was, he was gone.

'Rose? Are you all right?' Jamie asked.

She made herself laugh. 'Oh, yes, it's all quite enchanting. I'm having a hard time bringing myself into the real world!'

'Yes, this company is the master of Goldoni's work. Shall I fetch us some champagne?'

'No, I'll come with you. I would enjoy the stroll.'

She took his arm and let him lead her down the plushly carpeted steps to the lobby. She felt caught in a seashell of pale pink silk, marble columns and a long, polished bar serving prosecco, where they found the Fosters.

'Mrs Byson! How grand to see you looking so well,' Dr Foster greeted them. 'How have you been feeling?'

'Very well indeed, thank you. You were so kind after my silly behaviour,' Rose said.

'Nonsense!' Mrs Foster declared. 'I myself get so overwhelmed at all these grand sites, I'm surprised I didn't become giddy, too. Have you met Contessa Montadini? She is our one real Venetian friend. She once knew my mother!'

The Contessa was the formidably dignified lady who had sat with the Fosters in their box.

But she smiled after she carefully examined Rose and was not nearly so fearsome as she held out her gloved hand. 'How do you do, Contessa,' Rose said, wondering if she should curtsy.

The Contessa studied her with a diamond-framed lorgnette before nodding and smiling. 'You are the English *duchessa*, are you not? In the Palazzo Verini. I have heard of you. They say you are one of the greatest English beauties.'

Rose blushed and tried not to stammer. 'Well—yes, I am, I confess. An English duchess, not a great beauty.'

'A duchess!' Mrs Foster gasped. 'How silly of me to treat you so—so ordinarily, Your Grace.'

Rose gave her a reassuring smile. 'Not at all, Mrs Foster. My husband is here for his studies, so we are living very quietly.' And she had been glad not to always be 'the Duchess'.

'Well, I hope you can make an exception to your quiet life, Duchessa, and attend my masked ball. It is rather a well-known event in Venice,' the Contessa said. She didn't sound like a woman who was often nay-said.

'Oh, yes, we would not miss it for anything,' Mrs Foster said. 'It has a commedia dell'arte theme, such fun. We love to bring back a tale of something so quintessentially Venetian for our friends.'

Rose was very tempted indeed. She was so enjoying their quiet days, but something in her missed a party, too. Music, conversation, dancing. And costumes! She never missed a chance to dress up.

She glanced at Jamie, who was talking solemnly with a group of his scholarly friends. It would certainly be more of a challenge to get him dressed up and on to a ballroom floor. It had been that way throughout their marriage.

'I shall have to talk to my husband about it, but I think I can safely say we shall be there,' Rose said. 'How kind of you to invite us, Contessa. I do so love a masked ball.'

The Contessa smiled. 'Not at all, Duchessa. You are quite famous here, whether you realise it or not. The great beauty from London! Your portrait by Pagliei caused a great sensation when it was displayed last year.'

Rose was surprised and a bit dismayed. That portrait had been quite a daring one, with her dressed as Lucrezia Borgia with her hair loose. 'Oh, but we are meant to be quiet here!'

'I would not worry—there will be masks at the party. And you can hire a costume at this very theatre, if you like. It will be very Venetian,' the Contessa said with a laugh. 'I have an extremely old palazzo, one where Goldoni himself visited my ancestor. I'm sure your husband will enjoy that. Now, tell me, how are you enjoying our city thus far? Signora Foster tells me you met at the Miracoli. I married there, you see, many years ago...'

Rose chatted and laughed with the Contessa and Mrs Foster for several minutes, about the galleries and churches she had visited, her plans to go to Burano to buy lace, nodding at their advice at what she must see and buy. She was so enjoying herself, forgetting everything else in the delights of social engagement, when she caught a glimpse of someone in the crowd. That man again. Golden hair, a gold brocade waistcoat, an ironic smile—*could* it be him after all? She shivered with a sudden chill.

'Ex-excuse me a moment,' she whispered. She spun around and rushed through the thick crowd, the kaleidoscope of silks and jewels under the frescoed ceiling. She could barely breathe. She was sure it was him, come to haunt her again after all this time! She had to check.

Yet by the time she crept past the crowd to

the smaller, quieter outer lobby, no one like him could be seen. She shivered still, feeling very alone, very unsure. Transported back to that naive Rose she had once been.

She stumbled to the piazza outside the theatre and ran her gloved hand over her clammy forehead. Once again, the paper-delicate happiness she had tried to grasp was tearing away from her. 'I must be going mad.'

'Rose,' she heard Jamie say, his voice full of concern. 'Are you feeling ill?'

She glanced over the piazza again. No one. Only the Venetian night. 'No, I…' She swallowed hard, sure she did not want Jamie to know. She never wanted him to know just how silly she had once been. 'I needed a bit of fresh air.' She turned to him with a bright smile. 'I'm sure it's time for the next act to begin. Shall we return to our box? I can't wait to see what happens next!'

He looked doubtful, a frown creasing his brow, his eyes very dark, but he took her arm and led her back into the crowded theatre. She felt safer with him, his steady arm under her touch, but that unsettled chill lingered.

She looked back, shivering with the memories, wishing the past would vanish altogether. But she knew all too well that could never be. The past was always there, waiting.

Chapter Eighteen

'Well, Jenny, what do you think? Will I disgrace myself, the frumpy American girl in Venice?'

Jenny stared at Rose, wide-eyed. 'You know you are not frumpy at all, Miss R— Your Grace. Where did you find this gown?'

'At the costume shop of the Teatro Goldoni. Isn't it amazing?' She gave a little spin, making her gown flutter out in a bell. It was a Renaissance-style chemise of ivory-coloured silk, thin and soft, shot through with glistening gold threads that mirrored the high-waisted bodice and pleated skirt of gold lace over white satin. Sleeves of shimmering cloth of gold were tied on with narrow white ribbons twined with gold beads. Her hair fell loose, a dark red curtain down her back, tied with more gold and white ribbons.

'You look like the sun,' Jenny said, straightening the little train of the skirt.

'I feel like it!' And she twirled and whirled, laughing with Jenny.

As she tripped to a stop, giddy and gasping, she reached for her mask on the dressing table. It was from one of the famous mask-making shops off the Piazza San Marco, fine white leather in the shape of a cat's face, trimmed with gold lace. She held it up to her face and she understood why Venice did so love a masquerade. She no longer had to be herself, Rose Wilkins, scared and unsure. She could be anyone she wanted.

Just one night, she whispered. What could happen in one night? Except falling in love, as she and Jamie had at that long-ago garden party.

Suddenly, a delicate missile landed with a crack on the bricks outside her half-open window, and a burst of sweet, syrupy roses reached her nose. She laughed and ran with Jenny to the window to see bright confetti and bits of eggshell float to the cobblestones below.

Jamie stood there, also transformed by Venice and the night. A tall, lean figure dressed in a black velvet doublet and tall boots, a black cloak embroidered with silver stars and crescent moons tossed over his shoulders. Though he wore a mask, a silver half-moon and a black velvet plumed cap over his hair, she could see his mischievous smile. He, too, seemed so very different that evening.

'What on earth is that?' she said, laughing.

'A perfume egg! I was told by the man in the shop that it was an essential element of Venetian courtship.'

Laughter bubbled up again in Rose's throat, irresistible, like champagne. She clamped her hand to her mouth, but it wouldn't be held back. 'Are you courting a lady, then, Signor Moon?'

'Of course I am! What else may I offer my Lady Sun? Pearls, diamonds, parties, music…'

Rose tapped her chin with her finger, pretending to give it much thought. 'A dance, maybe.'

'Then I am at my lady's disposal! As many dances as she may want. Our gondola awaits.'

Rose shut the window and raced down the stairs. One could never keep a gondola waiting. Jamie waited for her on the landing and caught her up in his arms to spin her around and around, the two of them giggling like mad schoolchildren. It was going to be a magical night, she could tell.

The ball was already going strong as their gondola approached the edge of the Palazzo Montadini. The windows blazed with light, glimmering on the black water, fireworks shooting overhead in arcs of red and blue and green and silver. It was as brilliant as a noonday sun, glowing on the costumed figures crowded on the balconies, peering down at newcomers through their eerie pale masks.

A footman in sixteenth-century livery assisted Rose from the gondola and on to a carpeted walkway, lining the path inside with silver bowls of strong-scented tuberose.

Rose was utterly dazzled. Lines of small bonfires edged the flat rooftop and the docks, surrounded by pages dressed in rich green and silver satin. The whole place glowed golden, welcoming the costumed crowds alighting from their vessels to make their way, laughing, into the central courtyard. Pennants flapped in the breeze, red and green and gold, embroidered with family crests.

Voices and music floated on the breeze along

with the sweet scent of flowers, the tang of the fruit trees, drifting out of doors and windows. Long tables draped in Burano lace were laid out on the terrace, silver and faience platters of prosciutto and risotto, calamari, oysters, brightly coloured sweetmeats from the city's convents, goblets and goblets of prosecco.

Rose sat on the edge of the cushions lined up on the terrace balustrade, watching the stream of people depart from their gondolas, Pierrot and his Pierrette, Medicis and Borgias, ballerinas and acrobats, Columbines, cats and dragons.

Jamie sat down beside her. She didn't need to see him, as she knew his heat, his scent, as well as she knew her own now. No matter what strangeness happened tonight, he was beside her. She smiled. 'Are we really here?' she whispered.

Jamie laughed. 'Only until dawn breaks up the party. Is that a *unicorn*?'

'I do think it might be. I feel positively unimaginative.'

Jamie held out his hand, and she took it and walked with him into the palazzo. It seemed most of the guests had already arrived, their laughter and chatter loud everywhere she turned, down every corridor.

Inside past the open double door inlaid with etched copper, a page took Rose's cloak and handed her a small bunch of tuberoses as he bowed her into the party. Tall, silver-framed Murano glass mirrors hung on the green silk walls. Soaring ceilings crowned with frescoes of gambolling shepherds and shepherdesses looked down on the laughing crowds. Satin shoes clicked on floors of gold-veined marble, giggles muffled by faded old tapestries.

A footman offered them goblets of prosecco, which Rose took and Jamie refused, and she gratefully took a sip of the cool liquid. 'My mother would faint to see all this. She tries to be so grand with her Newport balls, but they'll never quite measure up to *this*.'

'How could they? No other place is Venice, no matter who tries to copy it.'

'No, of course not.' She laughed, her head light and giddy from the wine, the masked faces swirling around her. 'This is a dream!'

He laughed, too, and took her in his arms to twirl her around. 'Would you dance with me, Madonna Princess?'

'Of course, my fair prince.' She drained her wine glass and left it on a footman's tray before Jamie swirled her into his arms and across the crowded ballroom. Their hostess sat on a dais at the end of the ballroom, perched on a velvet, throne-like chair, dressed as the Queen of the Night in silver-spangled black satin and a diamond tiara. She nodded to them regally as they bowed to her and she waved them into the dance.

The music grew louder as they went deeper into the twirling crowd, the air warmer here, and scented with the bunches of white roses in the blue-and-white Ming vases and shallow bowls. Jamie slipped his arm around her waist, spinning her in time to the music, faster and faster until the crowd became a mere blur and her head was giddy.

She threw back her head and laughed helplessly, holding tightly to his shoulders as he spun her around in a graceful arc, as easily as if she was a feather. She'd never felt quite as wonderful as in that moment! She felt her body, that body that was always so foreign to her even though it was her own, was now filled with dizzy excitement. And it was all because of Jamie, so close to her, all hard strength, young and strong and alive, so perfect in her embrace. They had always fit together so well, as if created to be that way, Rose and Jamie.

He watched her intently through his mask, the flashing torchlight turning his dark eyes night luminous. A curl of hair fell over his brow like an inky question mark and her lips felt suddenly dry. She touched them with the tip of her tongue and his gaze sharpened.

'Rose…' he whispered.

People pressed them on all sides as the music ended, making Rose stumble against him. He caught her, holding her safe and steady against his velvet-covered chest. She could feel his warmth, smell his own lemony sea salt soap scent, and she felt as if she spun away again, straight up into the Venetian night sky.

'Shall we dance again?' he asked hoarsely.

'I think—I think I would like to sit down for a moment,' she whispered.

He held tight to her arm, steering her through the crowd, towards a quiet nook near the banks of flowers.

The laughter and music still reached out for her, beckoning, but for the moment they were a circle of two, quiet, warm, safe. Yet her heart pounded, and she felt too warm, too breathless. She pushed back her mask and drew in a deep breath.

Jamie loosened his own mask, letting it dangle down his back by its ribbons. He stared down at her, his face half in shadows, his expression unreadable. She was afraid her own emotions, that wild tangle of fear and need and longing, was written in her eyes.

Slowly, slowly, he raised her hand to his lips, placing a kiss to the tips of her fingers. He lingered over her skin, warm, embracing, leaving flames in their wake, burning and delicious. Then he pressed her palm to his cheek, a lock of loosened hair brushing her wrist.

'My sweet Rose,' he whispered. 'How have I become so lucky to be here with you now?'

Her heart fluttered wildly, and she couldn't answer. He softly kissed the pulse that beat in her wrist, touching it with the tip of his tongue.

'Oh, Jamie,' was all she could say, a hoarse gasp.

His arm slid around her waist, drawing her closer to him, ever closer. The lace of her gown caught on his velvet doublet and his lips were so very, very near…

'Jamie! Is it really you?' A man in a harlequin mask, clearly having enjoyed the Contessa's champagne greatly, bumped into them, laughing and merry. 'Whatever are you doing here?'

Jamie tightened his arm around Rose and said, 'My dear, you would not believe it now, but this is Signor Grattini, a well-known Dante scholar who teaches at the university.'

'Every hard-working academic needs his moments off, I vow!' Grattini grasped Rose's hand and bowed over it in an elaborate salute, making her smile. 'You must be the famous *Duchessa*, the great beauty. Rumours have not been exaggerated, you are a veritable Beatrice. Jamie here is most fortunate indeed.'

Rose laughed. So *this* was the sort of person her husband studied with so diligently. She couldn't help but like him, his bright dark eyes behind his mask, his lively smile.

'A group of us from the Accademia are here tonight,' he said, 'but we feel this ball grows dull. We were going to find another party. Would you care to join us?'

Rose glanced at Jamie, who raised his brow in question. She hesitated for a moment, that old shyness plaguing her, but then she remembered she was meant to be having an adventure here in Venice. Breaking out of her old life, finding new experiences. And was this not a grand promised adventure? 'That sounds wonderful, Signor Grattini. Do lead on.'

* * *

Grattini and his academic friends, along with their girls in red ruffled skirts and lacy shawls, led them down a narrow *calli*, the lane crowded so closely by damp walls of peeling stucco, the cobblestones slick and uneven under Rose's shoes. Above their heads, pale linen fluttered on their lines strung between windows, catching the breeze.

She stumbled on an uneven stone and Jamie caught her lightning quick. She laughed and wondered what trouble he'd led her into.

Sometimes, like tonight, that curiosity bubbled up inside of her, undeniable. She'd had only one glass of prosecco, but her head was light, her skin warm and tingling, her stomach fluttering with excited butterflies.

They stopped next to a door, pale yellow and peeling, and a tiny window set high above covered with a grate. Grattini gave a quick knock and silence followed that lasted so long Rose shifted nervously. She held close to Jamie's velvet sleeve. At last, there was a creak, a clink, and the door slid open. Grattini and his crowd led then down a steep flight of steps, and the air around them was damp and dank, as if they ventured far below the city itself.

At the foot of the stairs was another door, quickly pushed open, and Rose clung even closer to Jamie as they stepped beyond.

It was a large, square, windowless space, the walls hung with rich though threadbare tapestries that kept out the chill, along with braziers burning in every corner, giving out the green herbal smell of incense, turning the air silvery. Flickering torches were set high in the walls, illuminating large velvet cushions and carpets scattered across the floor.

Music played, strange, otherworldly pipes and brass finger cymbals, a soft rhythm that sent itself deep down to Rose's toes, making her long to spin and sway. Like at the ball, couples danced, a swirling tangle of skirts following the rhythm, hands and bodies meeting and parting, feet flying.

'See?' Grattini said merrily. 'Wasn't I right you should come with us?'

Rose smiled. She had seen two very different Venices tonight. 'Oh, yes, very right. That music is extraordinary.' She gave a little spin, laughing, and Grattini bowed and danced off with his own Gypsy maiden.

Rose twirled around to face Jamie. He watched her as if in fascination, as though she was someone he had never seen before. But she recognised that yearning, heavy, passionate look in his dark eyes so well.

He smiled in silence and held out his hand. She slipped her fingers on to his palm, and his clasp tightened on them, lifting them to his lips for a quick, sweet kiss. 'Shall we sit for a moment?' he asked, as if he feared she might faint again.

She *did* feel a bit dizzy. She nodded, and he led her to one of the cushions lined along the wall. It was thick and feather-soft beneath her as she tucked her legs under her skirts. Jamie stretched out next to her, sprawled lazily, his head resting on her lap. His eyes drifted closed behind his mask. She would never have imagined her husband would fit in so well in such a strange, wild place, yet he did, so perfectly. Her old Jamie, of the smiles and laughter, seemed to have come back to her from the drinking, and the working all hours, and the strains of unexpectedly becoming the Duke.

She stared down at him, enchanted. She watched his long fingers lazily toy with the cushion's fringes and she had a vision of that touch on *her*, tracing over her skin, lightly caressing the curve of her shoulder, the soft underside of her arm, circling a pebbled, aching nipple that longed for his kiss…

Rose sucked in a sharp breath, shutting her eyes tightly against the temptation. She smelled smoky jasmine, wine; the dancing grew faster, catching her deep in her heart. Closing her eyes didn't erase the scene, it only made it more intense, more personal.

Jamie reached up to gently touch her loose hair, tangling a strand around his finger as he'd always used to when they lay together in bed. Rose shivered, as if coming alive again.

'What are you thinking about, my Rose?' he asked softly.

She thought of *him*, of course. Their wedding and marriage, those glorious long nights in their chamber, their poor little baby, the tears and misunderstandings and confusions, but also the laughter, the love, the happiness. It was all there, all the time. She couldn't part from him, or any of it. 'That I'm glad we met Signor Grattini tonight and found this lovely place, I suppose.'

'You like it here?'

'Very much. The Contessa's masquerade was fun, too, but I've never seen anything quite like that.' She watched the dancers, a colourful swirl of steps she had never seen before, a wild tangle of music. Here they were free to dance as they wished.

She slid her fingertips slowly over Jamie's cheek, slightly rough with evening whiskers below his mask, along the sharp line of his jaw, a caress over his lower lip. He swallowed hard, but did not move an inch.

Her touch came to rest on his shoulder, strong and lean under the velvet, so warm. She pressed her palm to his heartbeat, absorbing the feel of it into herself.

He sat up and she rested her head on his shoulder as his arm came around her. His lips traced her brow above the edge of her mask, and his hand at her waist slid down, slowly, ever so slowly…

'Are you trying to seduce me? Your own wife?' she whispered.

He smiled against her hair. 'Is it working?'

Rose opened her eyes and stared up at him. He was as beautiful as ever, with his tousled dark hair, his night-black eyes. She *did* want him, more than ever, with a powerful force she had never imagined could exist. It was almost irresistible.

Almost.

She caught up his hand and pressed a quick kiss to it. 'I want to dance.'

'Your wish is always my command,' he said, helping her to stand.

They joined the dance and Rose twirled until she was dizzy and laughing helplessly, caught up in all the colour and drums and movement. For a while, she held Jamie's hand, but they were parted, and she lost sight of him in the crowd. Her head still whirling, she found a small, curtained doorway in the corner and gratefully slipped inside.

She peered carefully into the small room. It was dark, lit only by a few candles, the walls draped with heavy red cloth. A woman sat behind a low table, small and dark, her face deeply creased, dressed in a purple robe and gold turban. She studied a suite of cards spread before her, painted and gilded with fantastical scenes.

The woman glanced up to find Rose watching and smiled. 'Good evening, *signora*! Would you like a reading?'

'A reading, *signora*?' Rose said, curious.

'To see your future. Or to help you on your present path.'

'How fascinating,' Rose said and sat down

on the cushion next to the low table. 'I would very much like some help on my present path.'

'*Va bene*. I am called Maria, *signora*.' She gathered the cards up, fanning them into a neat stack. She handed it to Rose, watching as Rose reshuffled. 'Now, divide it into three stacks. Yes, just so. You have a specific question to-night?'

Only one? Rose laughed.

'I see you have many emotions,' Maria said. 'Let us try a simple five-card spread.'

Maria's gaze went to the first card. 'The Devil, reversed. You must let go of your fears and move into the future freed of old chains. Easier said than done, I fear. The High Priestess, also reversed. She is not entirely honest with us tonight. Something is not right.'

Rose thought of Jamie, of how dark his eyes were as he watched her tonight, the way his arms felt around her, so safe and yet so danger-ous. She didn't want to be hurt again, yet she couldn't resist him, any more than she could resist breathing. 'What is the next card?' she whispered.

'Death, upright. There is a reversal in your life. The past is gone, if you can let it rest.'

Gone? Rose shook her head. The past was

never gone. It always tried to drag her back against her will.

'Then we have the Hierophant, reversed,' Maria said. 'An unconventional way of living.'

Rose laughed. 'Very true.'

'And the final card, the Chariot, upright. An auspicious card, *signora*. You will find happiness, though it may be hard work and a difficult road to travel.'

Against her will, Rose felt hope rise up inside of her in a wave that threatened to overwhelm her. 'Is that not a good thing?' Once, she had thought she'd found happiness, only for it to slip out of her hands.

Maria nodded, her gaze still bent over the cards. 'If we can trust the High Priestess—let your heart open up again, *signora*. Don't let it remain closed and cold. The fate of the cards is up to you alone, *signora*. You need only have the courage to go forward.'

Courage? Rose sometimes thought she'd used up all her courage long ago, marrying Jamie when she was so young and naive, and now she had little left to spare. Her head ached and she was suddenly so tired.

'*Grazie*, Signora Maria,' she whispered and rose to depart, leaving all the coins in her purse.

A shadow shifted in the doorway and her breath caught as she saw Jamie, watching her intently, his mask in his hand.

'Are you well, Rose?' he asked gently, and she nodded.

'A little tired,' she said. 'Shall we return to the palazzo?' She wrapped her hand around his arm and followed him through the crowded party chamber. It was quieter now, everyone murmuring together, lounging on the cushions. Jamie steered her carefully past the sprawled figures dozing, the guitar player strumming a soft song, until they emerged from the steep stairs into the greyish pre-dawn light of the city.

She felt a bit like Eurydice, led out of an illusory underworld by her husband's sweet lyre. The narrow alley was deserted and she tipped back her head to draw in a deep breath of sweet, damp morning air.

'It's chilly,' Jamie said and swirled his cloak over her shoulders. She was enfolded in his warmth and scent, that feeling of safety.

'But you will be cold,' she protested.

He smiled wryly. 'Oh, no. I burn all too hot now, my Rose.' He took her hand again and led her along the damp stones of the walkway, taking her home as the Venetian sky flowered pink and orange and lavender above them.

Chapter Nineteen

'**W**herever are we going, Jamie?' Rose asked. They were having dinner at the palazzo, a lovely rare evening with just the two of them, with much laughter and talk of the glorious Venetian buildings they'd visited. Rose couldn't remember a time when she'd felt so very relaxed, and she hardly dared believe it was real. It was all she had once dreamed her marriage could be. Venice *did* hold a real magic.

And after they finished their gelato and espresso, Jamie declared he had a surprise for her. 'A surprise!' she cried happily. 'Whatever could it be?' Even on birthdays and anniversaries, Jamie had often forgot to mark the moment, only remembering with a bouquet or a box at the ballet days later. 'What is the occasion?'

'Need there be an occasion?' he said teasingly. 'We are in Venice and you are with me again at last! That seems the grandest occasion of all. Come, we will be late.'

'Late for what?' Rose giggled doubtfully, but she let him lead her from the palazzo. Signora Pollatini had waited in the *portego* to wrap her in her cloak, so obviously Jamie had accomplices. He tied a silk kerchief over her eyes, sending the world into shadows.

'And what is this for?' she asked, running her fingers over the silken hem. 'Such an odd game, Jamie!'

'I told you, Rose, it is a surprise. You'll like it, trust me.' He led her down a step. 'You do trust me?'

In that moment, Rose realised she *did* trust him. When had that happened? After everything standing between them, when had something so deep and wonderful shifted?

She nodded and held on to his hand to let him lead her onwards. She felt the rough stones under her satin evening shoes, the dampness of the canalside evening air. There was the creak of gates and windows, the salty scent of the city, laughter.

Jamie helped her into a swaying gondola and

the sound of water splashing against the sides of the boat was amplified behind the blindfold. She heard the toll of bells announcing the hour, music somewhere in the distance. The boat swayed beneath her, swinging out on to the water.

'Where are we going?' she asked again, trying to gauge their direction.

Jamie held close to her hand. 'You will see very soon. Have you always been so impatient?'

At last, the gondola lurched to a halt, and Jamie untied the handkerchief. They were adrift in the lagoon, surrounded by other vessels filled with merrymakers, drinking champagne, calling out to friends. The city glowed with pale gold light behind them, a fairyland in the night, surrounded by the bobbing lanterns of the boats.

She leaned against Jamie's shoulder, his arms wrapped around her, holding her safe. At last, a firework broke the dusty dark sky, an arrow of silver that broke apart into a thousand crackling pieces. Everyone applauded, the cries growing louder as more lights followed, faster and faster. Red, green, blue, gold, wheels and flowers and stars, exploding in a glorious display over the water.

As Rose watched, holding on to Jamie, she

suddenly felt alive again, truly alive, and resplendently happy, as if she was being born once more. She had never dared hope she would feel anything like it again.

'Oh, Jamie, it's wondrous!' she cried. 'How did you know about it?'

'The Contessa told me. It's to celebrate a saint's day, I think—everyone uses it as an excuse to feast and meet friends. As if Venetians need such an excuse! She thought you might like to see it.'

'Like to see it? It is glorious!' She gasped as a giant rose-like burst of red shattered overhead and she fell deep into the dreamworld of light and fire and Jamie. Only Jamie.

The palazzo was dark and quiet after the brilliant merriment of the fireworks, but Rose didn't mind. She still felt like a firework herself, fizzy, sparkling, afire from Jamie's touch. Without a word, she pushed his coat away from his body, letting it land on the floor, and took his hand to lead him through the *portego*, the enfilade of doors, to her bedchamber.

She wrapped her arms around him, holding him to her as her lips parted for his kiss. He groaned, a primitive sound of need, his tongue touching hers, their mouths and bodies and very souls enmeshed. He seemed caught every bit as much as she was, bound together as they had been ever since they first saw each other, never to be free. How he could make her forget everything else, every bit of the past, when he touched her!

Pulling him with her, Rose stumbled back until she fell across the bed, sinking down into its feathery softness. She drew him on top of her, their kiss becoming frantic. She wrapped her legs tightly around his lean hips, kicking her skirts out of the way. It wasn't enough, it wasn't close enough, not any more.

Rose let her head fall back on the satin cushions, revelled in the shivery sensations of his kiss against her cheek, the curve of her throat. The hot rush of his breath, the pounding of his heartbeat, all around her, part of her. How alive he was, how vital and real! She had lived too long in her own cocoon, trying to find safety, but now she wanted to feel again. No matter what might happen afterwards.

When she was with him, she knew real emotion, real pain, real joy. Maybe it would all be gone too soon, but she would hold on to it for that moment.

She closed her eyes tightly, absorbing every feeling and sensation. She slid her touch over his strong shoulders, his chest, until her trembling fingers found the pearl buttons of his waistcoat. She made quick work of them and unfastened his fine linen shirt. He groaned again, sounding almost pained, his face buried in her neck as she touched his naked skin again at last.

His heart pounded under her caress, his breath catching, but he didn't move away. He didn't snatch her control of the moment away from her. He let her explore him again, finding her husband once more.

She smoothed her palm over his warm chest, the sharp arc of his shoulder. She rolled him to the bed as she rose above him on her knees. She could hardly breathe, hardly think at all. All she knew was *him*, that deep drumbeat of need she had resisted for so long.

She didn't fight against it any longer. She couldn't.

He loosened the laces of her gown, his long fingers quick and nimble, and she pulled it off, discarding the expensive satin and lace, leaving her kneeling above him in her chemise and corset and silk stockings. She wondered if he still thought her beautiful, if he could still desire her as he once had, above all else. She had to resist the urge to hide from him.

'Rose,' he whispered in awe. 'My beautiful, exquisite Rose.'

He claimed her lips again, their mouths meeting in a desperate clash that held nothing of artful romance or subtle seduction. It had never been that way between them. There was only that urgent need that was theirs alone.

He pulled her forward and she tumbled down on top of him, stretched out against his body, their limbs entangled. There were no words at all now, no rational thought, just feeling. The joy of finding each other again.

He quickly shed the rest of his clothes, sliding into the eager welcome of her parted legs, his mouth at her breast. The delicious friction of damp, warm skin against skin, that need, always that need. She tensed a bit as they joined together again at last, it had been so long, but then she arched up to meet him in pleasurable wonder, sliding him even deeper, so deep they seemed as one.

'I've missed you so much,' he whispered.

'As I have missed you.'

He drew slowly out, then back again, faster, deeper, that wonderful glow expanding, growing, until Rose was sure she could soar up into the sun herself. As if she'd become the fireworks.

She held tightly to him, called out his name, until at last she reached the sun and flew apart in a thousand flying sparks. A shower of urgent release that sent her tumbling back to earth, weak and shaking.

He caught her as she fell, holding her safe again in his arms as she burst into inexplicable tears.

'Oh, Jamie,' she sobbed. 'That was—was *heavenly.*'

He laughed gently and cradled her against his chest, and she felt the deep rumble of that laughter as he kissed her hair, her cheek. 'Yes, my darling, darling Rose. Heavenly.'

It was still dark when Rose slowly swam up from her dreams, but the sky peeping past the edge of her curtains was palest, pearly pink. Almost morning.

She stretched her luxuriously sore body and smiled. For an instant, she wondered if that glorious night had been a dream, but as she rolled on to her side, she saw Jamie asleep beside her and she smiled even more. It was true, that lazy, delicious wonder of it all.

Once, when they were first married, she had watched him thus every morning, the dawn light glowing on his face, the shadow of his morning whiskers, his tousled hair, his bare skin in the twisted sheets. He looked so much younger asleep, so free of any care or worry. Just her Jamie. In that moment, that little fleeting moment, he was all hers.

Then he would wake and smile and reach for her, both of them laughing, rolling through the sheets, mussing them even more. Everything was just beginning for them then. What would she have done if she could have seen the future? The drinking, the quarrels, the loneliness, the lost baby, the separate beds that awaited them.

But things finally felt so very different after last night. She was floating on a cloud, the memory of every touch, every kiss sending her spiralling higher into the sky. She wanted to hold that feeling close and never, ever let it go.

She turned and glimpsed something new on her dressing table—the wedding chest she had looked at in the shop window. The box that had held the dreams of so many brides before her. A wonderful gift from Jamie.

Suddenly, his eyes opened and found her watching him. His smile widened, his hands reaching for her under the sheets, warm and strong and reassuring. She slid back beside him and gave herself up to his kiss.

Jamie watched as the rose-gold light of day slowly crept across the chamber floor, over the tangled bedsheets, finally touching Rose's face as she slept. He half wished it was still night, so that they could hide from the world again.

Where he could maybe even hide how very much he still loved Rose. Longed for her. He had always known he loved her, ever since the first time he saw her. He'd spent the first part of their long months apart trying to forget it, deny it, but some things just refused to stay buried. Refused to be denied. His heart was Rose's and would be until he died. So he'd worked hard on becoming a better man for her, for himself, so that they might have a chance together again.

If only he could know that she loved him, too, that she forgave him. Despite everything that had happened, surely the bonds between them could never entirely break?

He gently kissed her cheek and slid out of their warm bed. Rose murmured in her sleep, her fingers catching at the sheets as if she dreamed.

'Shh,' he whispered, leaning over to kiss her hair. 'Go back to sleep now, my darling.' She went still again, sinking back against the pillows, comforted by his murmurs. 'I will do all I can to make sure you are safe and happy.' Even if she could never forgive him and he had to let her go, he would do his best to find someone better for her.

Her eyes suddenly opened and she stared up at him. A smile started to form on her lips, but she seemed to see something in his face that concerned her and she sat up.

'Jamie?' Rose said, gathering the bedclothes around her as she sat up. He looked so sad there in the shadows, so very alone. 'Are you— Is it the drink? Cravings?'

He gave her a gentle smile and reached out to touch her cheek with the tips of his fingers, so gentle, so tender. 'Not at all. I hardly ever feel those any longer. I was just…remembering. Thinking.'

'Oh, don't do that!' she cried and wrapped her arms tightly around him. She buried her face in his shoulder and inhaled deeply of *him*.

'I do it too often and it never leads to anything of use.'

He laughed softly and held her, too, the pair of them alone in the morning silence. 'It's not terrible. In fact, it's vital. If our time in Venice has shown me anything, it is that I must be honest with you. Share everything with you.'

Rose thought of those days earlier in their marriage, when she had felt so alone, so cut off from him. 'That's all I've ever wanted. All I begged for when we were first married.'

'I know, yet I thought I had to protect you by hiding the darker parts of my heart. I was a fool to think I *could* hide them, for they chased me down in the end.'

She shook her head, confused. 'I don't understand.'

'I hadn't realised when we first married how much my own childhood still haunted me, the loneliness and fear of my father's indifference to me, the feeling I could never belong at Greensted the way my brother did. I never learned how to be a real partner, a real husband and father. My family's curse of drinking became my own curse, especially after we lost our child. Then I blamed the drink for my own inability to face fatherhood, my inability to help you when you needed me most. But it was not the drink. It was just my own damnable fear of not being good enough for you. Now, when I just let myself love you—it feels like anything is possible.'

Rose smiled as a ray of light, bright and shimmering and warm, pierced her heart, and she knew hope, real, true hope, again. 'Oh, Jamie. All I want, all I need, is that love! And for you to accept *my* love, my help. You take care of me, you always have really. Let me take care of you, too. We are not the people we were when we met, except the parts of us that recognised our hearts in each other. We've grown and learned. We can see clearly now, if we let ourselves. We can—' She broke off, wondering if that was all true, all possible. She could only hope.

His smile widened, warmed. 'Start again?'

'Yes. Exactly. Start again. That is, if you still want to? If you still want me.'

'My darling. How can you even ask that? It's all I ever want.' His lips met hers and they tumbled down to the bed once more, wrapped in each other, the pink Venetian light washing over them.

Chapter Twenty

'You have a visitor, *Duchessa*,' Signora Polla-tini announced. Rose glanced up from her book to see the housekeeper holding out a card on a silver tray. She shivered even before she read it, a feeling of foreboding coming over her. It had been a lovely morning, after all that had happened last night, the glories of it all. She had floated through a late breakfast on the log-gia after Jamie went off to his archival studies, then drifted, humming and twirling, through the house before she sat down to try to read. But now her heart turned cold.

She looked down at the card.

Gerald Mayhew. She had been sure this mo-ment would come, ever since she saw him at the theatre. She'd known deep down that it was him she'd seen. Several times she'd wanted to tell Jamie about what had happened in Newport. About how young and foolish she had been back then. Jamie would surely have known what to do.

But then he would take her hand, smile at her, kiss her and her resolve faltered. She was so ashamed of what had happened. She had flirted with Gerald, after all, even if she couldn't have guessed he'd do what he had done. She was finally on a path to regaining her marriage, but it was all still so very fragile. She dared not let anything mar it by allowing Gerald to convince Jamie she was some sort of artful tease who tempted men and then cried foul on them. She didn't want Jamie having any doubts about her at all.

She would have to deal with this herself. Thankfully, she was alone here for the moment and she didn't expect Jamie back for a while yet.

'Please, show him in, *signora*,' she said, amazed at how steady her voice was. 'Here to the salon.'

'*Va bene, Duchessa.* If you say so. Shall I send in tea?'

'That will not be necessary. The *signor* will not be staying long.'

As Signora Pollatini left, her keys jangling,

Rose carefully set aside her book and smoothed her blue silk morning dress, her hair, her pearls. She sat up as tall as she could, determined not to let him make her emotional or angry, and she folded her hands in her lap to keep them from trembling. She had so much to protect now; she was not that scared girl any longer. And she was determined that she, the famous American Beauty Rose, would let no blackguard threaten her happiness now.

Gerald swept into the salon and gave her an elegant, mocking bow, smiling his charming, gleaming American smile as if this was the most pleasant of social calls. Rose refused to smile in return.

'Your Grace,' he said, deep emphasis on those two words. 'How lovely you are looking. Marriage certainly agrees with you. I couldn't believe it was you when I saw you at the theatre! Little Rose Wilkins.'

'It is not the usual hour for calls in Venice, Mr Mayhew,' she said brusquely. She did not ask him to sit. 'To what do I owe this…honour?'

'You do wound me. Even though you are a duchess now, Rose, you surely remember we're old friends? Like Paul Adelman, who I met in London. He spoke so glowingly of you and your newfound fame. He and I have become quite good chums, he knows all the good gossip.'

'I have many friends in London.'

'Yes, so I've heard. But you've recently re-united with your husband, or so they say.' Despite the lack of an invitation, he sat down on one of the brocade chairs, carelessly crossing one foot over his knee, still smiling at her. 'We were so close once, weren't we, dear Rose? You were fond of me, as you showed so well. If the Duke found out anything about our little romance…'

Romance? Rose stared at him in revulsion, her stomach tight. *This* was the sort of man Lily had once warned Violet and Rose against so vehemently—selfish, grubby fortune hunters with no thought of anyone but themselves. And once she had so idolised his handsome face and charming ways! How very silly she had been; what a narrow escape she'd made. She saw now she had been very wrong to ever blame herself for her young, fumbling flirtations. She'd acted like any other young girl might have; he'd been the one at fault.

'What is it you want?' she said quietly.

'I merely ask the help of an old friend in my time of need. A few unfortunate investments, you see, and my father shows no understanding at all. A tiny amount to help me back on my feet…'

Rose nodded. Blackmail. Of course that was his game.

'Why come to me?' she said. 'My dowry went to my husband, I have only my pin money.' He didn't need to know about the investments Jamie had made for her. Her own money in the bank.

'Oh, my dear Duchess…' he laughed '…you underestimate your charms. You're very beautiful and clearly that has opened many doors for you. You'll easily be able to coax the money from your many admirers. You know, we really could have built a fine life together, you and I. Such fun.'

A life of lies and cons and games, apparently, no love or real home. She had a second chance for those things now. How could she let them slip away? 'Never. I would never have allowed you to use me to run your cons for you, running ten steps ahead of bailiffs and debt collectors, never safe or happy. No Wilkins would so lower themselves.' She almost did smile at that, remembering how once the Mayhews had been so snobby to her parents. But her father and mother, for all their faults, were always honest and gave that quality to all their daughters.

Gerald's manicured hands curled into fists, his handsome face contorted with fury, and he reached for her as if to grab her. Rose half stood, picking up the bell to summon the servants if she had to. But he quickly leaned away from her, his fists loosening, that tight smile back again.

'If you cannot help me, Your Grace, I must sadly tell your husband about your associations with Paul Adelman, and about what really happened between you and me in Newport. I am sure your reunion with the dear Duke would quickly come to a sticky end then. Such scandal!'

Rose swallowed hard. 'I told you, I have no ready money.'

'But you have so many other resources! Those pearls. That sapphire ring. And I'm sure you have a safe full of other pretties tucked away.' He gestured to her sapphire and diamond wedding ring and she instinctively curled her fingers inward as if to protect it. 'I'm sure you can find it in your heart to help me, Rose. Your dear old friend.'

He stepped closer, too fast for her to flee, and his arms came around her, tight as unbreakable ropes. Rose felt cold, suffocating panic welled up inside her and she was sure she would be sick. She landed her heeled shoe hard on his instep and took advantage of his surprise to shove him away.

He laughed. 'Oh, Rose. You really have become so thorny as well as beautiful. What fun. You have my card. Do send me word when you have the money for me, there's a good girl.' He strolled out, as if he hadn't a worry in the world. He only limped a bit.

Rose growled in fury and ripped the card he had left in two, leaving it on the ground as she whirled around and ran out of the house to the far end of the garden. How dare he come back into her life and resurrect that old torment, when everything seemed to be falling into place at last?

She sank down on to a bench, her fists clenched. And how could she ever hide this from Jamie now?

'Signor il Duca!' Signora Pollatini said urgently, her usually expressionless face tense. 'You are home at last. I fear the Duchessa had a caller, a man, and when he left—she was quite upset.'

Jamie paused mid-whistle, staring at the housekeeper in astonishment. He had a nice morning with his books, but had looked forward every moment to being with Rose again. Now the house seemed filled with a strange atmosphere. Who was this man? Someone who mattered to Rose?

'What do you mean, *signora*?'

She held out a card torn in two. 'This man. After he left, the Duchessa went out into the garden and she would not come in for luncheon. I do not know exactly what happened, but…'

Jamie looked down at the card. 'Gerald Mayhew, New York City, Newport.' With a Venetian address scribbled on the bottom. Someone from Rose's old American life, then? 'Thank you, *signora*. I will talk to her.'

He found his wife on a bench in the courtyard garden, staring silently out at the pretty flower beds, her hands twisted in her lap, her face white and frozen. She didn't seem to notice anything around her and that wonderful laughter she had only recently regained was nowhere to be found. He found himself terribly sad and angry, too. Angry at anyone who would hurt her, angry that she felt she couldn't trust him with whatever this was—though that was his own fault, as well. He had lost her trust through his own actions and it seemed he had further work to do to earn it back.

But he could never turn and walk away, leave her to whatever worries she had now. They had been apart for too long already. He had to let her know he was here for her, truly, at last, that he would not disappoint her ever again.

His Rose was a lady with a kind heart and the idea that some American brute would use that kindness against her made him burn with a raw fury he had never known before.

He forced that anger down, erased it from his expression and shook out his hard, curled fists. 'So here you are, Rose.'

She jumped up, startled, and spun to face him. 'I—yes,' she gasped, her eyes wide.

He took one slow step towards her, then another, his hand half-raised, palm up in entreaty. He didn't want her to run from him again. It felt as if this moment was so vital, as if their entire future depended on it in some way.

'Signora Pollatini says you had a visitor, someone who seems to have upset you.' He sat down, looking up at her. She looked so tense he feared she might shatter if he touched her.

'Is this a man you—you care about? Someone you once knew?'

Rose gave a bitter laugh. 'Quite the opposite.'

He couldn't help letting out a silent sigh of relief.

Rose sank back down on to the bench next to him. 'I just wanted to take care of it myself. Make it all go away.'

'Why? What is *it*?'

She looked away and the story came tumbling out. A girl in a secluded part of a night-dark garden, a man who took advantage of her youth and beauty. A man who'd just used that to threaten her with now, to make her afraid all over again. 'I—I did not want to burden you with this,' she finished with a sob. 'Not when things between us seem to be healing at last.'

Jamie thought of his poor Rose, young and vulnerable, and he reached for her hand, holding it tightly in his. 'Oh, Rose. You have never been a burden of any sort. Our troubles have been all on me.'

She swallowed hard and stared down at their joined hands. 'You are not angry? You believe me?'

'I do believe you and I am certainly angry. But not with you.'

'Oh.' She frowned, as if trying to fathom something new. He knew that feeling well. He had been trying to understand the rare gift of Rose ever since she'd landed in his life. Now he had a second chance with her. A way to help set things right. They had to learn to trust each other again and they would begin right here.

'I love you, Rose. I swear, you will never be alone again.' He took her in his arms and kissed her cheek as she cried on his shoulder, her back shaking as if she was finally releasing all the unhappiness and worry that had weighed her down for too many months. He vowed to himself he would never let her down again.

'I'm surprised you haven't run from Venice already, Mayhew,' Jamie said from the shadows. He had been waiting there on the narrow stairs of the cheap pensione for what felt like hours, his anger simmering. Now that fury was so cold it burned.

Mayhew spun around, fists clenched, panic flaring in his eye before he smothered it in a mocking smile.

'Surprised to see me instead of my wife?' Jamie said.

'So the little mouse spilled all, did she? Confessed?' Mayhew said with a smirk, trying to be casual. 'She is braver than I thought.'

'And you are even more foolish than I thought. Surely you should have known better than to have thought you could insult my wife even further than you already have and that there would be no reprisal from me?'

'What can you do to me? Even a duke can't bring me down any further.'

'I wouldn't bet on that if I were you, Mayhew—though they do say you enjoy a bet. A furious husband is worse than any duke could be.'

'So now you care about her, do you?' Mayhew sneered. 'Everyone knows you don't even bother to live with her. But now you suddenly want her, when so many others have feelings for her, including myself? Forgive me if I am not convinced—Your Grace.'

'I don't care if you are convinced or not,' Jamie ground out. 'I only care that you leave Rose alone from now on. Do not even look in her direction, or you'll see what a duke's power can actually do.'

Disgusted, fed up with having to even look at the swine, Jamie half turned towards the door to take his leave. He had to get back to what really mattered—Rose. But Mayhew suddenly lunged at him, catching him on the jaw with an unexpected blow that sent Jamie spinning against the wall. All his burning fury was rekindled and he finally let it fly free, grabbing Mayhew, slamming him against a closed door. All the emotions of the past year, his love for Rose, his despair at losing her, his anger that anyone would dare hurt her, bubbled up in him and overflowed like lava. He curled his fists hard in the man's coat, holding him pinned there like the bug he was.

'You call frightening and blackmailing a lady having *feelings* for her?' Jamie said, tightening his fists as Mayhew tried to squirm away. 'I call it being a damnable villain. Rose had a lucky escape from you all those years ago.'

'And she's so much better off with you, is she? Everyone says she ran away from you!' Mayhew kicked out at Jamie, driving him back, but only for an instant. Jamie remembered all the fighting methods he had learned at the saloon and came back with a sharp right uppercut that sent Mayhew to the damp carpet.

This man would never hurt Rose again. As Jamie grabbed him up before driving his fist back into Mayhew's face, he hoped no other lady would ever again fear this rogue. This lesson had to be for good and always.

'What is this?' a woman screamed in Italian. 'You tear up my pensione!'

Jamie tossed a bruised Mayhew aside and fell back against the peeling paper of the wall as a tiny, grey-haired woman in rusty black taffeta rushed at them. Her fury seemed to surpass even Jamie's in that moment.

She kicked at Mayhew, who tried to crawl away from her even though Jamie had blacked both his eyes and they were already swelling shut.

'You never paid your rent, Inglese Mayhew!' the woman shouted, kicking at him again. 'And now you bleed all over my floor!'

Jamie started to laugh and winced as his split lip twinged. He carefully touched it and saw he was bleeding, adding to the mess on the woman's floor. His knuckles were bruised, his ribs on fire, his cheek aching, but Mayhew was in a far worse state.

And certainly, Jamie thought as he watched the landlady finish the job on Mayhew's battered face, he would know better than to ever harass a woman again. Not a bad day's work.

The lady stopped beating Mayhew, who prudently lay very still, and spun to face Jamie. His laughter faded.

'And you, *signor*!' she shouted. 'I don't know who you are, but no real gentleman would brawl in a lady's home. Tsk-tsk.'

'You are quite right, *signora*,' he muttered through his bleeding lip. 'My deepest apologies.'

'Does he owe you money, too? It has been a nuisance, I tell you, people pounding on his door day and night.'

'He will be gone very soon, I promise you that.' Jamie dug out as much money as he carried and pressed it into her hand. 'Pay to have the room cleaned, *signora*, with my apologies again.'

A smile lit her wrinkled face. 'I will, *signor*, *grazie*.' She cast a bitter glance at Mayhew, who was slowly sitting up. 'What about him?'

'I will take care of him, don't worry.'

The woman cackled. 'I am quite sure you will!' She hurried away without a backward glance, clutching at the money.

'Get away from Italy, and from England, as fast as you can, Mayhew,' Jamie said. 'And pray neither I nor any of my wife's family ever sees you again, or this will all seem the merest trifle compared to what will happen to you.'

He turned and followed the woman out. She was nowhere to be seen, but Mayhew's pained whimpers followed him out the door.

His gondola waited at the end of the narrow canal, and he collapsed on to the velvet cushions with a groan. Only now could he really feel all the aches of a good fight, but it was worth it. Not very duke-like to brawl, maybe, as his brother had always done, but satisfying. And at least his dearest Rose was finally safe. She was the only thing in the world that was important to him. It had taken him far too long to truly understand that, but he knew it very well now.

Chapter Twenty-One

'So here you are, Rose.' Jamie's voice, harsh and hoarse, startled her and she leaped up from the garden bench where she had been waiting impatiently for what seemed like days, weeks. She took a deep breath and whirled to face him.

And gasped. His face, his handsome, dear face, was turning the most vivid shade of yellow and purple, his lip bleeding, his coat torn. Her Jamie—fighting?

'Whatever happened to you? It was Gerald, wasn't it?' she cried, running to him. He tried to kiss her, but winced, and she led him to the bench, calling to the footman to bring water and salve. When they came, she soaked a cloth in the cool water and pressed it gently to his bruised cheek. 'You fought him. You ridiculous, wonderful, foolish man!' She had to admit it was rather satisfyingly sweet to think of it. Not sweet that Jamie was hurt, not at all, but that he had gone out like a knight in a medieval *chanson* to defend his damsel. 'Where on earth did you learn to fight?'

He shrugged. 'When you grow up with a brother like mine, you learn to defend yourself. And after you left, I started going to a boxing saloon for lessons. It was wonderful for releasing all my frustration with myself.'

'As long as you never do it again.'

'What else could I do, when you told me what happened to you in Newport? I doubt he will ever pester a lady again now,' he said, gently touching her hand. 'I wish you had told me much sooner.'

Rose shook her head and wrung out the cloth again. 'I couldn't burden you with his awfulness. I thought somehow it had all been my fault then.'

He stared up into her eyes, so open, so filled with love. All she had ever longed for. 'Oh, Rose. Nothing that man could have done was possibly your fault. And you could never, ever be a burden to me.'

'You mean—you are sure you are not at all angry with me?' she said doubtfully, staring down at his hand against hers.

'I am certainly still angry. But not with you.

Never with you. I'm only angry with myself that you didn't think you could tell me about it long ago. I'm your husband. Not always the best of husbands, I admit, and I cannot apologise enough for that. But I promise to try my hardest from now on. We are together in all things. I can't bear to lose you again, my darling Rose. You are the kindest, sweetest woman I have ever known and I need you. I love you. That's all.'

He curled his hand around hers and she realised with surprise and delight and wonder that it was true. Such simple, perfect words, but they were everything to her. Now they had a chance to make a real life together. To learn to trust. To truly love.

'Oh, Jamie,' she cried and threw her arms around him. 'I love you, too. What fools we have been—*I* have been. I was young and silly when we married, but now I see so clearly! I see how together we can be, do, anything at all. I should have told you about Mayhew ages ago, but…'

'But I was not the husband you deserved and you needed, not then. I am now, I swear it. And I will always try to be. You are everything to me. You never have to be afraid again.' He held her so close, burying his face in her hair, and she knew they would never let each other go again.

Epilogue

A Lady in Society Tells All

Who would ever have thought it, my darling readers? The grandest house party of the Season will be held next month at Greensted, seat of the Duke of B.!

Those walls have not seen such merriment in decades, but now all promises to be glory and fun under the eye of the beautiful Duchess and her ever-so-devoted Duke.

I am sure we all wish them well in their domesticity and look forward to the new scandal. Who will it be, this Author wonders?

Greensted—1878

'Oh, do hurry, Vi!' Rose laughed, struggling to hold a wriggling little Hazel, her precious daughter, in her arms. The toddler chortled and reached for her cousins, Violet's twins and Lily's Little A., who were both racing past with Daisy Hammond, chasing through the gardens.

'You cannot rush perfection in art, Rose, you know that,' Violet muttered, squinting up at the light and then down at her photographic plate.

It was a perfect summer's day, all green and blue and gold, while the house, new windows sparkling, seemed to smile at its new life. Rose had worked hard on the gardens as well as the interior furnishings and she was rather proud now of the shady groves and the overflowing rose beds, spilling pink and red and white on to the new gravel pathways. There had been many months of garden designers, textile merchants, furniture deliveries from France, carpets and curtains and books, and now it was all as she had pictured. Something like the artistic haven at Pryde Abbey, where her friends could come to paint and write and laugh. And it all started now, with her family.

Violet glanced up again, frowning as an uncooperative cloud slid past. 'Just—one—more—moment.'

Rose laughed and held tighter to little Hazel, a tiny wriggle-worm in her lace and frills, her dark curls like her father's. They sat with Lily and her daughter on a bench by one of the walnut trees, the remains of a picnic lunch scattered on the blanket at their feet. Jamie, Aidan and Will walked nearby, Jamie showing off his plans for a new summer house to his brothers-in-law, and she smiled to see them all there, so handsome. She felt positively giddy with happiness, she had to admit. Love did seem to be on the breeze lately; she had even received an invitation to the wedding of Paul Adelman and Beatrice Madewell! Rose did indeed love a wedding.

Jamie threw back his head and laughed at something Aidan said, the sun shining on the unruly waves of his hair, his forearms strong and sun-browned under his rolled-back white sleeves. He looked so much younger now, lighter, full of smiles. At home.

'All right, now!' Violet cried and Rose and Lily smiled, doing their best to keep their offspring from blurring the image too much. Violet had won the Gold Medal at the Photographic Society's last exhibition and she would be furious if they spoiled it for her this year!

Violet saw to her tidying up, her chemicals and plates, and then ran over to collapse on the picnic blanket at their feet, her spring-green skirts puffing around her as her twins rushed to collapse across her lap. Rose poured her a glass of Venetian white wine in one of her swirling pink and blue Murano glass goblets, and Violet laughed as she reached for it. 'Thank you, Rose darling, I do need that.'

Lily sat back with a sigh, smiling as she watched her husband in the distance. She held on to her daughter with one hand and laid her other hand lightly over the small swell of her stomach under her blue-and-white-striped dress. Her third baby was on the way for her. 'Oh, it *is* a beautiful day. Who would have imagined we would ever be in such a place?'

'With me properly married again, you mean?' Rose teased. She let Hazel go to shuffle herself across the blanket, shrieking after her cousins.

'With all of us so very happy,' Lily said.

'The Wilkins sisters triumphant at last!' Violet said, raising her glass high.

They were giggling together as their husbands came back, Aidan plucking up a peach from the picnic basket and offering Lily a taste, Will saving Violet from the twins and carrying them off under each arm. Jamie scooped up little Hazel, his handsome face gleaming as he hugged her close. She reached up her precious, dimpled little fingers to tug at his hair. After their old loss, their painful parting and finding each other again, their baby was doubly precious. Rose's doctor had also revised his previous opinion and told them that she should have no problems bearing Jamie more children in the future.

Jamie sat down at Rose's feet, Hazel perched on his lap, and Rose reached down to smooth his hair under her palm.

'Triumphant,' Rose whispered. It *did* feel like a triumphant day, not in an overpowering, courtly way, but content, sunny, perfect. The future, which she'd seen as so shadowed, stretched before her in glorious colour.

'I love you so much, my Duchess,' Jamie said softly.

'And I love you, my Duke,' she answered and leaned down to press her lips to his. 'For always.'

'Yes. For always.'

* * * * *

Author Note

I hope you've enjoyed the adventures of the Wilkins sisters as much as I have! When I was very young, I found a biography of Jennie Jerome on my grandmother's bookshelf and was amazed at her bold, adventurous life. Later I discovered Edith Wharton and *The Buccaneers*, and wondered at the lives of young American women finding themselves in a whole different society and way of life than they had known and their various fates. The Wilkins sisters are the lucky ones, of course, and find true love and fulfilment in being duchesses!

The year 2020 was challenging in so many ways, so I loved being able to visit one of my very favourite cities, Venice, through Rose and Jamie. Rose's palazzo is based on the Ca'Doro and the Palazzo Gradanigo and she sees many real spots, such as the church of the Miracoli—Venice's favourite wedding church!—and the Teatro Goldoni. Hopefully I'll be able to admire them in person again soon.

Rose's artistic friends at Pryde Abbey are also based on real places and people—the Prinseps at Little Holland House and The Souls.

Violet got to visit Little Holland House as well, in *Playing the Duke's Fiancée*. Little Holland House was originally a dower house for the grand Holland House and was occupied by members of the powerful political family the Foxes. In 1850, H. T. Prinsep, director of the East India Company, moved in with his wife, Sara Pattle—sister of the photographer Julia Margaret Cameron—and it became a centre of artistic and bohemian life for over twenty-one years. The Prinseps moved out in 1871, so it couldn't be used in this book!

The Souls were an elite, social and intellectual group of society friends from 1885 to about 1900, including the Grenfells and Wyndhams, George Curzon, Margot Asquith and Violet Manners. Their children were known as The Coterie and included the famously beautiful Lady Diana Manners, though sadly many of them were killed in World War I.

A couple of interesting sources for these

groups are *Kensington and Chelsea: A Social and Architectural History* and Angela Lambert's *Unquiet Souls: The Indian Summer of the British Aristocracy, 1880–1918.*

Rose—quite against her will!—has found herself to be a Professional Beauty, or PB. They were the reality stars of their day. A trend arose in the 1870s and '80s for the images of beautiful society women, and also some actresses and singers, to be displayed and sold in shop windows and their lives were followed in newspapers. They were much sought after as guests of honour at parties, set fashions and could often build careers beyond society—such as Lillie Langtry. Other famous PBs included Lady Warwick, Jennie Jerome, Lady de Grey, Mrs Cornwallis-West and Mrs Wheeler.

I took a little historical liberty in allowing Rose to be called American Beauty Rose! The flower, a deep pink rose cultivar, was bred by Henri Ledechaux in France in 1885 and was called Madame Ferdinand Jamin. It was renamed when brought to America in 1886 and later became the bestselling rose in the US in the 1920s. I also took historical liberty with the Astor mansion, which was purchased by William Backhouse Astor Jr a little after this story takes place.

For more information, you can always visit me at www.ammandamccabe.com.

And here are a few more sources I enjoyed, if you'd like to read further:

Martin, Judith (2011) *No Vulgar Hotel: The Desire and Pursuit of Venice*
W. W. Norton & Company

Ackroyd, Peter (2010) *Venice: Pure City*
Vintage

Adby, Jane (1985) *The Souls*
Sidgwick & Jackson Ltd

Renton, Claudia (2018) *Those Wild Wyndhams: Three Sisters at the Heart of Power*
Knopf Publishing Group

Alonge, Roberto (2014) *Goldoni il Lbertino*
Editori Laterza

Goldoni Carlo *et al* (2019) *Goldoni on Playwrighting*
Wentworth Press

Davis, James C. (1975) *A Venetian Family and Its Fortune 1500-1900*
American Philosophical Society

COMING SOON!

We really hope you enjoyed reading this book.
If you're looking for more romance, be sure to
head to the shops when new books are
available on

Thursday 28th April

To see which titles are coming soon, please visit

millsandboon.co.uk/nextmonth

MILLS & BOON®

Coming next month

A DANCE TO SAVE THE DEBUTANTE
Eva Shepherd

Sophia rubbed her handkerchief across her eyes to wipe away the last of her tears. This handsome stranger was going to save her. It wasn't quite what she had envisioned for her first ball, but it was certainly better than being abandoned, left to cry all on her own.

And hopefully he was right. Once they had danced together the Duke would become her Prince Charming and her Season would be just as she had dreamed it would be.

'This really is kind of you,' she said.

Oh, yes, he most certainly was a handsome stranger. Even, dared she admit it, more handsome than the man she hoped to marry. His brown eyes contained so much warmth that staring into them was raising her body temperature, and despite the growing heat of her skin she found it impossible to look away.

Instead, she continued to stare at his lovely, smiling eyes. The way they crinkled up at the corners was so endearing, showing he laughed often. He was so obviously a kind man, otherwise she would feel uncomfortable being alone with this stranger, but she felt safe with him.

She quickly lowered her eyes when he inclined his head and raised his eyebrows in question. She had been staring at him for far too long.

'So, shall we?' Those brown eyes were still smiling but he did not appear to be laughing at her.

She waited, unsure what he was asking.

'But before we return to the ballroom and drive your beau wild with jealousy, perhaps we should introduce ourselves,' he said, standing up. 'I'm Lord Ethan Rosemont.'

She rose to her feet and bobbed a quick curtsy. 'How do you do? I'm Miss Sophia Cooper.'

'I'm very pleased to make your acquaintance.' He made a formal bow. 'And I would be honoured, Miss Cooper, if you would grant me the next dance, but perhaps you'd like to freshen up first.'

'Oh, yes, I suppose I should,' she said, and then to her mortification hiccupped. Her hand shot to her mouth, but he merely smiled at her, as if she had done something sweet rather than extremely gauche. She lowered her hand and smiled back in gratitude.

'I'll wait for you by the French doors just inside the ballroom.'

'Oh, yes, of course,' she muttered, embarrassed that she had got distracted and actually forgotten what they were planning to do.

'When you enter, I'll be so dazzled by your beauty that I'll simply have to dance with you immediately. That should make him sit up and take notice.'

She gave a little laugh and departed for the ladies' room. It was all make-believe, but for the first time since the Duke had abandoned her, she really did feel like the belle of the ball about to embark on an exciting adventure.

Continue reading
A DANCE TO SAVE THE DEBUTANTE
Eva Shepherd

Available next month
www.millsandboon.co.uk